Time seemed  pulled at my vest. All .... prairie. Even movement seemed to be discouraged. We were all held in the power of these peculiar lights, the deviant colors, and the chilly, gathering gloom on what had been a hot, sunny afternoon but a moment ago. The vast silence was broken by—of all things—the chirping of crickets in the grass. Then, off to the east, a lone dog began to bark.

3:28 p.m.

I turned at the barking of the dog and saw the ground shimmer with alternating waves of light and shadow. All around us these ripples of light raced across the broken ground. For a moment, I had the absurd urge to reach down and touch them.

I risked a quick sideways glance at the Sun. There was but a sliver of sunlight the Moon had not yet blotted out. I looked to the northwest where the black shadow of the Moon appeared. It had grown in size. It was coming our way. I couldn't see its edges now, and staring at the menacing shadow, it appeared like a giant black mouth about to devour us.

And then it did.

For a map of the 19th-century region
between Pueblo and Denver, Colorado,
please visit:
https://edwardmcsweegan.com/books/shadow-of-the-moon/

Shadow of the Moon

by

Edward McSweegan

Shadow of the Moon

Cover Art by *Jennifer Greeff*

The Wild Rose Press, Inc.
PO Box 708
Adams Basin, NY 14410-0708
Visit us at www.thewildrosepress.com

Publishing History
First Edition, 2023
Trade Paperback ISBN 978-1-5092-4832-2
Digital ISBN 978-1-5092-4833-9

Published in the United States of America

Dedication

To my wife, Sherrie,
who wondered what I was doing in the office
all those days and nights.

~*~

Acknowledgments

Thanks to the members of the Annapolis critique group—Jesse Ellis, Nancy Valdes-Franklin, and Nancy Budowski—who read every line of this story and made it better. And to Susan Moger, who provided endless encouragement and invaluable suggestions across every page. Thank you all.

~*~

Author's Disclaimer

"Does anyone suppose that any woman in all the ages has had a fair chance to show what she could do in science?"

*~Maria Mitchell, Astronomer,
Philadelphia, October 1876.*

~*~

"There is something romantic about him. He lives on horseback, as do the Bedouins; he fights on horseback, as did the knights of chivalry; he goes armed with a strange new weapon which he uses ambidextrously and precisely; he swears like a trooper, drinks like a fish, wears clothes like an actor and fights like a devil. He is gracious to ladies, reserved toward strangers, generous to his friends and brutal to his enemies. He is a cowboy, a typical Westerner."

~Walter Prescott Webb, The Great Plains, 1931.

Chapter 1

Davey heard it first. Whatever "it" was. A snapped twig? A boot kicking over a stone? The declarative click of a gun's hammer? Whatever it was, Davey woke with a start, jerking upright in his bedding, his duster sliding to his lap.

I was a few feet to his left. I opened my eyes to see him sitting upright, his mouth open, emitting a harsh whisper, "What's that?"

There was no time to reply.

A light flashed among the trees to our right. I heard a terrific bang. Davey's head jerked, and a spray of warm stickiness struck my face as Davey fell toward me. He hit the ground shoulder first. Then his head smacked the hard earth of our campsite. He didn't move.

Time seemed to stop while I stared at Davey lying on the ground. It had not. Flashes of light came from the trees, the noise grew louder, and the nervous whine of bullets cut through the night air. Brian, my younger brother, was on the other side of our low-burning fire. I yelled, "Brian! Stay down!"

I rolled to the left, away from Davey, to the deadfall at the opposite end of our camp. Along the way, my arm hooked the Winchester I had left propped against a fallen tree branch. I hugged it to my chest as a drowning man might hug a piece of driftwood and rolled under the trunk of a fallen pine tree.

Coming up on the other side of the pine, I felt safe for a moment, the tree trunk between me and whoever was shooting at us. I wasn't safe, of course, and neither was Brian, lying flat on the ground near the fire. I scrambled to my knees and laid the rifle across the top of the fallen tree. My heart was pounding. A tremor ran down the length of my body. A moment passed. The tremor faded. I fired back into the trees at the flashes of light.

I yelled to my brother, "Get behind a tree. Now!"

Brian got up on his hands and knees, kicking the fire as he did so, and ran in a crouch to a thick pine off to my left. He had his rifle, and I could have kissed him for thinking to take it along on his scramble to cover. Down a slight hill and deeper in the woods, our horses made a fuss about the unexpected din.

Brian fired at the muzzle flashes. I started up again too. Slower, though. I was about to run out of bullets. Clouds of gray smoke hung in the still night air. Lit from behind by our attackers' muzzle flashes, it looked like a tiny thunderstorm had formed but feet above our campsite.

Brian fired twice more. A yelp echoed in the trees. A branch snapped, and someone yelled in dreadful pain. Brian and I both fired again. I jumped up and ran to his tree.

"Sweet Jesus, what's happened?" Brian asked.

"We're ambushed."

The thin mountain air made me struggle for a steady, even breath. I pulled my brother away from his protective tree, and we backed deeper into the woods. We ducked behind a length of deadfall, and Brian asked, "What about Davey? We left him…"

"He's dead."

"Are you sure?"

"Yes, dammit. I'm wearing his blood and brains." I slapped at the sticky stuff on my face.

"What are we gonna do?" Brian strangled his rifle with both white-knuckled hands and looked around the darkness of the now silent woods.

"I think we hit one of them. At least the shooting stopped. For now."

"How many you think there are?" Brian asked.

"Two. Maybe three. Anymore, they likely would have just rushed in on us."

"Are they Indians?"

"No. We'd be dead in our beds." I searched the pockets of my vest and found two more bullets. The rest of our guns and cartridges, including Davey's, had been left behind.

"So now what? What'll we do?" Brian asked.

It was a good question. We were both bootless and probably outgunned. Everything we owned was back at the campsite. Our horses were behind us. Could we get to them and ride bareback through the night? But to where? And how far could we get in the dark?

I looked around at the quiet black woods, sniffed the drifting muzzle smoke, and said, "We should move down and behind the horses. Sit it out. Wait for dawn. We don't know who's back there, and they don't know where we are. So let's move now and hope they don't come looking for us."

I pulled Brian up, and together we padded in a clumsy bootless fashion down a slight grade to our four horses. One of them, Blue most likely—he was always a nervous creature around guns—snorted and shuffled

3

about. Brian calmed him, and then the two of us settled on a large rock, back-to-back, and waited for the creeping light of day.

It was my longest night. Fear kept me awake with the jangled, sweaty nervousness of someone with a fever. I felt the same restlessness from my silent brother as he shifted on our rocky perch and exhaled sighs of whispered air. I thought of Davey, lying dead up there in the woods. Perhaps his killers were standing over his body, picking through our gear and wondering where we might be. So we waited—for them or the miraculous appearance of a dozen lawmen or at least the dawn.

Nighttime in the Colorado foothills can be a noisy place what with the wind coming down off the Rockies, owls hooting, rodents shuffling here and there, and the occasional confident padding about of a bear or a cougar. We heard all of that nocturnal tumult. But slowly, the intimidating dark yielded to the reassuring light of a spring dawn. A bobcat stepped into the morning's gray light, showed its teeth, and faded back into the concealing trees. Squirrels moved about in the treetops. A pinecone dropped onto the needle-covered ground.

Brian stirred. "We should get back to the horses. We should ride outta here."

I stood up, stretched my hunched shoulders, and looked about the trees. "No. They might have heard the horses and decided to wait for us back up there. I think we should swing around to the camp. We need bullets and the rest of the guns. If they're still there."

"Davey…"

"He's not going anywhere." It was a heartless thing to say about him. But then I made it worse. "If we get a chance to get out of here, we may have to leave him."

4

Brian stared off toward the horses. "Okay."

I tapped him on the shoulder and signaled him to follow me. We crept back, slipping among the still dark trees, straddling the downed trees, avoiding loose rocks. It was like playing at soldiers again, but for the fact one of us was dead and the guns pointed our way were real. After a few minutes, we came up on the camp behind Davey's body and my bedding. Nothing seemed to be missing. We crouched down and scanned the woods, listening for unnatural sounds. It was quiet. We stepped over to Davey. Brian glanced at him and gagged. I didn't need another look at him.

"Later, Brian. Load your piece and get your boots." I pushed him toward his gear. The fire had burned to fine ash.

Trying to ignore the body at my feet, I yanked open a saddlebag, looking for a box of cartridges. I threw on my jacket, stuffed the box in my pocket, forced my messy stocking feet into my boots, and scooped up my pistol belt. A quick glance at the trees. Nothing. I ran over to Brian, who was pushing cartridges into the gate of his rifle. His hands shook, and he dropped several shiny brass rounds.

"Where's your Scofield?" I asked.

Brian alternated his attention between the woods and his rifle. "Saddlebags. I hate this."

I grabbed his bags and kneeled down beside him to load my rifle. In a minute, we were rearmed and ready to fight. But we seemed to be alone.

"Now what?" Brian asked. He looked scared.

I wondered if I looked scared too. I was, in fact. But whatever my face showed, I felt alert and ready to act. We had our boots on. We had loaded guns. The morning light was filtering down through the pines. We weren't two boys lost in the dark woods anymore.

"They may be gone." Glancing around the camp, I said, "Stay here. I'll go over to where they were shooting from." I stood, rifle at the ready, and crept toward last night's gun flashes. In a low voice I said, "Brian, don't shoot me in the back." He seemed more skittish than me. It was a good idea to remind him.

Stepping between the trees, I came upon a wide spread of spent .44 Winchester shells. Farther back, I found a smaller pile of .44 Henry brass. So perhaps three shooters—two with Winchesters, one with a Henry? I'm no tracker, but deeper in that side of those gloomy woods I found a clear line of drag marks. One of them hit and dragged back to his horse? That seemed to be the case. I found where they'd tied their horses. Fresh manure spotted the ground, and a barn-sized outcrop of lichen-covered rock appeared to have a smear of blood across its face.

I hurried back to my brother, calling out his name so he wouldn't shoot me when I emerged from the shadowy trees.

"They're gone." I sat down on his saddle.

"You sure?" Clutching his rifle, he glanced over at Davey.

"Yeah. Listen. We should bring the horses up and then take care of Davey. We can't stay here. We need the sheriff…and the undertaker."

If we pushed hard, we might make it back to Pueblo by nightfall. I wasn't eager to spend another night in the wilds. And we'd have Davey's body for another night. Overnight with the dead held no appeal, so Brian and I hurried back down to the picket line. We led the horses back to the camp and saddled our mounts. I got Davey's gear and a set of panniers and readied the other two horses. We'd been using the fourth horse as a spare ride and pack mule.

Saddled and packed up, we stood over Davey, dreading the next task and wondering how best to do it.

Brian looked pale. He turned away and said, "His head's all wrecked. How we gonna move him?"

Davey—we'd known him since the neighborhood primary school back in Chicago—was getting stiff. There is, I think, a kind of primal reluctance most people have about handling the dead. I felt that reluctance now. Davey's face was drained of its usual vibrant color. The left side of his head was black and blue and gaping wide from a bullet's violent exit. I wanted to throw up, but then I'd had no food since last night. All I'd do is choke up a dribble of acid and bile. I opened one of Davey's saddlebags and pulled out a clean shirt. Gently, I wrapped the shirt around his head and tied it in place with the sleeves. Now he appeared like a masked robber or a creature of Dr. Frankenstein awaiting reanimation and unwrapping by his creator. I would leave any future unwrapping for the undertaker.

"Empty his pockets," said Brian. "His parents will want his watch and other effects."

I stood up. Davey lay between us. "The undertaker can do it. Or the sheriff."

"No, Nolan. I plan to take him back home. To Chicago." Brian looked down at Davey and sniffled.

I was about to say…well, I don't know what I was about to say. Brian beat me to it.

"This is ended. I've had enough. The cattle drive. The winter in Denver scrounging around. Now this. This isn't some storybook adventure anymore. There's no adventure. There's just being dead in the cold hills. I'm going home, Nol. It's over."

I stared at Davey again and nodded. "Let's get him ready. We can talk later."

Brian lifted Davey's bootless feet. I lifted him from under his arms, the back of his head resting against my chest. We struggled with his weight, half-dragging him to his horse, and then stood there staring at the height of the saddle. Davey was as tall as me, but somewhat more solid. He'd been tough to wrestle down as a kid.

"Let go of his feet," I told Brian. "Grab an arm, and we'll lift him up."

Brian eased his feet down and then took hold of his left arm with me on Davey's right arm. "We'll push him up over the top of his saddle." I got my arm under Davey's cold, wet thigh and heaved him upward. The horse shied away, and we had to charge the animal with Davey clutched between us like a grotesque battering ram.

"Lift," I yelled to Brian, and we draped him across the saddle in one clumsy push. Davey's horse looked like he might bolt.

"He's gonna slide off." Brian grabbed the horse's bridle and looked away. "God, he's dead." There was a finality in his declaration. He dropped the bridle and brushed his hands along his pants as if he could wipe away death with a few frantic slaps on his corduroys.

I looked at our friend draped across the saddle like a shot antelope. That's pretty much what he was—a carcass that needed tying down and hauling back to town. Brian got some rope from one of the panniers, and we bound him hand to foot under his horse. I looped a length of rope around his waist and then around the horn of his saddle. Brian draped a blanket over him, and we tucked and tied it in place too. The result was our dead friend wrapped and tied to his horse like an unwieldy bit of baggage. That done, we burdened the fourth horse with the panniers and camp equipment.

We picked our way down out of the hills and woods. Brian led the packhorse, and I led the animal carrying Davey's body. It was slow going. We switch-backed our way off the foothills and led the horses across half a dozen cold, fast-moving streams. We stopped here and there to look around for imagined pursuers. I carried my Winchester across the front of my saddle. But the land was empty and quiet, and we saw no one until we reached the road. A Pueblo stagecoach hurried by, heading south to Colorado City. The drivers did not see us in among the trees.

On the main road again, we headed north as fast as two riders could manage four horses. I dreaded another night out of doors as much as I dreaded the telegrams we would have to send home to Chicago. The familiarity of the Pueblo road and the full light of day encouraged Brian to start talking again. And he did, blaming me for Davey's death and for putting the three of us in Colorado in the first place. He could blame me for the latter, but not for the former. Still, I let him vent his steam until he became repetitive.

I whirled my horse around at him. "Shut up. We've problems enough right now. You can bitch and whine all you want after we get to town."

"Yeah. I will." He kicked his horse and trotted away with the supply horse in tow.

****

9

Long past dark, we rode into Pueblo. A few late-night residents paused at the sight of us riding up the street. A body laid across a horse was a common enough exhibit, but it still drew a curious glance or two. The sounds of a Mexican guitarrón spilled out of a dimly lit cantina as we rounded the corner and trotted up the lane to the sheriff's office. Pale yellow light outlined a large office window. A deputy or two might be awake.

We stopped in front of the office. Brian leaned forward on his horse's neck and arched his back. Otherwise, he said nothing. I was grateful for his silence. I climbed down off my mount, started to fall over, and staggered about trying to get my legs working. Not bothering to tie the horses, I hobbled up the step, checked that my Colt was covered by my jacket, and knocked on the office door. I waited a second or two, then turned the worn brass knob and pushed the door open. The law doesn't like people rushing in unannounced, so I took my time walking through the doorway, my hands visible.

The sheriff was in, seated at a battered partner's desk, and eating a late-night dinner of chicken and beer. Two wooden armchairs were angled across from the desk. The sheriff looked up as I came through the doorway.

"I need to report a murder," I said.

The sheriff laid down a two-tine fork, wiped his mouth and squirrelly gray mustache, and leaned back in his chair. "Well, now, I'm guessing you're not the victim or the murderer." He glanced at the armchairs in front of the desk. I sat down, noting an area of the floor that had been scarred by a regular supply of spur rowels. My own cavalry spurs would not add to the damage, so I stretched out my cramped legs.

"It's our friend, David J. Tyler, from Chicago." I pointed to the door. "He's out front across a horse."

"Our friend?" the sheriff asked. "You and this Tyler weren't alone?"

Brian walked in at that moment. He nodded to the sheriff and propped himself against the far wall.

"My brother."

"Okay."

I told the sheriff what happened in the foothills. How we had been fired on in the dead of night, scrambled for cover, fired back, and rode out of the woods in the early dawn with Davey in tow.

"Just started shooting at you, huh?" asked the sheriff. "Seems odd to start blasting away like that."

I said, "They might have been trying to sneak into the camp, but Davey—David Tyler—heard something and sat up to look around. That's when he got shot and all hell broke loose around us."

"We didn't have anything worth killing and dying over," declared Brian.

The sheriff nodded as he opened a drawer and extracted a piece of yellow-tinted paper. He picked up the pen on his desktop and started writing. Now and then he looked up at Brian and me to ask about a particular detail or a name spelling. The scratch of the pen's tip across the rough paper almost lulled me to sleep.

He stopped writing and opined that we had had ourselves quite an exploit in the Colorado hills. I nodded in agreement.

The sheriff stood up, displaying a dignified paunch, and legs that had been re-shaped by years on a horse. He disappeared through a side door. Voices echoed, and then he and a sleepy deputy came back to the front office.

"That's a fine detail, fellows. One of them gettin' hit an' all. We can telegraph about the counties asking the local docs if they'd occasion to patch up a rifle wound amongst two or three fellas," said the sheriff. "Might get lucky trackin' these sneakin' cutthroats. Might have been Mexicans. Or miners lookin' for gold in someone's pockets instead of a mountain stream."

He sat down at his desk again. The sheriff eyed the remains of his dinner and said, "Deputy Franks, here, he'll take you over to the Cranston Undertakers office. Mr. Cranston'll take care of your friend."

The sheriff picked up the sheet of paper on which he had been jotting notes from our recital of last night's events.

I asked him if he wanted to see Davey.

"No. Seen enough gun-busted heads in my days. Undertaker can do the rest. You fellas need to sign your names to my notes here. I'll date it and sign it for the record." He looked up at me. "Any details need to change…well, then, we'll have us another talk and maybe sign another piece of paper."

I stepped up to his desk and picked up his proffered pen. I signed my name, and Brian came off the back wall to sign too.

The sheriff scratched at his mustache like there might be something hiding in it, and said, "Nolan and Brian Carter. Carter? You fellas at the Front Range Freight company over to the railroad station?"

Brian said, "We've been working there for a while now."

"Thought I'd caught the name around town. Well, Joshua here'll take you over to the undertaker. I expect I'll see you boys about before this matter is set to."

"Thanks. That sounds promising, telegraphing about a wounded man. I hope it helps," I said. I imagined two or three tough-looking riders hiding out in the hills, one of them bleeding to death in fear and pain.

The deputy opened the door to signal the end of the interview. Brian and I followed him outside to our horses and Davey's body, which now was but a dark bundle on a dark street. We followed the deputy, pulling the four horses behind us. Two streets over from the sheriff's office we found a sidewalk establishment with doublewide doors and prominent overhead signs advertising "Attractive Caskets" and "Scientific Embalming." The building was dark.

Deputy Franks stepped back into the street, searched around for some pebbles, and tossed them one at a time at the upstairs windows. That had no effect. So he dug a large rock out of the hard-packed street and heaved it at one of the upstairs window shutters. The impact shook the plank building. No one ever seemed to knock in Pueblo.

The rock was effective. A window opened and a heavy-set man in a nightshirt stuck his head out and yelled at the deputy.

Deputy Franks let him yell for a while and then identified himself and the nature of his late-night errand.

The man—presumably Mr. Cranston—turned away from the window, and a minute later a wavering light appeared at the doors. He opened the doors and stepped onto the walkway, holding a tin lamp high enough to see about.

Deputy Franks said, "Got a body for you, Cranston."

"It won't wait 'til morning?" the man asked. "Dead, ain't he?"

"No. We can't wait," shouted Brian.

The undertaker stepped into the street wearing his nightshirt, loosely buttoned pants, and worn carpet slippers. He reeked of cheap tobacco and sulfur matches. Easing around the horse carrying Davey, the undertaker pulled the blanket up from Davey and saw the stained shirt wrapped around his head.

The undertaker looked to me. "Head-shot, is he?" He glanced back at the deputy as if he suspected Brian or I might have been the assassin. "Well, bring him in. I'll clean him up and box him up in the morning. Too late and too dark to do much now."

His duties apparently limited to throwing rocks at windows, Deputy Franks disappeared down the street. Brian and I were left to untie Davey's body while Cranston held his lamp aloft and offered various opinions on the best way to remove a corpse from a tired horse. His knowledge of this task seemed to be theoretical since he offered no actual assistance in retrieving Davey in a gentle, dignified fashion.

We slid him off the saddle. I caught him under the arms, and Brian took up his feet again. Cranston led the way into the building, and I was thankful there were no steps to negotiate. We passed through a front room that smelled of wax and sawdust and varnish, and into a back room, which stank of a tangy ripeness and a harsh chemical. Brian and I wrestled Davey—one last time—onto a wooden table in the middle of the back room. Mr. Cranston drew a canvas tarp over his body and said, "He'll keep to the morning, fellas."

We followed him back through the front room, and I glimpsed the shadowy shapes of coffins set against the right wall and a small desk off to the left. Cranston saw us to the street and closed his flimsy doors. I watched the lamp's light fade from view as the undertaker returned to his second-story lair.

Brian looked up at the night sky. He stared for so long I thought he might be searching for something specific, but all he said after his silent survey of the stars was, "The boardinghouse will be shut tight at this hour. Best not wake Mrs. Sullivan. And the freight office too."

"The rail station is open. We'll sleep there. We'll let the horses in the livery. Leave the saddles and such on the corral posts. They'll be all right."

So we headed up the empty street, to the corral and then to makeshift beds under cover of the station platform canopy. We were both too tired now, and still too shocked by the ambush, to argue or speculate about the what and why of yesterday's events. So the well-schooled, well-bred sons of Jonathan and Mary Louise Carter settled down on the station platform like two penniless drifters to spend a fitful night on the edge of town.

****

Two days later, Brian and I watched the rail porters slide Davey's rough-cut coffin into a baggage car for the trip back to Chicago. Most of the passengers' valises and travel trunks were of a fancier make than Cranston's oblong box—as if shirts and socks and knickknacks were more precious than what lay in that crude container. The shoddy casket would outrage his parents. Yesterday's telegram telling them their son was dead by an unknown hand must have devastated them. Now they would have grief and outrage, and no good way to vent either pain.

Brian had most of Davey's possessions buckled up in his saddlebags. In his pockets he carried Davey's watch and money and the photograph of his family. He also had a bill from the undertaker. But for the coffin, he was traveling light, his own things in a small canvas satchel. I looked at his tired face and wondered again if I might find the courage to go with him, to face Davey's distraught family, and the not so thinly disguised accusations of our own parents.

I did not.

The steam whistle blew once. People milling about now began last-minute goodbyes and determined marches to the passenger cars or back into town.

Brian looked over and said, "Last chance."

"Any idea what you're going to do at home?"

"Mr. Price said there'd be a place for me at Ward's. They always need illustrators."

"Drawing top hats and ladies' shoes?"

Brian came alive again. "Well, at least no one will be shooting at me. It's a respectable job and good pay. You. You can keep the cold, the rain, the dust, the cows, the lousy food. Keep the whole damn West. Maybe you'll get lucky and get scalped. Write home about that."

He picked up his bags and hurried to the nearest first-class railcar.

I was right behind him and put a hand on his shoulder. He turned around, and I hugged him. I stepped back and said, "I'll write."

Brian nodded, almost to himself, moved away, and climbed aboard. As he stepped into the car, he said, "Don't get scalped, Nol."

The steam whistle blew again. Brian appeared in an open window halfway up the car. He leaned out and shouted, "You know what you're doing out here?"

"Looking for something," I shouted back.

Brian slumped back in his seat and gave me a look of exasperation he must have learned from our father. Before I could throw back some clever quip, the engine engaged, and the train pulled away.

I stood against the porch post and watched the train shrink into the distance. Long after the last traces of its coal smoke had dissipated in the warm morning air, I was still leaning on that post and staring off into the vastness of the Colorado prairie.

Chapter 2

Davey was dead. Brian was gone. With both of my companions absent in one form or another, the whole point of living and working in what was often described as the Wild West also was gone. What began as an adventure for three Chicago-born boys was done.

But I stayed on, more out of stubbornness than anything else, I suppose. It was summer now. I had two horses; one had been Brian's. I had a boardinghouse room and a job that paid hard cash. Not much cash, but then, not much was needed if you kept your head. The job, hauling freight up and down the road linking Denver and Pueblo and the places in between, was still a viable prospect. Unfinished rail lines and unresolved disputes between the various railroad companies kept wagon freighters and stagecoach operators busy enough throughout most of the year. But that would change as the steel rails and the copper wires spread across the immense prairie and the rugged Front Range of the Rockies.

I'd had two letters from Brian advising me of Davey's funeral and the recent activities of family and friends. My always-worried mother wrote begging me to come home before I wound up in a wooden box like Davey. It was hard to respond to the pleas of a worried mother. She meant well. I kept my letters short and sounding positive about my days in Colorado and the people with whom I worked and the wildlife I saw along the Front Range.

My father sent a single telegram that read, "Don't be a damn fool." It was a succinct message from a man who churned out a daily newspaper of long-winded denouncements, garish interviews, and large-print hyperbole. But he also wired five dollars to the First National Bank in Denver. I used some of the money to buy a new shirt and a restaurant dinner after we hauled freight up to the city one week.

Now, after breakfast and a violent jolt from Mrs. Sullivan's viscous coffee, I walked over to the Pueblo office and warehouse of Front Range Freight to see what business we might expect during the coming week. The early morning town already was alive with activity. People, horses, and carriages moved along the dusty summer streets. New telegraph poles were being planted near the rail depots. Overhead, a few large birds—eagles or hawks, I couldn't tell which—coasted on the invisible currents of air coming down from the mountains and rising from the warming prairie. The sky was a washed-out blue and cloudless, and later would take on a bleached aspect as the afternoon heat settled over the area, driving people indoors, to siestas, and to a slower pace of business and conversation.

I hopped across the railroad tracks and ducked under the water tank on my way to the company warehouse. The name of the company was much grander than the daily reality of its nature. There were four of us.

The boss, Thaddeus Gray, had spent decades in the territory fighting Indians, panning for gold, riding shotgun on stagecoaches, pilfering the occasional steer from cattle drives, and doing something mysterious for a

Mexican brothel outside of town. His partner was an older man named Charles—never Charlie—Banford who had led a less colorful life as a small-town accountant. There was Travis Sullivan—no relation to my landlady—who walked with a noticeable limp from a Union musket ball but could steer a wagon and cook a decent campfire meal. And then there was me.

I did the lifting and shifting of bulky freight, the packing and unpacking of the wagons, and the scouting about the rail stations for any business that might have been bumped by the bickering railroad men. It had been an easier and more enjoyable job while Brian and Davey worked here too. Now it was just me, and it seemed unlikely Front Range Freight would hire anyone to replace them ever again.

The building was small with a painted sign over the door advertising our existence as a viable business. I slid open the heavy side door and stepped into the office, which was but a walled-off section of the larger warehouse. Charles was at the only desk, reading a copy of the *Pueblo Chieftain* newspaper. He would be done in a minute; it was a thin newspaper. Thaddeus stared at a survey map of Colorado tacked to the back wall. He held copies of the new train schedules in his hand.

"Morning," I said to the both of them.

Charles looked up, flashed a yellow-toothed smile, and returned to his newspaper. Thaddeus, without turning around, said, "Roads and railroads. They're sprouting every which way. Pretty soon you'll have to stop every hundred feet and look around to keep from being run down by something."

I pulled a battered cane-bottomed chair up to Charles' desk and sat down. "We've been back in town for two days. Any new business yet?"

We had come back down from Colorado Springs after hauling three crates of printing press parts for the local newspaper. After that, I had been doing a whole lot of nothing in hot, dusty Pueblo. Hauling freight by wagon wasn't glamourous or exciting work, but it did get you out of town to watch the life of the prairie and earn a little money.

Thaddeus turned away from the wall and glanced at the train schedules he was holding. "Nothing local. Horses and mules aren't complaining, though. The AT&SF from Kansas City should be in around eight-thirty. Hop over to the station and see who and what comes in."

I slid the chair back and stood. "Okay. I'll see what I can find and stop back in with any promising leads." It might be another slow day for me.

Charles looked up from his paper. "Hot out there?"

"It will be," I said.

"You're young," he said and returned to the crinkled pages of the *Pueblo Chieftain.*

I walked back through the rail yards, kicking up bits of coal dust. From the shade of the station house platform, I watched the Atchison, Topeka & Santa Fe train pull into town five minutes late. A massive black engine with a battered cowcatcher on its front end slid by the platform, pulling three passenger carriages, an almost empty flat car, and a bright green caboose with its evening lanterns still lit. With a last expulsion of smoke, steam, and compressed air, the mechanical beast fell silent. The carriage doors popped open. Passengers spilled onto the platform or the hard-packed ground.

An assortment of salesmen and business types

stepped off with their sample cases and leather portfolios in hand. A local family I recognized alighted back onto familiar ground. Three Army officers stepped onto the platform and lit up pungent cigars. A small group of well-dressed men and women stepped down and looked about, wild-eyed. Easterners. My companions and I probably had the same look a year ago.

Two rough-looking drovers came off and made a beeline for the main street bars and cafes. Several eager-looking cowhands followed them. I imagined they all would be in the jail before midnight. Three Mexicans alighted and wandered off toward the livery. Farther down the track, I watched three young women step down, followed by an older woman.

Their mother? Mormon daughters?

They all gathered around a conductor who, after a bit of animated conversation, pointed them down the tracks to the offices and the siding of the Denver & Rio Grande Railroad.

I went looking for the head AT&SF conductor and found him inside the station, gulping down a glass of cold water.

"Mr. Fitzgerald. How's Kansas City," I asked.

"Ah, Nolan. Hard at work, are you? KC, well, it's the usual pile of vaqueros, Texans, coloreds, cows, more cows, drovers, and Easterners thinkin' they're already in the West."

"The usual, then." I asked him about the baggage his train had carried to Pueblo.

He scratched his graying beard and said, "Nothin' encouragin' comes to mind. But…there's a party of pretty girls travelin' with a professor all the way from Boston. Wantin' to go up to Denver on the DRG."

"Ah. But we're not so desperate yet as to be hauling ladies' knickers and corsets."

"They've equipment. Telescopes and such for the eclipse," he said.

"Telescopes?"

"For the eclipse, lad."

"Yes, I know. It's Monday afternoon. I was just trying to imagine freighting telescopes up the road."

"Best you catch them while the DRG and the AT&SF are still at each other."

"Telescopes and Eastern girls. Well, why not?"

So, I went looking for them. But with little enthusiasm. It was obvious to me that the railroads—even when they were not fighting over tracks and right-of-ways—were going to kill the freight business. I could stay here to watch that final death or I could go home and get on with a real job back in the city that was my source of friends and family. What really was the point of staying here? My shouted declaration to Brian as his train pulled away now seemed like empty bravado. Time to quit? One more trip to Denver? Then home? Before someone shoots me.

****

I found them in the DRG depot office arguing with the office manager. The DRG boss was a tough son of a bitch, in a neat brown suit and a yellow tie, who came down from the Denver offices to manage the Pueblo front in a financial and geographical war against the AT&SF. He was seen about town in the company of a former Pinkerton agent. That he felt the need of a bodyguard said much about the state of the competitive railroad business in Colorado.

Outside his office door, I heard an older woman's

voice, controlled but sliding into exasperation and desperation. "But we have paid tickets all the way through to Denver."

The DRG man was having none of it. His job probably was on the line, and he was not about to lose that well-paid job to an agitated grandmother and a couple of girls. "Madam, as I have stated, we are unable to transfer passengers and freight from the Atchison-Topeka line."

"Why not?" demanded the older woman.

"There have been…business complications of late," said the DRG manager.

"Complications, whatever their nature, do not negate our prior arrangements or our costs, sir," said the woman.

"I'm afraid, madam, they do. Now, this office will sell you additional tickets direct to Denver. Or you may wait until circumstances change. Or you can find another conveyance up to Denver."

That seemed to end the deliberations. It was quiet for a moment, and then a heavy wooden door closed off to the left. I stepped away from the station door and walked to the end of the platform. I watched the four women step outside, clutching their valises and carpetbags. They stood in the late morning sun, talking among themselves and looking unhappy.

Two of the girls were young—as young as me, I supposed—and dressed in the heavy attire of proper Eastern girls. They were attractive in a prime sort of way. The other woman was a mousey-looking thing who might have been preparing for a career as a schoolmarm. She reminded me of a grammar schoolteacher I had endured back in Chicago not so long ago.

The grandmotherly woman—the professor—looked both mad and exasperated, like my mother sometimes looked at Brian and me when we were younger and doing something of which she did not approve.

The professor was a solid-built woman with a mass of large gray curls upon her head. She wore a black dress that provided a stark contrast to her skin, which was as pale as a summer day's cloud. Her face might have been handsome on a man, but on this colorless, elderly woman, it appeared odd and out of place. She did not look at all like what I imagined a college professor to be. A feisty public-school teacher perhaps, or an unmarried aunt, but not a professor steeped in the knowledge of obscure arts and sciences. She was looking along the tracks as if searching for someone to bite.

I stepped up to her, tilted my hat back, and said, "Good morning, madam. Ladies. I understand you're having trouble with your tickets to Denver. Perhaps I can help."

The conversation stopped, and they all looked at me. The professor stared at me for a moment, then began a head to toe, and back again, examination of my person as if I was an odd bit of museum sculpture she wanted to memorize, or perhaps some suspicious-looking delinquent for whom she was planning an appropriate punishment.

Her long and silent scrutiny was unwarranted. After all, I had had a bath two days ago. The local man who called himself a barber had cut my hair and shaved my face. The cuts had since healed. My clothes were clean enough and common enough for Pueblo that I drew no attention on the dusty summer streets. My appearance was both harmless enough and respectable enough. Yet this stern-faced professor seemed to think otherwise on both counts.

Her examination finished, she said, "Young man, unless you are able to transfer our baggage and our persons to the next Denver-bound train, you cannot be of any assistance to us. Thank you very much." She turned back to her colleagues.

"Ma'm," I started to say, but was cut off.

"This is Professor Maria Mitchell," said one of her young flock. "From Vassar College in New York."

"Professor. Excuse me, but you're unlikely to find yourselves on the next northbound train unless you're prepared to pay for new tickets and freight charges."

"We cannot and should not. We have tickets paid all the way through from Boston to Denver," said the professor.

"Yes, I expect you do. But the DRG—the Denver Rio Grande Railroad—and the Atchison, Topeka & Santa Fe train you alighted from this morning are not honoring each other's tickets or accepting the transfer of baggage and freight between them. You have stepped into the middle of a lively railroad war."

That got their attention. To keep it, I explained what was happening between the DRG and AT&SF railroad companies.

The two railroads had been fighting over exclusive access to a mountain pass connecting Colorado and New Mexico. Most of the fight over access to the pass was being carried out by railroad lawyers in courtrooms, far from the heat and the dust of the territory. But the local workers and engineers for the two railroads thought the lawyers should not have all the fun, so they sabotaged each other's equipment. Bare-knuckle brawls in the rail yards were common events that kept the sheriff busy. By February, the AT&SF had had enough of the lawyering and the brawling and hired a few local gunmen to better represent their position in the dispute. That worked out well enough; the DRG had no interest in, or money for, a shooting war and ceded the pass to the AT&SF.

"This is the most outrageous behavior among civilized men. Imagine hiring killers over a business dispute," said one of Mitchell's young companions.

"Yes, Mr. Lincoln said the railroads would bind us together, not have us shooting at one another over a few tracks or the price of a ticket. It's outrageous," said the mousey-looking woman in the group.

Professor Mitchell shook her head and said, "Then this silly little war of conductors and lawyers is ended now. The Santa Fe railway has the Pass, does it not? Why cannot we board the train and be on our way?"

I shook my head. "Well, ladies, I'm afraid hard feelings linger. And those feelings may be inflamed anew. There are rumors of a silver strike up in Leadville—it's in the mountains south and west of Denver. There may be another fight over who gets to lay track through the Royal Gorge area and then on to Leadville. This time, there could be a real shooting war between the D and the Santa Fe. So right now, they have no interest in helping each other with the transfer of one another's passengers and freight."

The professor and her group fell silent, no doubt considering their predicament.

I filled the silence. "My name is Nolan Carter, and I work for a freight company back up the street. Perhaps we can haul your equipment and baggage up the road to Denver and get it there in time for Monday's eclipse."

Mitchell looked at her companions and said, "Oh, we've come so far to be stopped but a few hours from our destination. This seems a cruel joke."

The last girl in the professor's group said, "Perhaps we could remain here for the observation. Pueblo is within the path of totality."

"No, Cora. Emma and Cornelia will be waiting for us in Denver. And Dr. Avery is expecting us at her house. Everyone will be in Denver, and we must be seen in Denver by our peers and by the newspaper people." She turned to me. "What do you propose, Mr. Carter?"

I didn't know why she wanted to be *seen* in Denver, but I left that mystery for later. I took off my dusty black gambler's hat and looked at this dejected foursome from back East.

"Well Professor, I propose we gather up all your baggage and make sure it's safe. Then we should walk over to our office and consider various options for getting all of you up to Denver in time for the eclipse. There's little point in standing here in the hot sun worrying over the greedy antics of the railroad managers and lawyers. With luck, we'll have your things in a wagon and on the road this afternoon."

Professor Mitchell nodded to herself. "Yes, perhaps an alternative plan is preferable to no plan at all. We shall be most interested to learn how you propose to get us to Denver in a timely fashion. It is one hundred miles, is it not?"

"More like a hundred and twenty along the road," I said.

I led them back to the AT&SF station house. At the far end of the platform, they found their two remaining carpetbags, three large wood-and-brass tripods lashed together, a rolled canvas tent, and three long wooden cases containing the telescopes. The long cases had brass handles at both ends and were closed with several brass latches.

I glanced at the professor and asked, "Your telescopes?"

"The three of them, yes. These must get to Denver. In working order. With us," she said.

"That shouldn't be a problem. Did you remove the optics?" I asked.

Surprised, she said, "Yes, I have the lenses, along with a chronometer." She lifted the bag she was carrying to show me.

The young woman named Cora said, "A chronometer is a delicate, but highly accurate type of clock."

"Yes." I pulled on the watch fob hanging from my vest pocket. "I have one too."

I wanted to let her know I wasn't an illiterate drover, but I didn't want to be too sarcastic in my reply. She might have blushed at my response, but under the shade of the platform roof it was hard to tell.

Professor Mitchell said, "I was concerned the lenses and the chronometer not be subjected to rough handling in the baggage car." She turned to the other two girls. "Phebe, would you and Elizabeth be so good as to watch the telescopes and bags? I will take Cora along and investigate these freighting options by the Denver roads."

She looked at me. "Mr. Carter..."

"Nolan," I said.

"...please direct us to your offices."

So I did.

On our walk to the warehouse office, I asked her what she did back in New York.

"At Vassar College, I teach mathematical astronomy, spherical trigonometry, the computation of orbits and the prediction of eclipses," she replied, eyeing the slow-moving denizens of Pueblo.

From behind us, her younger companion said, "Professor Mitchell discovered a comet and was awarded a gold medal by the king of Denmark. Now she is the director of the Vassar Observatory, which is equipped with the third largest telescope in America. I'm Cora Harrison, by the way. Vassar class of '76."

I tipped my hat to her. "Welcome to Pueblo."

The professor stopped in the middle of the street to stare at three Indians walking to our left. They were dressed in dyed wools and worn leather. Their long black braids were tied in place with bright ribbons and silver rings. One of them gripped a Spencer rifle. I did not know what tribe they might have come from—Pueblos up from New Mexico maybe—but the occasional Indian in town during the summer was not unusual. Still staring, Mitchell pulled a small notebook from her pocket and began to scribble a penciled note. She muttered the words, 'untutored Indian' as she wrote.

After a moment, she looked up and said, "Remarkable. Mr. Carter…your office?"

I waved a hand in the general direction of our building and we set off again in silence.

****

At the warehouse, I introduced Professor Mitchell to Thaddeus and Charles. She gave them a curt nod and took hold of the cane chair near Charles' desk. She tipped the chair forward and leaned around to examine the stenciling on the back of the chair seat. It read, "L. Hitchcock. Hitchcocksville, Conn. Warranted," with the N letters printed backwards. Perhaps satisfied by the chair's New England pedigree, the professor sat down and pulled out her notebook again.

From the throne of the old cane chair, she demanded to know everything about the quality of the roads to Denver, the state of our wagon springs, the health of the horses, the cost per pound of freight, and the facilities available at every little railroad town we might pass on the route north. If the hiring of our freight company had been a boxing match, then both Thaddeus and Charles would have been clinging to the ropes, too beaten down with questions and financial calculations to continue.

Cora stood to one side, watching this combat play out. Perhaps she had witnessed similar scenes in the past, or maybe, as a student, she had been on the receiving end of a similar Socratic inquisition. I took that moment to better examine this girl with the fancy college education who had traveled almost two thousand miles to watch a three-minute eclipse.

She wore short brown hair done up in tight curls and had clear gray eyes that seemed to wander but missed nothing of import. Her lips were full and presently trying to hide a smile. She looked like she was posing for a photograph or a painter's canvas. She wore a black skirt and a white ruffled shirt dotted here and there with soot from the train's smokestack. I liked her face, and the rest of her.

She turned to find me staring at her. Now I felt a blush spreading across my face, but I was saved from outright humiliation by Thaddeus.

He said, "Nolan, see if you can roust Travis and get

the light wagon rigged for a fast run to Denver. Eclipse aside, when you get there, do scout about the depots for southbound freight we might haul. Then send a wire advising of such."

"Sure." I nodded to Cora, "Miss Harrison," and stepped into the deeper reaches of the warehouse. I hurried past the two company wagons and through another doorway that led to a double corral. Travis was watering the mules that pulled the bigger wagon.

"We're heading up to Denver today. Thaddeus wants the express wagon rigged," I said.

Travis hung his bucket on the pump handle and limped my way. "What we haulin'?"

"Telescopes and baggage belonging to some lady astronomers from Boston."

"So, a light load," he said.

"Very light, I'd guess. Telescopes…they're just hollow tubes."

"So are cannon," Travis replied.

I couldn't decide whether Travis was being funny or difficult. Often it was hard to know. I looked back at the warehouse and asked, "Will you get to the wagon? I need to get my horses and gear."

"Righto," he said, and followed me back into the building.

****

I did not see Thaddeus again. I assumed he had acquiesced to all the professor's demands, and a financial deal had been struck. Not needing to know the specifics of the freight billing, I instead hurried to my boardinghouse to pack some clothes and collect my guns. Mrs. Sullivan, the house owner, was in the kitchen. I told her I would be gone for about a week and would pay her for the week's rent on my return. She looked up from sorting garden vegetables long enough to mutter, "Yes, yes, fine."

I left thinking I would be paying for a room I wasn't occupying, and she would take advantage of my absence to rent it to some tourist looking for a place to stay during the eclipse. There was little I could do about it.

At the livery, I gathered my tack. Old Man Frederick must have seen me and ambled out of his hatbox office. He was, in fact, only thirty-one years old, but had acquired the "old man" moniker by way of his slow gait, hesitant speech, and a painful indecisiveness. I thought to stampede past him with my gear, but since the matter was one of money, he showed an unexpected liveliness.

"Headin' out, Nolan?" he asked.

"I am." I stepped into the corral with a saddle.

"Need to pay up for July, then."

Walking to my horse, I said over my shoulder, "I'll be back the first week of August."

"Your brother left. Your friend got himself killed. You might not come back for one reason or another. Best settle accounts while we're both here and now."

I wasn't going to get away. "All right. I'll stop in the office as soon as I saddle up." That satisfied him, and he shuffled back to his little hideaway among the tack and bales.

I rigged Barley, my red-and-white paint horse, and then Brian's mustang. The mustang—named Blue—was a light brown creature with a long black mane. Lately, I had established the habit of taking both animals with me on trips up to Denver and south into New Mexico. The two animals liked each other's company, and being able to switch from one mount to another, I found I could ride farther and faster without playing out either horse. And I could not yet bring myself to sell off my brother's horse, whatever the added cost to me.

In the livery office, Frederick presented me with a bill I only glanced at before dropping two dollars on his desk. "I'll be back in August." I was out the door before the Old Man could construct and deliver a reply.

As I led the horses to the AT&SF station house, someone called my name. I looked around to find the sheriff mounted on a white appaloosa splattered with random patches of black hair and a mane as shaggy as the sheriff's mustache.

"Carter. Headin' out?"

"I am. Freight haul up to Denver."

The sheriff tipped his voluminous hat back on his head and stepped his horse around my own two. "About your late-night encounter last month. Just thought I'd mention there's been no word from any town doctors patchin' up a gunshot of late. Looks like your ambushers 're gonna remain anonymous."

"So then, the one we hit either died or got better on his own?"

The sheriff nodded. "I suppose. Probably they're still out there somewhere. Two or three of them. Sleep light on the road." With that, he gave his horse some invisible signal, and the animal moved off.

"We're sticking to towns and hotels," I called after him. Yes, well-lit towns and hotels with locking doors. No more muzzle flashes in the night.

****

At the station house, I tied up my horses. Travis pulled up behind me in our green-painted express wagon. A yellow cigarette hung from his dry lips. He puffed out a white cloud of Virginia smoke and said in his Georgia voice, "So then, a fast trip up to Denver. We should take the slow road back. Hotels and all." He tilted back in the wooden seat and stretched his lanky legs over the scuffed footboard.

"We have to get there first. I'll see about the freight."

I walked behind the station and found Cora Harrison and another of the Vassar girls sitting among the crated telescopes and other baggage. They were looking at a charcoal sketch of a girl sitting on a telescope case with the station house in the background.

"That's a fine drawing," I said.

They stood up and Cora said, "Hello again. Mr. Carter, this is Elizabeth Abbott."

Abbot stuck out her hand, and I gave it a gentle shake. "Are you also an astronomer?"

Elizabeth said, "I'm a schoolteacher now, but I was one of the astronomy students in the class of '73." Then she held up the drawing and said, "It's Phebe's work, Professor Mitchell's sister. She's the artist among us."

"She's very good," I said.

Cora said, "She came with us from Boston to do drawings of the eclipse." Cora looked at me looking at the drawing and asked, "Do you sketch, Mr. Carter?"

"My brother is the artist in the family, but I can rough out the difference between a cat and a cow." I looked about the platform and asked, "Where's Professor Mitchell and her sister?"

"They've taken their bags and gone in search of rail tickets. She asked us to oversee the loading of the telescopes and then be on our way."

On our way?

I was puzzled. Where were they going? To find their professor? They couldn't mean a train; they didn't have train tickets. The next stage coach? No, that was another day off. The two of them stared at me like they were expecting a response. Enlightenment was slow in coming.

"You're coming with us!"

"Yes. Professor Mitchell thought it best the telescopes be accompanied," said Cora.

I could not believe this was part of the agreement Thaddeus had struck with the professor. We hauled freight, not people. I should have stopped back in the office to talk to Thaddeus about the particulars of this job, but I assumed it was a straightforward haul to Denver with a drop-dead Monday deadline for arrival. I had seldom involved myself in the business details of previous trips up and down the road.

What was the cost per Vassar student? Was it by the pound? Like any other freight?

"We don't usually take passengers," was all I could think to say to the two girls.

"You don't usually transport telescopes either, I'll bet," said Cora. "But this is a unique moment in time. We must adapt to the circumstances."

Before I could think of a response to Cora's declaration, Travis came up behind me. He tipped his hat to the girls and said, "Burnin' daylight, Nolan. These the fancy telescopes?" He lifted one end of the larger wooden case. "Like to see these all set up in Denver."

I still was thinking about the problem of the girls as passengers when Cora said, "Take a quick look now, if you wish. Mine is in the middle-sized case."

I stared at her. "You own a telescope?" I had a small

square of blue-tinted glass through which I planned to glimpse the coming eclipse.

She swung her beaded handbag over her shoulder and said, "Well, I'm an astronomer. My parents thought I should be equipped for the job."

"Yes, I suppose…" Curious girl.

Travis lowered the end of the larger case, so I bent down and popped its three latches. I eased the lid back. Cradled inside was a six-foot tube of shiny brass. The mouth of the tube was maybe four inches across, tapering off toward the eyepiece, which was absent. A finderscope was bolted to one side of the lower end, along with a thin plate that read, *Alvan Clark & Sons, Cambridge, MA*. Farther up from the finderscope was a brass arrangement of hinges and bolts to secure the tube to its tripod.

Travis leaned in for a closer look and said, "Probably see all the way to Atlanta with that kind of spyglass."

"A beautiful instrument," I said to Cora.

I closed the solid wooden lid and snapped down the brass latches. Travis picked up one end of the case again and said, "Let's get these loaded."

I hurried to the opposite end, lifted the case, and followed Travis as he limped down the platform steps to the wagon.

We placed padded canvas tarps in the wagon bed and then set the three telescope cases on top of the padding. The Pueblo-Denver road was well-traveled, but it still presented a vast number of dips and bumps, exposed rocks and deep ruts, and debris from occasional springtime washouts. Professor Mitchell was wise to have removed the glass lenses from the telescopes. A cracked lens would render a telescope useless.

Travis and I packed their tent and the three tripods between the cases. The two women came around the station house carrying the last of their luggage. I took their bags and placed them in the bed and shut the wagon gate. Looking back at Cora and Elizabeth, I wondered how we were to carry the two of them in this small wagon. This was supposed to be a fast, light trip, not a church picnic.

Cora saw my horses and walked over to them. "They're lovely animals. This is a beautiful mustang. Are they yours?" she asked me.

I nodded.

"You're bringing two saddle horses?"

"Two are handy for scouting ahead and off into the prairie," I said. I was busy imagining when Travis would realize we had passengers and what he might say about this remarkable fact. I cursed the railroads for their greed and for the daily inconveniences they created.

"Wonderful," said Cora. She reached into the wagon, pulled her carpetbag free, and headed into the station. "I'll be right back," she said and disappeared inside.

Elizabeth watched her go off, and then she walked down to the left rear wheel of the wagon and asked, "Mr. Travis, is this a Mormon roadometer? I've never seen one like it before."

Travis tipped ash from his cigarette into the dusty street and limped over to look at the boxed brass gears bolted to the side of the wagon bed. "Yes, a fine mechanism. Very consistent. Like the Mormons themselves."

Still staring at the mechanism, she said, "Is it

consistently correct or consistently wrong?"

Not waiting for an answer, she touched the dusty brass worm screw and traced her fingers along the face of the gear wheel and down to the trip arm. "So, if this is a sixty-tooth gear wheel and this rod rotates one time per six revolutions of the wagon wheel, then three hundred sixty revolutions of the wheel will yield one mile of distance traveled. Yes?"

She looked at the two of us. I had no trouble believing she was a schoolteacher.

Travis was at a loss for words, so I said, "It seems to be accurate enough. Most times it agrees with the measures of the Colorado Springs stagecoach and our bigger freight wagon."

"Well, that is reassuring. If you set it to zero here, we shall have an accurate measure of our journey from town to town." She disengaged the worm screw from the sixty-tooth gear wheel and set the wheel back to its zero starting point. Travis emitted a puff of aromatic smoke.

Cora reappeared before Elizabeth found any additional computations with which to quiz us. But her appearance was almost as surprising as Elizabeth's math and mechanics. She had changed her clothes. Now she wore a tan riding skirt—which, actually, was a pair of lady's pants baggy enough to contain three pairs of legs. She wore a matching vest, a black Spanish riding hat, and low-heeled boots.

Cora came down the steps saying, "I hoped for a chance to ride somewhere in the Colorado range. It's so unexpected that you have two horses for the trip. You won't mind my taking a short ride now and then, will you, Mr. Carter?"

I didn't know what to say at this point. I snapped my

head around, looking down the street and hoping Thaddeus might appear to make sense of what was unfolding here.

Travis dropped his cigarette. He pivoted about on his good leg to face me. "They're coming with us? Does Thaddeus know about this? All of 'em?"

"Yes and no," said Elizabeth. "Professor Mitchell decided she and her sister should remain here in Pueblo and try to get our original train tickets refunded by the Santa Fe or honored by the DRG rail company. Cora and I are to ride with the telescopes in case they fail."

Cora came down the platform steps and said, "The professor and your Mr. Thaddeus agreed to have our telescopes and related baggage transported by wagon. She and Phebe will try to get aboard the next train to Denver. If they succeed, they will send a telegram ahead and have your wagon stop and await the train's arrival. Then the telescopes and our baggage will be transferred to the train and Front Range Freight will bill for whatever distance has been covered by the wagon. If Professor Mitchell and Phebe are forced to buy new tickets outright, then they will head to Denver, meet the others in our party, and await the arrival of us and the equipment. Your Mr. Thaddeus assured us the wagon would reach Denver with time to spare."

Elizabeth turned to us and said, "It's the best we can do, given the time, this nasty little railroad war, and our limited funds. We cannot all buy additional tickets or pay for hotels. There are people waiting for us in Denver. And a free house and a splendid viewing site. We must get there. Otherwise, all our work will have been for naught."

I looked at Travis, who appeared as confused and

agitated as I felt. The eclipse would occur late Monday afternoon—it was Tuesday now—so there was plenty of time to make the trip. The road to Denver followed the railroad, occasionally crossed the tracks before resuming its parallel march, and passed through half a dozen towns where a telegraphed message could be received and the wagon halted. The plan seemed simple.

But it fell apart in a commonplace fashion, leading to events no one could have imagined.

Travis glanced at the two women, then back at me. "This is a pile of inconveniences. How are we…?"

I knew what he was thinking. The road was rough in places. It was hot. There was only so much water between towns. Travis liked to smoke his rolled cigarettes along the road, and when a piss came on, he often stood up between the seat and the footboard, unbuttoned his pants and announced to the world, "I'm irrigatin' the prairie." Now he'd have to find a less dramatic way to relieve himself. So would the women. Embarrassment seemed like it might be our first stop on this trip.

I glanced at Cora and then said to Travis, "We'll just have to adapt."

Travis said to the women, "Where y'all to sit? This ain't a stagecoach." Without waiting for an answer, he climbed up in the wagon and sat down, taking the thick leather reins in hand. He looked like he might ride off by himself.

Elizabeth and Cora looked at each other. Cora said, "Elizabeth can sit up front with…Mr. Travis. Perhaps I could ride your mustang for a while?"

The day was wearing on. I looked at my watch. "Maybe once we're out of town. For now, we can use the tent to make a more comfortable seat in the wagon bed."

This seemed agreeable to the two women. Cora climbed into the wagon to unroll the tent. Elizabeth, dressed in a long skirt and short jacket of gray-green cotton, stepped up on the wagon's iron foot peg. Travis extended his hand for support, and she stood up next to the seat. From there she helped Cora lay the tent across one of the telescope crates and over the wagon flare-boards to make a kind of padded seat.

I got Blue and tied a line from his halter to the wagon gate. Then I brought Barley up to the wagon, tightened the cinch, and slipped my gunbelt out of the left saddlebag. I strapped it on, tossed my jacket on, and swung up in the saddle.

Glancing again at our two passengers nestled in the freight wagon, I nodded to Travis.

"We're off," Travis said, though he sounded ambivalent about it. He flicked the reins and the two-horse wagon team stepped forward.

I nudged Barley with the rounded brass knobs of my cavalry spurs, and we started up the road. The sun was at its peak—I gave a moment's thought to the idea of it vanishing during the upcoming eclipse. The newspapers said the world—our little part of it, anyway—would go dark for two-and-a-half minutes. Feeling the sun on my back in bright, hot Pueblo, it was hard to believe that fiery orb would wink out in the middle of a summer day.

We passed a water wagon rolling into town, and I waved to a local farm family on a buckboard. We left the last of Pueblo's buildings behind us, and Elizabeth said, "This is almost as exciting as the coming eclipse."

She was right.

Chapter 3

On the road north of a hamlet called Cactus, I relented and let Cora ride Blue for a while. She said she grew up in Kansas and knew how to ride. Certainly, she knew how to dress for a ride. She untied Blue's lead line and climbed up on the saddle before she looked over at me. "Why do you have McClellan saddles?"

Travis heard this and said, "Cause he's a damn Yankee and likes to ride like a damn Yankee general."

I shrugged. "Cheaper. Lighter for me and the horse. I'm riding, not working, so I don't need a Texan's horn or a high pommel and cantle to keep me seated. Barley likes the fit." I gave him a pat on his muscled neck.

Cora leaned side to side, testing the saddle, and then swung her booted feet outward to check the stirrups. Satisfied, she squeezed Blue between me and the wagon and trotted up the dusty brown road. I rode after her.

As we passed by the front of the wagon, Travis muttered, "It's a damn derby."

Cora riding off like that gave me some worry. Colorado was not always the stuff of dime store novels, but any number of things could go wrong. I learned that hard lesson but weeks ago. The occasional robber lurked between the towns. Random prairie dog holes might trip up a horse. A rattlesnake might spook a horse and throw a rider. Weather off of the mountains changed the landscape in minutes. On a cattle drive last year, I was thrown from my horse by a lightning bolt. It hit another rider a few yards from me. He and his horse were killed instantly. That was not unheard of. On the empty prairie, a man on a horse often was the only tall target for a stray bolt of lightning looking for the shortest distance to the ground.

I caught up to Cora. She laughed and pointed to a small herd of pronghorn antelope at a gully spring. "It's delightful to be out here riding about. It's an extraordinary vista, don't you think? All this empty land."

The land was not empty. It had never been empty. The Indians had been here for who knows how long. The Spanish had been here since the 1600s. Still, her carefree smile got me smiling too. She was lost in the moment, and I was content to wait her out and watch her face. It might have been then—watching her watch the pronghorns—I realized she was beautiful. She turned to catch me watching her again. I would have to stop staring or be less obvious about it.

"You carry a pistol?" She saw the Colt holstered on my left side.

"It's a handy thing to have against the occasional snake." I reached down and tugged on the stock of the Winchester resting in the saddle's scabbard. "And a rifle," I said. Pointing to the antelope, I pulled the rifle free. "How about lunch?"

She looked alarmed and said, "No." Then, "You're joking with me."

"Yes, I am." I dropped the weapon back into the scabbard. "We'll eat in the next town."

"Why two guns? Is it so dangerous on this road?" She looked around the dry and scruffy landscape, taking

44

in the short grass, the gray rock, and the green scrub.

"We have three, actually. Travis has a shotgun hooked under his seat. But, to answer your question, no, the road's not dangerous. On the other hand, if there is trouble, the Denver police are a long way off, and we're in between town sheriffs. You do want us to protect your telescopes?"

I had a sudden memory of Davey lying dead on the ground and the whine of invisible bullets in the night air. I blinked a couple of times and heard Cora's voice again.

"Well, I hope there will be no occasion for any gunplay. The newspapers back home are full of stories about murderous bandits and wild Indians and other such perpetrators."

Travis and Elizabeth came up behind us, and we eased the horses to the side of the road to let them pass.

Cora waved and said, "Lizzy, would you like to ride?"

Elizabeth turned and said, "Not for your life. I'll stay safe on the wagon."

****

Considering our late start and our unexpected passengers, we made good time. We passed through the towns of Nada and Cactus with only brief stops to water the horses and make use of such facilities as the local cantinas and boardinghouses could provide. At Piñon we had come almost twelve miles and decided to stop rather than try for Wigwam, which was another five miles north.

Piñon was a Mexican place too small to warrant calling it a town. It was, in fact, only a loose cluster of whitewashed adobes, a church, and a tiny station house that could send and receive a telegram, if you could find the operator. And he was nowhere to be found. We parked the freight wagon in front of what passed for an inn and cantina. Travis climbed down, stretched himself this way and that, and proceeded to assemble a cigarette with the deliberation of a miner mixing nitroglycerine.

I led our two passengers inside to a low-ceilinged cantina. Two old men in rough white cotton sat in a corner drinking raw tequila and spooning up a watery chili. The woman who ran the place came over to me; she recognized me from prior stopovers. She didn't speak English, but with a few Spanish words and a pantomime of sleeping and pointing to the two women, I got her to understand we needed food for four and a bedroom for the ladies.

I don't know what Cora and Elizabeth thought of this peculiar stage play, but the old woman found it amusing. At one point she stared at the women, pointed to me, and said something in Spanish. The two old men glanced at us. I didn't follow what she was saying, but I heard the word, "Mormón."

I gave her a pained smile and said, "No." They were not my wives.

I looked back at Cora and Elizabeth. They were unaware of the joke, and I turned back to the amused proprietor and said, "*Comida, por favor,*" and held up four fingers.

We got a meal of corn tortillas, chili, and sangria without any further innuendo from the old lady. The girls were suspicious of the chili and mystified by the warm, round tortillas. Travis and I sat across from them, and I gave them a quick lesson in tortilla tearing and chili dipping.

"Table etiquette out here is a little more forgiving

than in New York," I said.

"Mind those Mexico chiles, though," said Travis. He held up a spoonful of them. "Otherwise, we'll need a couple more pitchers of this sangria."

Elizabeth and Cora began as hesitant diners but soon took to pulling apart tortillas like they were doing something novel and fun but slightly scandalous.

Fatigue settled in before we finished dinner. Soon after the last drops of sangria vanished, I followed the old woman and our two passengers down a short hallway to a room that might have passed for a monk's cell in a monastery. The proprietor left, and I placed the girls' bags on the raw wooden floor.

I gazed about the tired, whitewashed room and said, "Well, it's not the Palmer House, but it'll do till morning."

On the way out of the room, I pointed to a heavy wooden chair in the corner and said, "Put that against the door."

Travis was waiting outside, having downed a generous shot of tequila. I followed his wagon with the telescopes up to the public barn. We knew the stable was as comfortable as the cantina's rooms and so settled ourselves in the hayloft.

Looking down from the dark loft, I saw the dim outline of the wagon we had backed into the barn with its cargo of brass telescopes. I thought about the coming eclipse. It had been publicized in the Colorado newspapers off and on for years. Now it was daily news. I expected to watch it from Pueblo or wherever I found myself on Monday, the twenty-ninth of July. But here was an unexpected opportunity to see it through one of these telescopes.

I rolled over and asked Travis, "Think we'll get a chance to see the eclipse through one of these telescopes?"

"Maybe," was all his shadowy form had to say on the matter.

I rolled away from the edge of the loft and thought about the girl who rode Blue this afternoon, and who owned a telescope. She was different. I was intrigued.

****

In the morning, I searched for the telegraph operator, but failed to find him. The tiny town did not get enough telegraphic traffic to warrant someone sitting in the office all day listening to other people's clicks and taps.

A northbound train rolled through the town but did not stop. Watching it disappear around a bend, I began to worry about missed trains and telegrams, and I envisioned a long run all the way to Denver with our two passengers.

I walked back to the cantina and ate a breakfast of beans, cornbread, and coffee with Travis and our two passengers. Elizabeth and Cora appeared rested, though not as neatly dressed and made up as when I first spotted them at the Pueblo train station. But then neither was I. Already, I wanted a shave and a bath. I was hoping to maintain an obvious contrast between myself and Travis, who often maintained an air of indifference regarding personal grooming and public opinion.

The two women had seen the train too, and I told them what I knew about it, which was nothing more than they knew. I said, "Colorado Springs is a big town with a proper telegraph office and a fair number of rail lines. We should have some word from your professor or our boss about getting you two on a train with your equipment."

Travis did not seem convinced. We walked back to the livery to rig the wagon and horses. He said, "In the war, every plan I ever heard about fell apart before it ever got started. Looks to me like we're in the middle of a plan."

"Well, I assumed there were two possible plans: deliver them to Denver before the eclipse or get them on a Denver train somewhere between here and there," I said. "Either way, we'll see the eclipse somewhere along the way and get paid for watching it."

Travis rolled another cigarette and let me collect the tack and hitch the wagon. When I was finished, he climbed onto his seat and sat waiting and smoking while I saddled my horses.

We collected the girls at the cantina and rode out of town, which took but a second or two. We hugged the Little Fountain Creek on our left. A few hundred yards beyond the creek was the DRG rail line. Despite the water trickling down from the mountains, the land was purple sage and dry red sand, amongst which hid jackrabbits and prairie dogs and the occasional orange-faced prairie chicken. It was getting hot. Cora angled her riding hat against the sun. Elizabeth dug a green parasol out of her carpetbag and opened it up. Travis glanced up at its lacy pattern and bamboo handle but refrained from comment.

Cora, sitting in the wagon bed again, took a small brass telescope from her bag. She and Elizabeth took turns scanning the landscape and trying to get a view of Pikes Peak to the northwest. I rode up alongside the wagon and handed Elizabeth a pair of Army binoculars from my saddlebag. My father had carried them during the war. "Here, try these. You'll get a decent enough view of the land about."

"Thank you," she said.

About fifteen miles south of Colorado Springs, the Little Fountain Creek flowed into the larger Fountain Creek. The railroad track cut across the creek and the road, so now we traveled with the track to our right and the creek to our left. We stopped here to water the team.

I climbed off Blue; I'd been riding him since leaving Piñon. Cora wanted to ride again, so I handed her Blue's reins and cinched up Barley. I welcomed Cora's company away from the wagon and thought we might trot ahead or fall behind the wagon as the mood took us.

Settled on Blue's saddle, Cora scanned the pine-covered hills with her telescope. Finally, she focused the little scope on Pikes Peak with its persistent patches of snow and its long, narrow ridgeline. I came up behind her and she turned in the saddle to offer me the telescope. "Twist the outer adjustment screw to focus."

Turning the screw, I was rewarded with a crisp view of that towering pile of rock. "Excellent view, even from here," I said.

She asked, "Have you ever been up there, Mr. Carter?"

"Nolan. Mr. Carter is an annoying parent in Chicago. But yes, I was up there a year ago with my brother and a friend of ours. It'll take your breath away. Literally. It's over fourteen thousand feet."

"Nolan," she repeated as if she were tasting the name and wondering if she might try it again. "Well, Professor Cleveland Abbe is up there right now. He's the chief meteorologist for the Army Signal Service in

Washington."

Travis climbed back up to his seat, stuck his damaged leg over the footboard, and said, "We'll be getting to the Springs late as is." This was his way of saying, "Stop talking and start riding." Which we did. I tucked Cora's pocket telescope into one of my saddlebags.

Walking over to Barley, I said to Travis, "Go. We're right behind you." I swung up in the saddle, looked to Cora, and we started off behind the wagon.

The roadometer. I wondered if Elizabeth had checked it this morning before we started.

I glanced at Pikes Peak again and said to Cora, "This Abbe fellow, he's an astronomer too? Did he haul a telescope up the Peak? I don't recall the Army having one up there."

"Oh, yes. I'll bet he has the best view from that height. But I think most of the professional astronomy groups are headed to Denver. It's supposed to be a big town with plenty of accommodations and excellent rail connections. We didn't know about any railroad wars."

Before I could comment, she said, "But there are other academic groups scattered about the West. Henry Draper from the University of Pennsylvania is up in Wyoming with Mr. Edison. He—Edison—has a new invention called a tasimeter with which he hopes to measure the heat of stars."

The heat of stars? This seemed unlikely to me, but I supposed if anyone could do such a thing it might be Tom Edison.

"And there's James Watson from the University of Michigan. He's in Montana hoping to find the planet Vulcan during the eclipse. It's too close to the Sun to see except during an eclipse. Assuming it even exists. Do you know of Vulcan?"

I shook my head. "No, I have not heard of it before. I know of Mercury, Venus, the Earth, Mars, Jupiter, and…Saturn. And Uranus and Neptune. Do we need another planet?"

She threw a quick glance at the Sun and said, "Yes, because there's something wrong with the orbit of Mercury around the Sun. It isn't quite what the math predicts."

"Maybe the math is wrong?" It often is.

"No, the math is correct. Numbers don't lie. The orbit is wrong." She turned to me and asked, "Have you ever heard of Urbain Le Verrier? He was the director of the Paris Observatory years ago."

"*Je ne le connais pas,*" I said.

"*Oh, tu parles français?*" Cora smiled at me. "How delightfully unexpected."

I wanted to say, "Hey, I can read and write too," but the churlish urge came and went. She was calling me Nolan and using the familiar French "tu." The barriers of formality had fallen.

"It was French or Latin. Thought I'd run across more French-speaking peoples later in life than Roman priests."

"*Un bon choix.* Well, Monsieur Le Verrier, he discovered the planet Neptune. Guess how he did it."

"Big telescope?"

"No. Like Mercury, the predicted orbit of Uranus was not what astronomers were observing. So, Le Verrier, sitting at his desk, did some math and calculated the size and location of an unknown planet affecting the observed orbit of Uranus. And when astronomers looked again, there it was: Neptune."

That stopped me. The idea that someone could draw symbols and equations on a piece of paper and have a real planet emerge from those hand-drawn squiggles was something new. Was math a kind of exploratory science that could make real discoveries? Like chemistry or physics? Did this girl riding beside me know how to do such things? What else did she know?

"Well, that is a neat trick, to conjure something real out of...abstract numbers."

"Perhaps it means numbers are as real as the things they describe," she said.

This was getting too deep for me. Numbers were real only if they conveyed how many miles one had to ride or how many dollars one had in a bank account. Numbers, alone on a piece of paper...well, they were just invented symbols and swirls of ink and graphite. Were they not?

"Will you and Professor Mitchell search for this Vulcan planet too?"

"No. We're here to concentrate on the eclipse. Besides, I'm not sure Professor Mitchell believes there is another planet to spot."

Earlier, Cora had told me Professor Mitchell discovered a comet—its faint tail had been visible to anyone with a telescope and the patience to use it. Now, riding along behind the wagon, she told me the professor once worked for the Navy calculating the movement of stars and planets as an aid to navigation on the trackless oceans. She had the job of "computer" or mathematician for the *Nautical Almanac* and did calculations for the transit of Venus across the face of the Sun. Observations of the transit by different observers at different points on

Earth were then used to calculate the distance between the Earth and the Sun.

Cora tilted her Spanish hat back on her head and nudged Blue up alongside my horse. She said, "Professor Mitchell was in Iowa for the last total solar eclipse in '69, and just this May she photographed a transit of Mercury. Now we're all gathering in Denver for this eclipse."

"Busy woman. I suppose she keeps you busy too."

"Indeed, but it's fun." She looked over at me again and asked, "Have you ever read *Popular Science Monthly?* The Vassar Observatory contributes a regular astronomy column. So, anyone wanting to look for Jupiter some night or know what time the Moon will set can check our column."

Nodding, I said, "Sure. I read it sometimes for those controversial articles by Darwin, Pasteur, Huxley, Edison…"

How odd to think I might have glanced at the astronomical columns written by the woman now riding beside me.

Cora reined Blue and stared off to the east to watch three black-tailed jackrabbits sitting among clumps of shortgrass. "Isn't it strange to see three rabbits sitting together like that? What do you suppose they're doing?"

I glanced over. "Gossiping, perhaps. With those gigantic ears, imagine all the things they might hear during the day."

She laughed. I took a moment to study the happy, relaxed face of this woman who had come out here to watch an eclipse.

"You're not tempted to shoot one for lunch are you, Nolan?"

"At that distance, they're safe from me."

****

We rode on, getting dusty from the road and uncomfortable from the growing heat. Cora's brown riding clothes had taken on a tinge of red from the prairie dust. After a while, we caught up to the wagon. Travis had pulled into the scrub to let the horses drink from the creek. I expected him to complain that I should be riding point, checking the road ahead. Instead, he was sitting in the wagon with Elizabeth, staring at a magazine. He looked up at our approach and waved the publication at us.

"Got here instructions on how to see the eclipse." Travis waved the paper pamphlet in his hand and said, "Never imagined it to be so darn complicated."

Elizabeth said, "I was showing Mr. Travis the Naval Observatory's booklet on the eclipse and the best means by which to observe it safely."

"I've got a square of blue glass wrapped up in my saddle bag for Monday," I said.

"Me too," said Travis. He held up the booklet and said, "Lotta words here for a three-minute show."

Travis seemed to have come to terms with our "inconvenient" passengers. He was enjoying Elizabeth's astronomy lessons. Perhaps as much as I was enjoying Cora's company.

"Two minutes and forty seconds. In Denver," said Elizabeth. "It may seem a short time, but you'll remember it all the rest of your life."

"Our lives may be as short as the eclipse if we don't reach Denver with the telescopes," said Cora.

That was cold water in the face, but it was true. The clock—the celestial clock hanging over our heads—was ticking at an unstoppable pace. We had the telescopes,

55

but Mitchell and her sister had the optics. Neither party knew where the other was at the moment. And both parties would be disappointed if they did not meet in Denver before the appointed time when the Earth, the Moon, and the Sun aligned themselves in a movement that might be mathematical to the clan of science but would be magical for most of the people in its path, and perhaps a fearful reminder of how small all of us were before the silent, majestic workings of a greater Nature.

Word of the approaching eclipse first appeared in *The Denver Post* back in March of 1876. Since then, the *Post* and other Colorado newspapers regularly updated the literate public about the coming event and what to expect when it arrived. Published maps showed the route of the eclipse across the western states, and the swath of land—119 miles wide—that would be plunged into darkness as the shadow of the Moon spread across the plains.

I wondered what the illiterate locals would think. The lone woodsman high in the mountains who lacked any news? The single family out on the prairie? The Ute Indians up north? What would they think was happening? The end of the world? It might seem like it. The Earth inexplicably grown dark, silent, and cold. I listened to a street preacher in Colorado Springs tell a corner gathering it was God's preview of things to come.

Yet, towns and stations within the path of totality were filling with curious tourists and learned scientists. The tourists brought their pieces of blue or smoked glass through which to view the event. The scientists brought their telescopes, cameras, spectroscopes, and chronometers.

But for all the news and diagrams and explanations

of the eclipse, and the knowledge and technologies available to the scientists, when the darkness came, would we still feel a vestige of irrational fear? A fear not entirely extinguished by the reason of our modern world?

And I wondered how I would react when the Sun was blotted out next week. Would it be difficult to stand there on the open land, beneath the distant stars and planets, watch them in their eternal movements, and not feel a twinge of primordial panic at the sudden altering of the everyday world?

I would find out on Monday.

****

We reached Colorado Springs in the early evening. Travis stopped the wagon in front of the train depot. The telegraph office was next door. Elizabeth and Cora climbed down and went into the station house. I tied Blue and Barley to an iron hitching post.

"Well, I'll head over to the West Springs Hotel and see if they have rooms and storage for the telescopes," said Travis.

"Okay. I'll see if we can find our missing professor and then decide how to proceed with our passengers and equipment," I said.

"Ya know, we're not even halfway there and this little plan's already feelin' like it's at the mercy of crapshoot chance," said Travis. "Waitin' on trains that ain't comin.' Huntin' around for telegrams not sent. Or that we plain missed."

I didn't disagree. Not out loud. I lifted my arms and shoulders in a shrug, but otherwise avoided arguing the point. Travis gave me a look, flicked the reins, and headed down the darkening street toward the hotel.

The Sun slipped behind the mountains. The red rock

pillars of the Garden of the Gods faded into blue-black shadows. I stood by the horses, watching the last light of the day vanish behind the cold slopes of Pikes Peak and thinking Wednesday was ended.

Tomorrow, Thursday, we would either ride again or put our freight and passengers on the morning train. I liked riding with Cora. To tell the truth, I didn't want her to leave. But I wanted her to succeed and to see the eclipse with her telescopes and her friends. How could I make sure that happened?

Cora and Elizabeth came out of the station looking distressed. "But for the one we saw from the road, there has not been a train through today. There may not be one tomorrow either," said Elizabeth.

Cora said, "The railroad war is still on."

I nodded. I knew there had been no train. We'd been paralleling the track and even out of sight of the rails we would have heard a train or seen its smoke. "We'll go next door and see if there are any messages from the rest of your party."

They hurried down the sidewalk. I followed.

A lone telegrapher sat in the Western Union office. Cora asked him for any messages from Professor Maria Mitchell. He rooted through a small pile of half-sheets and said, "No. Sorry. No professors."

"Any mention of telescopes in the day's messages?" I asked.

Again, he flipped through the recent messages and said, "Just from the Army weather station on Pike."

The two women looked at me as if I might know what to do. I shrugged and said, "She's either back in Pueblo or ahead of us. Perhaps she's on the train we saw pass us at Piñon this morning."

"Well then, we should send telegrams back to Pueblo and ahead to Denver. Let her know where we are now. We can check in the morning for any replies. Then decide what the best course of action should be," said Cora.

"Seems reasonable," I said. There was, in fact, nothing else to do.

Cora handed Elizabeth a blank half-sheet and said, "Lizzie, write to the Pueblo Western Union for Professor Mitchell. Tell her where we are. The telescopes are safe. Ask what we should do. I'll write to Denver, care of Dr. Avery."

Cora took a half-sheet and pencil and asked the telegrapher, "Can a telegram be delivered to a Dr. Alida Avery at Twentieth Street in Denver?" She turned to me and said, "We're staying at her house."

"If it's urgent and you pay the charge," said the Western Union man.

"It is and we will."

They printed out their brief messages and handed them to the telegrapher. He read through both notes, made a change in word length here and there, and crossed out other words all together. Then he added up the cost.

Cora paid him. I stepped to the counter and asked, "Any notices come through about the train schedules? There should be a regular run north in the late morning."

"Haven't seen anything recent. But sure, the DRG schedule up and down has been hard to predict of late. Bunch of rich men arguing over who's gonna be richer. Makin' all the rest of us wait on the outcome."

"True enough," I agreed.

I opened the door for Cora and Elizabeth. They

stepped out to the still warm air of the evening. I told the telegrapher, "If there are any responses, we'll all be up to the West Springs. Name's Carter."

We walked up the busy street, dodging foot and carriage traffic. The dust and the crush of movement forced us up onto the covered sidewalks. At the big brick-and-stone hotel, we found a well-lighted lobby busy with guests and locals looking for an in-town dinner.

Travis had claimed the last available rooms, but he and the wagon were not about the premises. I assumed he had gone up the street to the livery we used when we were in town. Leaving Elizabeth and Cora at the front desk, I stepped outside onto the hotel's wide-planked porch. Hotel chairs were scattered about the porch, and I sat down in one to watch the evening activities of Colorado Springs.

After a minute, Cora appeared on the porch. She pulled an armchair over to my chair and sat. I straightened up in my chair.

"You look tired," she said to me. "It's been a long day riding in the heat."

I juggled my hat in my hands and said, "I'm not so much tired as I am worried about getting you and your gear up to Denver. Where's Elizabeth?"

"She's upstairs waiting for a pitcher of hot water and some towels. I need the same. I must present a fright after traveling all day."

I glanced at her pretty face and thick brown hair and said, "You look fine. A bit dusty, perhaps, but none the worse." In fact, in her company, I worried about my own appearance. Days in the same dusty, sweated clothes, unshaved, and beginning—I imagined—to emit an aromatic blend of man and horse.

"Thank you for that. And for worrying about our getting to Denver. It is important to be there. To be seen by the others and all the reporters. And to be seen as competent, capable astronomers with our equipment."

I tilted back against the wall and said, "Professor Mitchell said much the same about being seen in Denver. What's so important about being 'seen'?"

She leaned in my direction. "Oh, it's so important for women everywhere. All of us in school and studying the sciences. Have you ever heard of Edward Hammond Clarke? He was a physician in Boston. A few years ago, he wrote a terrible, outrageous book called *Sex in Education: Or, A Fair Chance for the Girls.*

I smiled at her and said, "I think we must travel in different circles. I don't ever seem to know any of the people you mention."

"In this case, ignorance of the man is bliss. His terrible little thesis is that too much education for girls is bad for their health, dooming them, in fact, to a lifetime of sickliness, and eventually dooming the human race to extinction by the decreased fertility of so many educated women."

She gave me a hard stare and asked, "Do I appear sickly to you?"

I had a vivid memory of her riding atop Blue and gracefully climbing in and out of the express wagon. "No. You look just fine to me."

Did I grin as I said that? I hoped so. I wanted to defuse her obvious indignation. But she took my statement literally and continued her angry history of Dr. Clarke.

"He's dead now, having himself lived a brief, sickly

life—perhaps *he* was too educated—but his thesis lives on. And too many people are eager to believe it and use it as a rationale for keeping women out of universities and medical schools and out of the sciences. It's hard enough to get through life on your own terms when so many barriers are put up before you. It isn't fair. It isn't right."

"This seems an easy enough notion to disprove," I said. "Aren't there plenty of university-educated women who married subsequently and raised children?"

"Yes, of course. We're not 'Vassar victims' succumbing to overwork and overstudy. Professor Mitchell's friend, Doctor Alida Avery, proved that after compiling and analyzing nine years of Vassar student medical records. And many other prominent women have responded to Clarke's book as being more about generating hysteria than providing quantitative evidence of his suspect thesis. In a word, the man is all nonsense. Two years ago, at the Woman's Congress, Professor Mitchell gave a very well-received speech about how important it is to have more women in the sciences."

I tipped away from the wall and said, "'The Need of Women in Science.' It was printed in the Chicago papers. I remember that. I remember the article because it was reported from Philadelphia."

"Oh, were you at the…?"

Travis' high black boots knocked on the porch. He came up to us and said, "The team's set for the night, and the hotel has the telescopes in the storeroom. Any news from the telegrapher?"

Cora and I stood up. I shook my head. "Guess we'll have to wait until the morning and see what comes over the wire or up the track."

It was dark now, and Travis took a moment to assemble another cigarette by the light of the hotel's glass doors. He looked up and said, "Gonna go over to Dan's Café for beer and beans. You gonna be up to the telegraph and the depot in the mornin'."

I wasn't sure whether he was asking, ordering, or simply stating an already established fact. "Yeah, I'll be up and around."

Travis nodded, tipped his sagging hat to Cora, and climbed back down the steps. We watched him limp across the street and disappear around a corner.

I said to Cora, "You and Elizabeth should get something to eat before the kitchen shuts down. We need to get an early start if the train doesn't come through."

"All right, then. Thank you for getting us this far." She stepped back into the hotel lobby.

I watched her walk away and wanted to follow after her. She was a curious girl. Woman. And not like any of the Colorado or Chicago girls I knew. Those girls were either frontier rough and often illiterate, or city-bred snobs looking to marry well and live better. Cora was college-educated, could ride a horse, do math on an astronomical scale, literally, and had willingly ridden off into the prairie with two strangers in order to deliver telescopes to waiting friends. She probably knew any number of famous scientists and equally educated men of her age and background.

What did she see when she looked my way? A dusty cowboy who hauled freight between local frontier towns? If so, that was a fiction she was seeing. But absent the horses and the guns, what was left to see of me or to admire?

I stood on the steps for a moment, looking at the

bright half-moon and listening to the people walking by. After a minute or so, I went in search of Travis and dinner.

Chapter 4

I was up before the sun, having spent a restless night with images of Davey and my brother, shiny telescopes, and idled trains. Also, Travis' snoring encouraged an early exit from the hotel room. The Western Union office was still closed, so I walked over to the livery and spent an hour harnessing the wagon team and then saddling my horses. I paraded them back up the street, stopping at the hotel to load the three crated telescopes, and then walked the team to the telegraph office. The door was open, and I found the same clerk from last night behind the counter gluing lengths of ticker tape to telegram forms.

"Any of those from a Professor Mitchell?" I asked.

He scooped up two telegrams and a mug of coffee from his desk. "Right here. Came in late last night, but I didn't see any sense in bothering anyone about them."

I snatched them from his thin-fingered hand and read through the contents. Mitchell and her sister were in Denver, having arrived there late on Wednesday. Two other Vassar alumni had joined them there, and now they wondered where Cora, Elizabeth, and the telescopes were situated. An immediate response was to be sent care of Alida Avery. I stuffed the telegrams in my vest, grabbed a message blank and wrote, 'All in Co Sprg. Details to follow. Cora & Liz.'

I pushed the message across the counter and said, "Send that right now," and headed for the door.

65

"You've got to pay for those and this," said the Western Union clerk waving the sheet.

"We've more messages to send. We'll be back to settle up."

I found Travis on the hotel porch smoking a breakfast cigarette and told him about the missed telegrams.

"Well, now, guess they should have all gambled on the DRG getting out of Pueblo. So, what's the plan now?"

"They up yet?" I inclined my head in the direction of the hotel doors.

"Yep. Just finishin' breakfast. Peculiar girls they are. I don't understand the half of what they're sayin'. Like they got their own private language or somethin'. Seems there are eclipses all the time, but most of them occur over the oceans. No one around to see them but the fishes."

I held up the two telegrams and said, "I'll show them these messages and see what they want to do. Would you go down to the depot for any news of another DRG coming through today? If there's a train they should get on it with the telescopes."

Travis pulled himself off the chair and stood up to flex his legs. "If there's a train and they can get a ride, what are you goin' to do?"

It was a good question. I had not thought so far ahead. "Me? Ride back down to Pueblo with you and the team, I suppose."

"You'll see the eclipse but miss the girl. You can see both in Denver." Travis smirked. After a moment, he turned away and limped down the steps.

Embarrassed by Travis' insight, I went into the

hotel, cut through the carpeted lobby, and headed down the hall to the rear dining room. Elizabeth and Cora sat at a table cluttered with breakfast dishes and notebooks. They waved me over.

"Good morning." I laid the telegrams on the table. "Professor Mitchell's in Denver." I sat down in the chair vacated by Travis.

Elizabeth snatched up the telegrams and read them out loud. I poured myself some warm coffee and picked up a stray piece of toast.

Elizabeth looked at me and asked, "What should we do?"

"Is there a train that will take us up today?" asked Cora.

"Travis is at the depot checking," I said. "If one stops, it might be best to get on board whatever the additional costs. You'll get to Denver in hours instead of days."

"We have little money to spare," said Cora. She whispered "Damn" and said, "The government provided funds to other astronomers—eight thousand dollars. And the railroads even sold some of them discount tickets to Colorado and Wyoming. But not a penny for us."

I didn't have any cheerful or clever answers for them. The three of us were silent for a moment, and then I said, "Train or wagon, you need to send some assurance to your professor about the telescopes arriving on time. Why don't we go over to the telegraph office, see if any news has come in, and then send a message off to Mitchell and company? And maybe Travis will have some news of the train schedule."

Elizabeth got up and said, "I'll get our bags from the room and meet you in the lobby."

I gulped another mouthful of coffee. Cora picked papers and a notebook off the table. A fat-looking wood-and-brass ruler lay beside her plate, and I picked it up out of curiosity. There were two internal pieces that slid back and forth and a series of scales that were not inches or the French centimeters.

I looked at Cora and said, "This is a very elaborate ruler."

"It's a slide rule. I use it for logarithms and trigonometry."

"I use my fingers. Toes too, if the math is really hard," I said.

She laughed at my poor joke. I handed over the mysterious ruler.

"Well, I can't very well unlace my shoes in public every time I need to do a calculation," said Cora. "And I don't believe you need to use your toes for any serious thinking."

"Is that what Monsieur Le Verrier used to find Neptune? A slide rule?"

"I'm sure he did. Professor Mitchell and her students, for example, used them in calculations of the transit of Mercury last May."

"You've mentioned transits a couple of times. Are they important in eclipses?"

"No. But they're critical to being able to measure the size of the solar system and the distance between the Sun and the Earth," she said. "Did you ever do trigonometry in school?"

"I doodled in some geometry for a year or two," I said.

She looked at me and said, "It's easier than you might imagine." She laid a piece of paper on the table and started to draw. "Imagine drawing lines on a piece of paper as big as the solar system," she said.

She drew three circles with two intersecting lines between them. The Sun, Mercury, and the Earth. "Now, if we have two observers in different locations on Earth, they will see Mercury move across the Sun's face, the transit, at different angles and times. And if we know the distance between the observers—we'll call it 'd' for 'distance'—then we use trigonometry to find the distance between Earth and, the planet Mercury. The triangle formed by 'd' and the two observation angles is an isosceles triangle. If we divide that triangle down the middle, we then have two right triangles, so we use basic trig to calculate the distance between the Earth and Mercury. Knowing this, we can then find the distance between Earth and the Sun. And then, using Kepler's Third Law, we can use this information to determine distances to the rest of the planets."

I sat back in the chair, amused at the math lesson and humbled by her easy familiarity with such complicated matters. She looked up from her drawing.

"I wish you'd been my math teacher in school. I would have tried to be a better student."

"Were you a bad student?" She gave me a curious look, as if she hoped for some unexpected revelation from me.

"I was a lazy student." Tapping her drawing, I asked, "Is this something that takes innate talent? Or is it a craft—something many people could learn to do through practice?"

"Well, I think it's a craft that may be taught to most people. But there are other people, special people, for whom this kind of thinking and calculating is child's play. They're the born geniuses of the world."

Cora looked over to the doorway and waved at Elizabeth, who had stuck her head back in the room. We stood up, and I asked her if I could keep the drawing of the transit.

"Of course." She picked it up, folded in half, and handed it to me.

"Thank you. For the lesson and the drawing."

I stepped away from the table and followed her back to the lobby to settle the two bills and collect the bags. Cora wore her riding clothes again, so there seemed a good chance she and I could ride ahead this morning and…what? Talk? Stare at each other? Or would there be a train today and then a goodbye wave from an open window?

Outside, I carried their bags, and the three of us walked around the corner and headed up a second street to the DRG depot office. The morning sky was a brilliant blue vault arching over the mountains and the town. A faint breeze—drifting down from the mountains—carried a hint of moisture. Patches of snow were visible on Pikes Peak and among the shadowy ravines of the mountains. Clean cold water would be pouring down the rocky slopes to fill creeks and streams all along the road and rail lines.

Travis and a few hopeful passengers stood around outside the office. We walked up. He lifted his palms. "No word of a train yet," he said. "Just headin' over to the Western Union."

"Oh, dear," said Elizabeth.

We followed Travis farther up the street—guided by the telegraph poles and the tangle of wires spread like spider webs between them—to the telegraph office and to where I'd left the horses and wagon in the reluctant care of the telegrapher. In the office, we found another telegram from Professor Mitchell asking of our immediate travel plans.

"What should we say?" asked Elizabeth.

Cora turned to the telegraph clerk and asked, "Is there any word regarding a morning train? Heading to Denver?"

"There's been no notice of one, or for that matter, of any routine train scheduling. I'm not sure what's happening," said the clerk.

Cora came over to Travis and me. "Should we continue on, then, or stay and wait for a train? Oh, this is so frustrating. The uncertainty of all this…"

I tipped my hat back and looked around the room as if the answer might be tacked on a wall. "I don't know. The train's a gamble right now. Your professor caught one, but there's no telling if you might do the same."

I looked at Travis, who didn't seem to have an opinion one way or the other. Turning back to our two passengers, I said, "The wagon will get you and the telescopes to Denver. Later than you want, yes, but you'll get there. That's the one thing we know this morning. What might happen this afternoon or tonight is anyone's guess."

The clerk said, "I could query the Pueblo office to see if a DRG is coming up this way."

"You should have done that first thing this morning, damn it," I said. I leaned on the counter. "Tell them we need an immediate response. We've got plans to make depending on what the hell the trains are doing."

The clerk asked, "Who's to pay for all this traffic on the wires? You already owe…"

"Just send the message." I fished a five-dollar Half Eagle from my vest pocket and smacked it on the countertop. "Start clicking."

While he sent the query sparking down the wire to Pueblo, the four of us stood against the wall of the battery room and tried to decide what to do and what to tell Mitchell.

It seemed obvious in the absence of a train today we should continue to Denver by wagon. But if the DRG sent a train to Denver, would they honor the AT&SF tickets the two women still were holding? Elizabeth had both of their tickets in her handbag. If Cora and Elizabeth needed to buy new tickets and pay additional freight charges, did they have the money? I already was offering my own money for telegrams here and there. I didn't have enough hard cash to buy train tickets too. Besides, what kind of freight business was I participating in if I helped the customers pay for the transport? I was sure Travis would have a comment or two about my unusual business acumen. And later, he did.

The telegrapher finished his message and sat at his station, chewing at a pencil and waiting for a reply from Pueblo.

"I don't know if Professor Mitchell can wire us additional funds for tickets," said Cora. "And would a train be willing to wait here for confirmation of that wired money? We have limited monies for this trip, but we have free room and board with Dr. Avery."

Elizabeth said, "Who would guess the eclipse might be the less dramatic part of our entire trip? Just getting to Denver now has become a nail-biting escapade."

I said, "We might continue up the road, and if a train does come along during the day, we could try to flag it

down. They do sometimes
such."

Travis leaned on the bac
resting on his good leg. "Lik
highwaymen and run right by

"With two women and a
robbers we'd be."

Travis pushed himself of
like on his good leg. "Now   ... idea for some
enterprising bandits: dressing like women to stop trains
and coaches. 'Course, they'd need to get off with a big
score to justify wearing bonnets and hoop skirts and all."

We chuckled at the image of desperados in dresses,
and I tucked the idea away until I could write to my
father again. It would be the kind of thing he'd like to
report in his newspaper—whether it ever happened or
not.

The telegraph came to life with a series of sharp
clicks. We all walked over to the counter to listen to the
metallic chatter. The clerk chewed at his pencil and
watched the receiver tap out its coded news. When the
mechanical chatter ended, he penciled a brief note.

He turned back to us and said, "Bit of a crew fight
in the railyard. There's no train been scheduled
northbound yet."

"Well, that's it, then." Travis left the office. I
watched him through the plate glass as he checked the
rig and started up a conversation with the wagon's two
horses.

"So, we'll have to continue riding," said Cora.

I nodded, still staring out the window. I turned and
looked at the two women. They were distressed. I
suggested they now send a telegram to Professor

73

g her we'd be late, but we'd be there. It
ensible to wait in town for a train that might

lizabeth wrote out a message which the clerk
ed to a manageable format before sending it to
Denver, care of Dr. Avery. He and Cora discussed the
bill for the messages; she picked up my Half Eagle to
give it back to me, but I waved it off and stepped outside.

Travis worked on another cigarette. He glanced up
from its construction to say, "I like Denver well enough
to keep rollin' up the road. 'Course, by the time we get
there, you may be short on cash. You know the idea
behind the freightin' business is to make money, not
spend it on the customers."

"You worry about your money. Let me worry about
mine." I walked around the wagon to check my horses.

I cinched up Blue and Barley. Cora and Elizabeth
came out, looked up and down the street as if they hoped
a train might appear magically from around the corner,
and then they climbed into the wagon. Travis noted the
odometer reading and checked the lashings for the
telescope cases. He climbed onto the wagon seat, said
something to Elizabeth, who was sitting beside him
again, and flicked the reins. We rode out of town with
me trailing Blue on a longline.

The sky was clear, and the view of the Peak and the
surrounding mountains was enough to make anyone
want to stop and stare for a while. Elizabeth and Cora
surveyed the range with Cora's telescope and my
binoculars. On a low mesa in front of the Rockies was a
jagged line of red sandstone spires and outcrops that
looked like a set of broken teeth. Cora asked about the
formation, and I, riding alongside the wagon, told her it

was an area called the Garden of the Gods.

"How poetic. Is it an Indian place? A sacred site?" she asked.

"No. Not that I know of. The Utes—a tribe in the Utah-Colorado border area—used to come here sometimes, but it was mostly to hunt elk."

Travis said, "Couple of surveyors, before the war, come through. One of them thought it'd be a fine place for a beer garden. Though who'd climb a mesa for a beer?" He looked to Elizabeth as if he expected a serious answer from her. "The other fella—he was the poet of the two—said it'd be a fit place for the gods to assemble. So, garden...gods...Garden of the Gods."

Cora smiled and said, "Elk or beer or gods, perhaps we should pray to all three for a speedy journey to Denver."

Everyone was silent for a moment. Praying, perhaps? If so, it was another disappointing reminder of how seldom one's prayers are received and granted.

****

Travis had ambitious plans for reaching Larkspur before it got too dark to see the road and its nighttime hazards. That was about thirty-two miles of travel. The road through this area was in good condition with few ruts or washouts or flashflood debris. Our wagon load was featherweight—we carried two slim girls and three tubes of thin brass. The horses were young and healthy. It did not seem unreasonable to expect we'd reach the town early enough to find a meal and a bed for our passengers.

We followed the creek and the rail line and passed through two empty towns. The railroad had left them off the station stop list and the miners who first settled here had since moved on. All that remained of once hopeful communities were clusters of weathered buildings and dry wells. If anyone still was in these almost vanished places, they did not show themselves, and we did not stop except to let Cora ride Blue again.

The creek twisted off to the east, and we found ourselves riding between rolling hills and stands of pine. We stopped in the shade of a cottonwood grove to take water and let the horses rest. Birds chirped among the tree branches, and I caught a flash of a fox's red-brown fur on the opposite hillside. Elizabeth climbed down to stretch her legs, and Cora swung off Blue to walk about and ease her own saddle pains. Ahead, the road curved sharply to the right, but a light current of warm air and the general topography of the spot brought to us the sounds of an approaching wagon. The horses' ears swiveled around at the sound, and then a single-horse wagon appeared.

It was a paneled patent medicine and eyeglass wagon. The driver—a salesman or perhaps a self-described doctor—pulled to a stop alongside of us. Bearded, bespectacled, and dressed in a garish checkered suit, he tipped his hat at the women. Travis and he conducted a brief discussion about the road ahead and behind. I eased Barley behind his wagon and came around on the opposite side of him. He mentioned a stagecoach he'd seen in the distance and which seemed likely to overtake him before long.

"Saw the tail ends of a couple of cows wandering up the hills. Loose or herded, I couldn't say," said the man. Then he gave a wave and headed off in the direction of the Springs.

A few minutes later, we saw an oncoming

stagecoach pulled by four big horses. Travis moved our rig to the right. The coach hurried by us, the driver giving us a wave, and his passengers looked out the windows at us. The coach line had a schedule to keep, and the driver seemed determined to hold to it. These were the only people we had seen on the road to date.

We rode on through the hot afternoon. Cora took to Blue again. Her wide-brimmed hat was pulled low to shield her eyes from the afternoon glare. Elizabeth made her way from the front bench to the wagon bed and Cora's usual seat on the folded tent and telescope case. Travis smoked an occasional cigarette and seemed content with the trip, the passengers, and the passage of time.

I watched Cora fiddle with the reins and then noticed the raw redness of her palms. "How are your hands?"

She raised one hand and said, "Too delicate now from holding too many pencils and pens, and too little riding. But they're fine."

I pulled off my riding gloves and handed them to her. "Here. They're a bit worn, but they'll stop any further chafing."

She reached for them, brushing my fingers with hers, slipped them on, and then laughed at the flaccid, unfilled fingertips. "Thank you. This feels better already."

"Good. One less pain on the ride to Denver."

****

The day wore on and the Colorado heat climbed toward intolerance. I unbuttoned my vest and loosened my bandana. My jacket was rolled and tied across the front of the pommel. I rode up alongside Cora and said, "I think Blue likes you." *I know I do.* "He may want to head back East with you." *I know I do.*

"He's a fine horse and an easy ride. I wish I had him in Kansas growing up. Or even last week in Kansas City. A quick ride would have been nice." She looked at the undulating knolls topped with pine and fir and the flat stretches of open scrub between them. "Can we ride up that way? Surely, we will not lose the road."

"No. We'll not get lost." I watched the wagon rolling up ahead. Usually, I ride close. Still….

"It would be nice to get off the road for a bit of sightseeing," I said. "Most trips, I have neglected the sights in favor of a fast run between towns. I don't suppose a quick detour will matter so much over the course of the day."

Travis and Elizabeth were ploughing up the middle of the road at a good pace. I rode up alongside the wagon and leaned in to tell them Cora and I were going to cut east through the woods, and we'd meet again farther up the road.

Travis stared straight ahead. "This ain't a Sunday jaunt." Then he moved his head like it was set on a swivel and looked at me from under the frayed brim of his sagging Georgia Boy hat. "How far east you ridin'? New York, maybe?"

Elizabeth giggled at the question and looked back at Cora where she trailed in the wagon's dust.

"Not so far as it'll matter to our time. We're in between towns. In between trains. In between telegrams. Half an hour won't matter at the end of the day. We'll ride fast to catch up if need be. Though likely we'll come out ahead of you."

Travis shook his head but held his tongue.

I pulled Barley away and waved to Cora. We peeled

off the road and trotted onto the Colorado plains, scaring up a prairie dog and some frantic ground squirrels as the horses thumped the dry ground.

We rode up a gentle slope of light brush and well-spaced pine trees. Under their aromatic cover the air was cooler and the bright afternoon light was filtered and diffused. It was quiet in the grove without the creak of the wagon and the regular impact of horseshoes on a well-traveled road. We let the two horses wander between the trees, giving them a slight nudge to the north and east now and then. We passed on opposite sides of an ancient bristlecone pine that now was a sun-bleached pillar of cracked wood, and I remembered something Cora had started to ask yesterday.

I pulled alongside Blue. "You were about to ask me about Philadelphia the other night? When we were on the hotel porch."

She turned to me with a smile. "Oh, yes. The Centennial Exposition. Were you there?"

"I was, but I witnessed no lectures about science and suffragettes. Too many other things to see and do and not enough time to see and do them all. But we did find time to see Bell's telephone machine and Edison's automatic telegraph. And my brother and I managed to down a lot of free root beer and popped corn."

"I saw those too. And the Corliss steam engine." She laughed and said, "My family and I waited in line in the agricultural hall to get a banana. By the time we received one, the hall had run out of plates and dinnerware with which to eat it. So, we shared a single fork. Did you ride the monorail?"

"Yes. An odd train. It might work for a big city like New York, but I can't see such a thing connecting cities or running across the states. Did you ride it?"

"Only once. In the early evening when it was not so hot," she said.

With that, she pushed her hat off the back of her head and let it slide down her back until the chin cord stopped it. She ran her fingers through her hair, and I watched, imagining those fingers were my own. A low branch ended my fantasy, and I refocused myself by asking about Mitchell and her "Women in Science" speech.

"It was after the Expo ended. At the Fourth Congress of the Association for the Advancement of Women. Most of her students took the train down from New York to attend the Congress," she said. "The point of her speech—well, you read it in the newspaper. Women have to be free to work outside the home. We need a 'fair shake' in the sciences. Personally, I think men are fearful of the competition. Bad enough they have to struggle for fame and fortune among themselves. Imagine if they had to struggle with women too. I should think the idea intolerable for most men."

She gave me a hard look. I found an unexpected fierceness in her stare. I knew what I said in response would affect things between us for the rest of the trip. And maybe beyond.

"I'm sure that's true. But Cora, I'm not in competition with you. I'm not a scientist or mathematician. I'm just trying to get you and Elizabeth to Denver to be 'seen' with Mitchell and the others."

No, I wasn't a scientist or mathematician. In fact, I had no idea what I was. Today, I was a faux cowboy with two horses, two guns, a little money, and fading chances of earning any more. And tomorrow? What would I be tomorrow? Sooner or later, I would have to decide.

"Well, thank you for that. And I hope you'll come 'see' us at work on Monday," she said.

"Yes, I'd like that very much. Perhaps you or the professor can tell me what I'm looking at when the full eclipse occurs."

Then she said, "Strange, isn't it, we might have walked right by each other two years ago in Philadelphia. And now here we are riding together through Colorado."

Maybe we had walked past each other in Philly. I had read about Mitchell's speech. And I sometimes glanced at the astronomy column Cora and her classmates wrote for *Popular Science Monthly*. Then the railroads stranded her right in front of me. Was the cosmos weaving a web pulling us toward one another? Chance is a funny thing. Ask any gambler.

I almost suggested these tenuous connections to her as evidence of a mutual destiny, but then thought better of it. She might think it melodramatic nonsense, or worse perhaps, she might pull out her slide rule and prove it mathematically unlikely. Which would be a worse response?

Heading north again, we rode on through the late afternoon. Overhead, a rich blue sky stretched from the mountains to the prairie's horizon. We crossed a rocky stream of sparkling water and stopped to let the horses take a mouthful. Beyond the stream, we headed up another timbered knoll. Chirping finches and warblers crowded the tree branches until a passing hawk silenced them. Near the top of the rise and sheltered by a thick stand of old fir trees, Cora pulled up Blue.

She glanced at me and said, "Would you mind a moment's rest? I'd like to soak my feet in the little creek back there. Only for a quick minute."

I hesitated, but then relented. "Sure. Soak away. But then we might have to trot the horses to the road and the wagon. Are you game for a little fast riding?"

"I think that should be fine," she said. "In fact, it should be exciting to do so through this lovely country. Perhaps a full gallop on the road again?"

"Well, okay then. I'll mind the horses here. They'll appreciate a minute's rest."

I swung out of the saddle and took the reins of both animals. Cora climbed down, hung her hat on a broken tree branch, and started down the slope with the grace of a deer gliding among the trees. I wondered what her legs looked like beneath her skirt and boots.

"Mind where you step down there," I called after her. It seemed safe enough. We'd just ridden through there, scaring off any vermin with the heavy thumping of shoed horses.

She disappeared between the trees. I eased the cinches on both animals and let them nibble at the brush and wildflowers. Groping around in one of Barley's saddlebags, I pulled out a hardcover notebook. Tucked in its pages was a pencil, and I sat against a tree to jot down notes about our trip, the missed train, and our flurry of telegrams up and down the wire. I stopped for a moment, thinking I might write something about Cora. But I hesitated to commit my thoughts about her to paper. Instead, I scribbled a reminder to send a letter home.

Everyone would be interested in the eclipse— Chicago was hundreds of miles from its path—and my father might use my notes and comments in a news story. Likely though, dear old dad the editor would add a lot of vibrant adjectives, imaginary quotes, and even a few tall tales about Denver citizens blinded by the mysterious light of the eclipsed Sun. He enjoyed coloring the otherwise black-and-white details of the daily news. I once suggested he take up fiction writing, but he insisted it didn't pay like the newspapers.

I dropped the pencil in the notebook. Then I walked over to my horse and tucked the book in the saddlebag. Through the trees, I noted the slant of the sun. I checked my watch. It was getting late enough that we should head back to the road.

Barley and Blue stopped eating and raised their heads. They looked down toward the creek, their corncob ears twitched around to catch some new sound. Big wet nostrils flared open at an unexpected scent. I stopped moving too and listened for what they were hearing. Then I heard a man's voice.

I stopped breathing and tilted my head to catch the voice.

A hunter? A miner?

I took a breath and started down the hillside after Cora. More voices. Then a laugh. Spanish words rolled up the hill and echoed off the tree trunks. I froze in mid-step. My raised foot sank back to the ground, and I touched the revolver at my side.

How many? No matter, this probably was trouble with one or two or ten.

I ran to Barley and yanked the Winchester from its scabbard. I levered a round into the breech and started back down the hill, moving from tree to tree.

Fifteen rounds in the rifle, five in my pistol. Another six on my belt.

I glimpsed the stream again. Three horses stood off

to the left. A light laugh and garbled Spanish words reached me. The tone sounded disarming. To me, it sounded deceptive—like a man with a hatchet tucked behind his back calling gently to a barnyard chicken—and it made me mad. I cleared the last bit of foliage in a rush and saw Cora. She was barefoot and standing beside the creek. Three vaqueros stood across from her.

Stiff brown sombreros, sheepskin chaps, and short-waisted deerskin jackets. Decorative silver conchos here and there, and three pistols. Real cowboys. Riding up from Mexico or Texas. They must have cattle around. And other riders. They were all easy smiles and light words and edging toward Cora, not wanting to spook her yet. I slid up against a thin birch tree about twenty feet from her, raised my rifle, and shouted, "Cora."

She spun around. Before she even focused on me, I yelled, "Grab your things and get up to the horses."

The three Mexicans saw me now. One of them was directly across the creek from where Cora stood. The other two were off to my right, standing close together. The one near the creek smiled at me and waved, but I was more interested in the other two.

Cora grabbed her boots and stockings and came my way. I didn't look at her, but when she got nearer, I said, "Up the hill. Get ready to ride." She hurried past me without a word.

The man in front of me stopped smiling and lowered his hand. His cover—Cora—was gone now, and he was the closest and clearest target. He knew it. Thirty feet from me, with me behind a tree, he wasn't going to pull his pistol yet. Not until he was desperate.

There was a long silence.

I suppose they were thinking about how to take me.

They weren't walking away, so it looked like someone would die here. And for what? Why? Why couldn't they just wave and ride off? No. They wanted Cora. I was in the way.

Chapter 5

I didn't have to think about our situation. I knew I was going to have to shoot them. I couldn't turn and head back up the hill. They'd start firing the second I moved to walk away. So, I kept to my narrow cover and keep my rifle trained on the two dusty vaqueros to my right. This was my ambush. It would play out my way this time.

One of the two men broke those seconds of silence with a smile and casual tone in his voice. I didn't understand what he was saying—my Spanish was limited to a few words about cows and beer and a few handy curses. But I didn't care what he said. I only cared that as he spoke, he took a step in my direction, blocking the right hand of his companion.

I shot him.

I hit him high in the chest. His legs collapsed under him and he went down like a scarecrow cut from its post.

I levered another round and aimed at the second man. When his companion stepped forward, he'd taken that little flicker of time to reach for his pistol. When his friend fell away, he already had his gun out of its holster and coming up fast.

I shot him.

I hit him in the shoulder. He twisted around from the lead slug's punch, and I shot him again in the upper back. I think he died on his way to the ground.

The first vaquero I shot moved on the ground. He was alive and maybe ambivalent about being so. He wailed and thrashed until a gagging sound stilled him.

I swung around on the third man. He threw his hands up and shouted at me. I had no idea what he was saying. I didn't care.

"Your pistol. Drop it. Pistol. Down. Bajo!" I shouted at him. Then I thought to shoot him and be done with it. I'd shot the first two. Why not three? I felt mean now. And safe. I had the upper hand here. I wasn't going to die.

But then he nodded his head like a charged telegraph key and said, "*¡Está bien! ¡Está bien!*" He lowered his left hand to his pistol. Like my own holstered pistol, his gun was on his left in a reverse holster. He eased it free with two fingers and tossed it on the stony ground. The vaquero stepped away from the abandoned gun and looked over at his two friends.

I moved away from my protective tree trunk and stepped onto the hard-packed bank of the shallow creek.

The man on the other side of the creek was young. Younger than me. His cattle drive beard couldn't hide his youthful face. He watched my approach, rifle at the ready. "*¡No dispare! ¡No dispare! No hicimos nada! Nada*," he shouted at me.

"*Cállate*," I said. Shut up. A handy word in this part of the world.

He shut up and stood still. I stepped into the creek, shuffled across the pebbled bottom and stepped up onto the opposite bank.

"Back up," I said and waved my rifle at him. He stepped back a few feet, and I stooped to pick up his discarded pistol. I tucked it into my belt and edged away, heading toward his two shot friends.

One was dead; a neat bloodless hole in the back of his leather jacket announced his status. I yanked the pistol out of his Slim Jim holster and stuck it in my belt. The other vaquero was alive—for the moment—and coughing up blood. His right arm seemed paralyzed, and his eyes were as wide as Half Eagle coins. I pulled his pistol with my left hand, keeping the Winchester steady in my right. His head moved.

Was he looking at me? Maybe. But I didn't care. He started this violent little dance, and now he had to pay the fiddler.

"It was me and Cora, or you and your friends. You lost, amigo," I said to his coughing face and staring eyes. I walked away. I slid past the first man again, holding my rifle with both hands. We stared at each other.

Their horses were three small, solid-colored animals. *Galicenos*, I think they're called. They carried charro saddles and rifles. I pulled the long guns, stacking them under my left arm.

Glancing back at the standing Mexican, I watched him edge toward his two prone companions. He put his hands down and dropped to his knees beside the wounded man. He cried out and repeated the same words over and over. I stepped away from the horses and placed the rifles on the ground. Then I yelled and waved my hands at them. They backed away. I fired two shots in the air. Spooked now, they bolted back up the creek to the road and the rail line. They ran past a couple of longhorn steers that now were wandering into this little ravine.

Cows. So, they're drovers. Up from Texas or the other side of El Paso? How many cows? They might have a chuckwagon. More riders with them?

I couldn't wait around to find out. I was lucky with these three. I couldn't keep trusting to luck. I gathered up the rifles again and splashed back across the creek. The bearded man kneeled beside his friend—or maybe he was a relative, a brother. In any case, he wasn't a threat now, so I hurried back up the slope without looking back.

It was slow going. I was carrying forty-five pounds of guns. I hoped one of them wouldn't go off accidently. It would be ironic to survive the Mexicans themselves only to get killed by one of their confiscated weapons.

I was breathing hard, and my hands were shaking. The tension of the encounter was wearing off, leaving only that afterward feeling of shaky cold and fear. A handy thing, that after-action fear. It should serve as a reminder not to do again what caused all the clammy fear in the first place. But it never seems to work that way. And now I wondered: *How did this happen? I just shot two men.*

I stumbled, looked up, and saw Cora coming toward me. Her sun-kissed face now was pale and grim-looking.

"Are you all right? The shooting..." She stepped back up the hill. I followed at her heels.

"I'm fine. The horses?"

She glanced back to me, looking like she was about to confess to some terrible crime.

"Blue. He's run off. He bolted at the noise of the guns. I couldn't catch him."

I let the rifles slip out from under my arm and looked around like a desperate man lost in the woods. "Damn that cowardly horse. I'm gonna find him just to shoot him." I looked at Barley. "Is he cinched?"

"Yes, I'm sorry. He's ready to ride. I was setting

Blue…he just ran," she said. "I'm sorry…for everything."

I thought of the three horses I'd just chased off. Damn it. Damn it all to eternal hell.

Gazing down the hill again, I half expected to see a horde of vaqueros charging at us. But there was no one to see and nothing to hear. I looked back at Cora. "It's okay. It's okay, but we have to go. Right now."

I handed my rifle to her, then picked up one of the Mexican rifles and slid it into the scabbard. I gathered up the other two and lashed them to the back of the saddle where my duster was rolled. Then I dumped the three confiscated pistols in a saddlebag and strapped it shut. Barley was a four-legged armory. I looked back at Cora. She had my rifle in one hand and her hat in the other. I took back the Winchester.

"Hop up." I caught her booted foot in my hand and helped her swing up to the saddle.

She looked down and asked, "What about you?"

I searched among the trees and down the hill. "I'll guide."

I took Barley's reins and led him and Cora through the trees and brush. We climbed a little higher in among the trees and turned south and east. I wanted to put distance between us and the Mexicans and whoever else might be near the road.

"The road is behind us."

Cora had a good sense of direction. But then someone who knew the planets and the stars like she did wasn't likely to get lost on a clear day in Colorado.

Not looking back at Cora, I said, "There may be more of them back that way. They may be pushing cattle along the road. Easy ground and water for a chuckwagon. May still be another rider or two, or more, with them."

"What happened…down there?"

I glanced back at her and said, "Later. Right now, we need to put some distance between them and us."

****

The ground flattened out, and I guided us between lonely trees and scattered boulders. We were getting farther from the road. I wasn't sure which was the best direction to head yet. Back near the road we might run into more drovers. But riding across the prairie would take us farther from Travis and Elizabeth. Going north, on a parallel track with the road and the rails, seemed the best course until we were clear of any Mexican cattle drive. Whichever way we chose, I couldn't walk the whole way. Time was as much an enemy as any cowhand we might meet. It would be dark soon, and the prairie night would present other problems.

I pulled Barley over to a pile of half-buried rock. I hopped up on the mound and said to Cora, "We should ride now. Put some distance between us and the drovers and catch up with Travis and Elizabeth. But first we need to repack this poor horse."

I untied the two rifles and my duster to make room behind the saddle for Cora. Then I got my jacket from the pommel and slipped it on.

Cora watched me shuffle the guns and gear. "Should we leave the other guns? Four seems too many to carry."

I nodded. "It does, but they may come in handy if we run into anyone else out here. They're expensive, too. It would be throwing away good money." I glanced her way. "Which we will do if we absolutely need to."

I wrapped the two rifles in my duster and tied the

awkward bundle under the pommel. Barley was patient enough with this repacking. Then I asked Cora to slide back off the saddle and onto the back edge of the blanket and the saddlebags. The seat was free now. I picked up my Winchester, swung a leg over the top of my steady horse and settled on the saddle. We were ready to ride. I pointed us north and west, and we headed through the late afternoon prairie.

Cora was quiet through most of our jog away from the creek and the drovers. Now she put her gloved hands on my shoulders, and she said, "I'm sorry."

I reached up to her left hand and said, "It's not your fault. It was theirs."

"They appeared…so unexpectedly. And right away, they seemed too friendly. Smiling faces, but they felt…wrong," she said. "It's my fault you had to shoot."

I wanted to stop. I wanted to take her in my arms. Comfort her. But this was the wrong time and definitely the wrong conversation for such a bold act. Instead, I replied, "They were looking for trouble. They found it. It's not your fault. It's not my fault. And it's over. We needn't worry anymore about it." But I wondered if we did.

****

We chased the last rays of the prairie sun as it sank behind the mountains to wash the western slopes with warm summer light. We rode back into a stretch of rolling land with a gurgling creek. The shortgrass and brush got thicker. I wondered if it was the same creek we'd left earlier. Ahead, I spotted a dozen longhorn steer taking advantage of the water and the grass. We'd ridden farther and faster in the direction of the road than I imagined. We stopped near the wandering cows.

"Cora, can you dig my binoculars out of the right saddlebag?"

"Yes," she said.

I felt her move away from me to root through the leather bag. After a moment, she passed the glasses around to me.

In the growing darkness, I searched the area for riders. I didn't see anyone. I didn't hear anyone, and Barley was not reacting to the scent of other horses. These longhorns must have wandered off. There might be either a single Mexican left alive to tend to them or a few others busy with their dead and dying friends. We probably were safe from any further encounters.

Cora whispered, "Do you see anyone about?"

I gave her back the binoculars. "No. I think it's only us and the cows."

I nudged Barley. "Listen, I'm going to scatter these beeves. If anyone is riding out this way, I'd rather they spend time rounding up stray livestock than tracking us. Let's keep the Mexicans busy and then be on our way."

With that, we rode toward the cattle. I kicked a boot free of its stirrup. Mindful of the six-foot horns on these creatures, I worked my way close enough to give one of them a good kick. It bellowed and hurried away. I pushed us in among them and made as much noise as I dared, kicking any animal that came within range of my boot. They didn't like my horse or the noise, and after more bellowing, they trotted off in different directions— anywhere away from my boot and my horse. Pistol shots would do a quicker job of scattering them, but the noise would carry. I didn't want to attract the attention of anyone looking for these longhorns.

With the cows scattered, I turned away and pushed

Barley hard to put more distance between us and the creek. Cora wrapped her arms around my waist—a pleasant spark of energy ran through me.

After a short burst of speed, Barley slowed to a walk, burdened as he was with two riders and too many guns. The sun was gone now. A few bright stars were out in compensation of the lost light. The light breeze ended. The prairie was fast giving up its daytime heat.

I said to Cora, "You'll have to be my navigator now. We should be heading north."

"We are."

We rode in silence—hooves and the creak of the saddle the only sounds. Later, a coyote barked off in the distance and broke the quiet of our passage.

Cora placed her hand on my shoulder again, and asked, "What happened down there? I heard the shots. I was so worried. You. Alone. Against those three men."

"They didn't give me a choice." Even now, thinking about it, I was shocked at the suddenness of it all. And the pointlessness of it. They could have mounted up and rode off. Instead, they decided they'd kill me and take Cora. "I shot two of them," I told her. "One's dead. The other…possibly."

"I'm so sorry," she whispered.

"It wasn't your fault. It was them. It was their choice. And they chose wrong."

"Should we tell someone? A sheriff or the Denver police, perhaps?"

"No. Not immediately anyway. Maybe I'll have a word with a sheriff I know back in Pueblo. He might be interested. Otherwise, I think you and your friends should do what you came out here to do and not get caught up in some big investigation or news story. We're

94

in the right. No drover back there will be coming to charge us with a crime. That's not how things work out here." I twisted around to look at her and said, "This isn't New York or Boston."

We rode for a while, lost in our own thoughts. I didn't know what Cora was thinking about, but I kept imagining how things might have gone if... If this or if that. I envisioned a dozen scenarios in which I was dead and Cora was taken. But I shot first. I won. It's done.

Cora leaned out and around to ask, "What of Elizabeth and Travis? They'll wonder what's become of us."

"I'm sure they are wondering. But I expect Travis will push on to the nearest town and wait for us, thinking we're off seeing the Colorado sights or something."

Likely, he's stewing and muttering about the fragility of all preconceived plans. I'll never hear the end of this.

"Are we going to keep riding? Can we find the road or a town?" asked Cora.

"I hope we can. We should hit the road soon," I said.

But I wasn't sure where we were. Back on the road with Travis and the wagon, we'd passed the pond known as Palmer Lake and then the remnants of a town called Divide. Were we still near Divide? Or did we ride far enough north to find the almost abandoned town of Greenland, the next town before Larkspur? Any town, with however many inhabitants and amenities, would be welcome at this point. I was worn out. Barley needed a rest. Cora, I'm sure, was tired—more likely traumatized—from the day's deadly events. And where was Travis and the wagon? By now, Elizabeth might be worried too. She'd be on a dark road, in the middle of nowhere, with a strange man. Travis would keep his head. I hoped Elizabeth would do the same.

I untied the canteen from the saddle and passed it back to Cora. We rode by an abandoned house and a lean-to stable. I considered stopping there for the night, but I imagined Cora would be nervous—for all kinds of reasons—about doing so. It was tempting shelter, but anyone else passing by might have the same idea. I didn't want any late-night visitors. We rode on. She handed the canteen back to me, and I drank the last mouthfuls of our water.

We struck the road again. But riding on the road wasn't much better than traipsing through the prairie given the darkness. In the distance, the glint of steel rails reflected the light of the quarter Moon. A line of slender telegraph poles stood between the road and the distant rails and faded away in the gloomy distance. I wished I could tap those copper wires hanging between the poles and call for help.

"We're back on the road," I said to Cora.

"That's good, isn't it?"

"Well, it means we know where we are again, more or less," I said.

She surprised me by shaking my arm. "The Palmer House. The Chicago newspapers. An annoying parent in Chicago. You're from the city. What is a man from Chicago doing on a horse in dark and dangerous Colorado?"

"Playing cowboy. Rescuing damsels in distress. The usual dime novel stuff," I said.

"Yes…thank you for that. But seriously, how is it you're out here and not back in the city living a more…comfortable life?"

"Oh, I don't know. Youthful adventure, perhaps." An easy, empty lie. I did, in fact, know. Well, I thought I knew.

"Ishmael went to sea," she said.

"Look where that got him—floating in the middle of the ocean on someone else's coffin."

I had Davey's coffin. And my brother's accusations. "Besides, Chicago doesn't have an ocean. I couldn't have sailed much farther than Wisconsin or Canada."

"Did you have adventures here in Colorado? Without a white whale?"

Did I? No. Stepping back now to take a long view of things, no, it wasn't adventurous at all. Not in the storybook notion of fun. It was long weeks of grueling work. Then an ambush. And a murder. Now this. Whatever this turned out to be.

"No whale. Just out here to see the elephant. That's the expression, out here to see what's what. See the frontier before it's all fenced in and cut up into farms and towns."

Cora asked again, "So, did you see your elephant?"

I told her about the cattle drive.

****

The high school teachers confirmed we had little more to learn from them and so they set us loose upon the adult world. We were not ready for that world. Instead, we enjoyed the frivolities of the city and paid for those amusements with sporadic employment at my father's newspaper, the *Chicago Daily Tribune*. We traveled here and there, safely attached to the city by the lengthy umbilicals of the railroads. But in those travels we looked more and more to the West and to the stories and photographs from that tantalizingly close frontier.

Eventually, we went.

Davey, Brian and I took the train to Denver. Davey, watching the passengers come and go from station to station, observed the population of travelers was getting younger. The farther out we traveled, the fewer gray-haired men we saw. By the time we reached Denver, no person onboard was older than forty. Did the elderly avoid the frontier territories, or did people not live as long in the western regions of the country? Perhaps we should have given Davey's observation more thought before alighting on the Denver platform.

We arrived looking like "Eastern dudes." Even we knew we looked "wrong" for this part of the world, so we set about blending in with the locals. All three of us hurried to buy sturdy clothes and riding boots. I found us three saddle horses in a public corral between East Denver and the South Platte River. We paid a good price for them and somewhat less for three used cavalry saddles. A gunsmith sold us three used Winchesters. We contemplated buying revolvers to fully arm ourselves, largely against our own imaginations, but the gunsmith discouraged the purchases. He pointed out, correctly, that for one, we did not know anything about revolvers, and we each might therefore be a menace to ourselves and each other; two, the Denver police discouraged the carrying of concealed weapons within city limits; and three, the effective range of the pistols was only about forty feet, even for an experienced shooter. The Winchesters would keep trouble farther away than any pistol. It was sensible advice, and we held to it for some months. Later though, Brian and I went "full Western" and bought two pistols.

In the spring of 1877, we rode south with no

particular destination in mind, watching railroad tracks being laid as we wandered and stopping in towns both prosperous and dying along our route. We passed through Pueblo, heading to Colorado City, and thinking we might wander into the New Mexico Territory. In a café south of Colorado City we fell into conversation with a trail boss moving cattle up to Denver. He was looking for riders for the drive north, and we were looking for something to do.

We had no idea what we had signed on for, aside from twenty-five dollars in pay after we reached Denver. We knew the trip north was a bit less than two hundred miles—an easy enough ride—but we did not know eleven hundred longhorn cattle only moved twelve or fifteen miles a day. It would take at least two weeks to push them to the Denver railhead which, ironically, would deliver them to the slaughterhouses in Chicago. Riding out to the herd, we soon discovered we had been hired to replace three colored drag riders who had had enough of moody cows and alkaline dust and headed off to look for something better. Now the drive consisted of four Negros, two Mexicans, a Texan who wasn't happy about the company he was forced to keep but kept his mouth shut about it, four other white men, and three city boys who were clueless about what they were doing.

Eleven hundred cows, and the horses needed to herd them, made up some forty-six hundred hooves that filled the air with endless clouds of fine prairie dust. As drag riders, we were stuck behind the herd, watching for bovine stragglers, and being coated in choking layers of fine prairie dust. It settled on clothes, horses and saddles, and crept through our damp bandanas to suffocate all of us. We stayed mounted all day and sometimes into the night chasing cows, looking for cows, rescuing cows, and counting cows.

A few days of dust and uncooperative longhorns and we were on the verge of quitting, pay or no pay. But then one of the swing riders and the wrangler—the guy who took care of the *remuda* of reserve horses—were both killed in a lightning storm while they rode through open country. I was close enough to one of them to have felt the energy of the lightning bolt wash over me. After the scattered herd was pulled back together and the dead men were buried, the trail boss elevated us to the exalted status of flankers and swing riders. It was less dust, but the same long hours in the saddle. Thanks to the *remuda*, our horses got a regular reprieve, but the riders did not. And it was the same bad food, snakes, ticks, hailstorms, wolves, river crossings, and every other kind of inconvenience one could imagine. We reached the Denver stockyards. We took our pay and took our leave of the cattle business.

We came to Colorado to see the West, and we saw an important part of it. Davey, being an optimistic companion, insisted someday we would look back on the drive with fond memories. I didn't think I'd live long enough for it to happen. Davey didn't.

****

"So, you were a real cowboy," said Cora. "It sounds…awful. I'm sorry. It's not like any of the stories I've read in the newspapers and magazines about working and living out here."

"Nothing's ever as good as it sounds from a distance," I said.

Then I told her about the ambush in the Colorado foothills last month.

She was quiet for a while. Then she leaned against me and whispered, "You're very lucky to have escaped. I'm so glad. And now you're alone in Colorado. Will you go back to Chicago after this?"

Was I lucky? I didn't feel lucky. Yes, I'd survived the cattle drive and the ambush and the vaqueros this afternoon. How long could a person blunder from one danger to another before he ran out of...luck? I didn't believe in divine intervention or my own invincibility. And Chicago? Right now, it didn't even seem like a real place.

I was riding a tired horse in the dark and undecided about what to do. Keep riding? Stop and camp in the open? We seemed to be getting farther from Denver, not closer.

I reined Barley to a stop, tilted my hat back, and looked around at the dark scrub and the mountains to the west. It was quiet. There was no wind.

Cora shook my shoulder. "There's a light off to the right."

I looked to where she pointed and saw the faint flicker of a campfire about two hundred yards from the road.

"Should we ride out to see what it is?" she asked. She was animated by the sight of the fire and the possibility of friendly company.

I was more suspicious. Not many people choose the prairie to camp when they might find a town with an available bed. That's what I was aiming for. But then a town seemed less and less probable tonight.

"Could you pass me the binoculars again? Let's see who might be there."

Cora retrieved the glasses, and I focused them on

that bit of firelight in the distance. I saw the contained flames, and in the background, a wagon. Then a figure in a dress walked in front of the fire. A woman. The sight was reassuring. Few bandits or homeless drovers traveled with women, though Travis' idea of stagecoach robbers dressing up like women came to mind. Then, for a moment, I wondered where he and Elizabeth might be at this hour.

I passed the glasses back to Cora and said, "A woman walked in front of the fire. They might be homesteaders. Or a small wagon outfit out of Kansas or something."

"Should we ride over and inquire about them?" she asked.

No one likes strangers riding into their camp in the dark of night to make inquiries. But the company of others seemed better than riding and walking through the night or sitting on the open ground to await the dawn. We had no food or bedding. Either way, it would be a long night.

I said, "Yes, but we need to be cautious about approaching them. It's dark. They don't know us, and we don't know them."

I moved us off the road toward the distant fire. About halfway there, we stopped, and I climbed out of the saddle, careful not to knock Cora to the ground. I looked up at her. "I'll lead Barley close to the camp and then call out to them. If things take a turn for the worse, just ride out of here back to the road. Head north. You'll hit a town sooner or later."

"And what about you? I can't leave you here."

"Yes, you can. I've my rifle and pistol. It's dark. I'll be fine." I looked around and said, "I won't be happy about it, but I'll be okay. I'll get back on the road at some point."

With that, I picked up the reins and led Cora and the horse toward the fire.

Chapter 6

We were close now. I counted three men, two women, and maybe two kids. A short wagon covered over for sleeping and a loaded buckboard were stationed off to one side. I saw some mules farther back. They began to shuffle on their tethers. We stopped. They had caught our scent. Their owners would notice in a second or two.

I called to the camp. "Hello, the camp."

From my vantage point outside the circle of firelight, I watched everyone stop for a moment. Then one of the men ran to the wagon and snatched up a long gun. He stayed on the other side of the fire and called out, "Who's out there?"

"One rider. One on foot. Can we come in?"

"Take your time 'bout it."

Shapes and shadows gathered behind the voice in the camp. I spun my rifle around, so the stock was pointed forward. I jingled Barley's reins and we stepped into the flickering light of the campfire.

Their camp was on flat, open ground. I stopped a few yards from what was a cook's fire with a kettle of stew hanging above the flames. Off to the side was a covered pot and a covered frying pan set on a large flat stone. Beyond the fire was a group of dark-skinned men and women.

They stared at Cora in her Spanish hat and riding

clothes. I glanced back. Even tired and dirty, she was a striking sight in this middle-of-nowhere place.

The man with the gun broke the spell of surprise and said, "Whacha wantin' here?" He stepped closer to us and I saw the double-barrel shotgun he held. It appeared old, but at this distance it surely would kill me.

Brief is best in most situations, so I said, "We're lost." I looked back at Cora and then said, "We need a safe place to sleep. And some food."

One of the other men said, "Fairly demandin' for a beggarman."

"We can pay."

"How much?" asked one of the men.

I held up my rifle—the barrel pointing down—and said, "I've got three good long guns and two pistols you can have." I might need that third pistol for Cora.

I walked around Barley and helped Cora climb out of the saddle so she would not get tripped up by the Mexican weapons lashed to the front of the pommel. She straightened up, looked around, and then said hello to the homesteaders on the other side of the fire. A young girl standing near the buckboard gave Cora a cautious wave.

I passed my rifle to Cora. Everyone seemed to relax a little now that I wasn't holding it. I untied the two rifles and pulled the third one from the scabbard. Cradling the weapons, I stepped around the fire to the three men on the opposite side.

They were dressed in rough-spun clothes and old shoes in need of a cobbler. One of them wore a straw hat. Another man wore an old bowler perched far back on his head. The man with the shotgun was bareheaded. He had a messy beard and badly cut hair. Maybe he had a run-in with the Pueblo guy who shaved and cut my hair.

I held up the Mexican guns and said, "Two Winchesters and a Henry." I moved to hand them off but stopped in mid-step.

Two Winchesters and a Henry? I remembered the piles of shells left at the nighttime ambush where Davey died. Shells from a Henry rifle and more from a couple of Winchesters. Was this a coincidence? Or were the men who ambushed us the same ones who tried for Cora this afternoon? Colorado is a huge place, but there aren't all that many people in it yet. It could have been them, heading out to a drive or leaving one and taking their time heading home.

Today, the vaquero kneeling beside the first man I shot...what was he saying? *Otro*? No. *Otra vez*. "Again." In cafes, sometimes I would see a Mexican hold up a glass and say to the bartender or the server, *Otra vez*. Again.

What did *otra vez* mean today? Brian or I must have hit one of the ambushers. There was a yelp in the woods and blood on a rock. The first man I shot today, was he the same one we hit in June in the foothills? The sheriff never heard from any doctor about a gunshot patient. That bushwhacker either died or recovered on his own. So, was the young vaquero lamenting his friend getting shot *otra vez*, again? An amazing coincidence, if true. And maybe justice served. For Davey and for Cora.

"Sometin' wrong?" asked the man with the shotgun.

I focused on him again. "No. I was just reminded of something." I held up the rifles, and the two unarmed men took them from me.

"They're loaded." I walked back to Barley and opened the saddlebag. I got the Mexicans' pistols and walked back to the three men who now were occupied in examining the rifles. The old shotgun lay at their feet.

I held up the revolvers. "Two Smith & Wesson .44s. Be careful. They're loaded too."

Another man stepped up to take the pistols. The bearded man who had been holding the shotgun looked at me and asked, "You always travel so gunned up?"

I shook my head. "No..."

Cora stepped up beside me and said, "There was some trouble on the road."

"Three vaqueros wanting to make trouble." I glanced at Cora. Then I waved my hand at the guns and said, "They were reluctant to give up their guns. But I insisted."

I left the story at that. Sometimes less is more, and I let them imagine how I might have taken five guns from three drovers.

"You've got $150 worth of guns there. Will that buy us dinner and a place to sleep?"

A woman in a tattered skirt of blue and green stripes, her black hair loose, walked over. "And breakfast too." She smiled at Cora and said, "We got a jackrabbit stew, beans in molasses, and fry-pan cornbread. Much the same come mornin'."

"That sounds wonderful," said Cora. "I've not had rabbit since I was a child."

I agreed. It might have been rattlesnake stew. Stringy jackrabbit sounded just fine.

"Is there water about?" I asked.

One of the men used his new pistol to point beyond the buckboard. "Back thataway. Nice little spring."

"Thanks. We could use a cool drink." For some reason, I reached over and took Cora's hand. She was surprised but didn't pull away. The two of us headed around the buckboard, trailing Barley.

We cleared the camp and she asked, "Was it wise giving strangers all those guns?"

"Normally, no. Never. But we don't have much money left, and the horse can't keep carrying all that weight. Besides, those are probably the first real guns those men ever held. They're more likely to shoot themselves or each other than shoot us." I was parroting the Denver gunsmith who had discouraged my brother and me from buying pistols last year.

"You took six guns from those men," said Cora. She looked over her shoulder at the camp. "The other pistol…"

"…is for you. In case we get separated," I said.

I stopped and turned to her in the dark. "Listen. That gun. If there's trouble, just pull it out and pull the trigger. Don't wave it around trying to threaten someone. No one out here is intimidated by that." I mimicked someone holding a gun with two hands. "Two hands. Pull the hammer back. Pull the trigger. No one will blame you or charge you for shooting someone. You're on the frontier."

I hoped she was convinced of the necessity of maybe having to use the pistol. I didn't know how else to emphasize my point, so I just stepped closer and said, "Please."

She pushed down my hands holding the imaginary gun. "Let's not get separated."

Ahead, water bubbled over rock. A pool of shallow water emerged from the rocky ground and ran off in the dark. I looked at Cora and said, "Careful where you step."

I eased the cinch and bridle on Barley and let him at

the water.

Cora looked up at the starlit sky. "Where do you suppose Elizabeth and Travis are now? Professor Mitchell must be worried sick. For us and the telescopes."

I untied the saddle canteen and dug an enamel cup out of one of the saddlebags. "Travis'll keep his head. He knows the road. He's got a shotgun. He'll get Elizabeth and the telescopes to Denver. By train or road. Now we need to worry about getting you there."

"It's more important the telescopes arrive," she said.

I looked at her. "Not to me."

I wondered if she blushed in the dark. But then she said, "Thank you, but I'm only half the agreed-upon freight. There're the telescopes and Lizzy to be delivered."

"Travis will get it done."

I filled the cup upstream from Barley's greedy slobbering and passed it to Cora. Then I filled the canteen, drank half its contents, and refilled it. I handed it to Cora and rooted through the saddlebags for my camp lantern. I struck a sulfur match from my vest pocket. The oily wick took the match flame, and I slid the front panel closed and flipped up the lens cover. A bright yellow light emerged. I held the wire handles and waved the light around the spring looking for any nighttime creatures not already scared off.

"That's a convenient little light to have," said Cora.

"Good thing it wasn't in Blue's bags. Of course, he still ran off with my clean shirt and socks and a few other useful things."

Lamp in hand, I rooted through the remains of my belongings to find a rough hand towel, a soap tin, and a small packet of Bromo Paper. I handed these things to Cora along with the lamp and said, "The area's clear of any pests, so you may want to stay here a while and…freshen up. If you want." I pointed back to the camp and said, "I'll be just up there by the buckboard."

"Thank you. That would be a welcome diversion." She shined the lamp across the scrub and rock and said, "I'll be back in a moment."

I took up Barley's reins and led him back to the homesteaders or settlers or whoever they planned to be. Along the way, I diverted into some waist-high scrub and unbuttoned my pants. Travis' regular benediction—I'm irrigatin' the prairie—came to mind as I did the same. The irrigation continued for so long Barley got impatient.

****

At the camp, I pulled the McClellan and blanket off Barley, hobbled him with a short line, and left him to munch away at the available foliage.

The man with the bowler hat came up to me. He had an old face, but what looked to me to be a young body ready for any kind of work. He asked, "Where the lady?"

"Washing up at the spring."

He pointed to the buckboard, saying, "She can sleep there. Some those sacks make a good 'nough bedding. There's no room in the covered. You her husband?"

I shook my head, wishing I was. "Just a hired hand getting her up to Denver."

"How come you're on one horse? Hard way to travel."

"We lost the other mount dealing with the Mexicans."

He glanced at the pistol grip protruding from my

jacket. "They all dead?"

"Two of three," I said.

"That third fella…he comin' lookin' for you?"

"He's minding cows and burying the dead." I hope.

Bowler hat looked at me, nodded, and walked away.

Now I wondered if there was cause for concern. We found this camp easily enough. Might someone else?

Their fire began to smoke, and the smell of green cottonwood trying to ignite drifted my way. A light moved beyond the wagon and Cora reappeared. I met her at the buckboard. Her clean face shone in the flickering light as she said, "No bandits."

"Good. We're running out of horses." Bullets too, truth be told. Blue had run off with the box of cartridges that fed both my guns. I pointed to the flatbed wagon. "Your bed awaits. You can sleep on the wagon. It'll keep you off the ground. I'll be right underneath, so you've nothing to worry about but a bit of snoring."

"Bunkbeds. More or less. Won't you be uncomfortable on the ground?" She bent down to look under the wagon.

If only that was an invitation. "I've my duster to spread out and my jacket for a blanket if there's a morning chill. We'll ask about a spare blanket or canvas for you." I took off my jacket and tossed it on the buckboard. Cora placed her hat and my trail kit on the wagon too.

The little girl appeared beside us. She stared at Cora for a second and then said, "Mama says suppa's 'bout ready."

She took hold of Cora's hand and led her to the campfire. It surprised me. I followed, thinking, Hey, the handholding is my job.

Some planks were set atop two boxes and some grain sacks to make two benches. An old milking stool stood beside the ring of stones that contained the cooking fire. The three men sat, admiring their new weapons, but stood up when we approached. It was time for introductions.

I stepped up beside Cora and said, "Thanks very much for your help tonight. My name is Nolan Carter. I'm from down in Pueblo. And this is Professor Cora Harrison all the way from Vassar College in New York." Cora glanced in my direction, but I continued. "She's come out to Colorado to observe the eclipse with other famous astronomers."

They all looked baffled by my announcement. The other woman, older and dressed in gray and dirty white, stirred the stew and asked, "What's aclipse?"

And here it was: An actual example of people out on the prairie, lacking news, almost certainly illiterate, who were going to be shocked, if not terrified, by the spectacular darkness that would occur on Monday afternoon. How would they have reacted? Dropped to their knees and prayed? Hidden themselves under the wagons, wondering if the Sun and the light would ever return? I'd given them guns to defend themselves against the everyday dangers of the frontier. Now, perhaps, Cora might give them a bit of knowledge against the primitive fear of the unearthly spectacle to come.

Cora stepped around the edge of the makeshift bench and sat down. "Eclipse," she said. "An eclipse is when the Moon gets between the Earth and the Sun and creates a shadow. On Monday afternoon, when the Sun is still out, the Moon's shadow will turn this whole area dark as night."

They looked at her as if she had flown into their camp on a broomstick.

Cora must have sensed something similar because she turned to me and asked, "Do you have something to write on?"

"I do." I walked back to the buckboard smiling. Professor Cora was about to launch into another lesson on mathematical astronomy. I'd had my lesson this morning...

This morning? Was it still today?

So much had happened today it now seemed more like a week since Cora had waved her slide rule at me and drawn diagrams at the hotel breakfast table. This was the longest Thursday of my life. Tomorrow was Friday, and Denver was still a distant goal. I opened a saddlebag, pulled out my notebook, and walked back to Cora's circle of new astronomy students.

I flipped to a blank page at the back and handed her the book and my stubby pencil. She took them, looked around, and moved over to the milking stool. "The light is better here," she said. They gathered around her, leaving me out of the circle of spectators. I tilted my head back to look at the bright stars sparkling between thin wisps of gauzy clouds. Did anyone know how far away the stars are? I'd have to ask Cora.

She was drawing on the back page, saying, "This is the Sun, and this circle is us, the Earth. Now on Monday, this circle, the Moon, is going to move in between the Sun and the Earth, and block some of the Sun's light."

I leaned in and watched her draw a quick triangle between two circles, the Moon and the Earth, and shade it in with the pencil.

"The Moon will make a shadow on the Earth." She

pointed at the sky. "Right above us. This entire area will become dark for almost three minutes. Then the Moon will move away, and the Sun's light will return. Monday afternoon. That's..." She looked at me.

"It's still Thursday, believe it or not."

She turned to the wide-eyed faces around her again and said, "In four days. Tomorrow is Friday. Monday will be the solar eclipse."

Her audience seemed incredulous. The two women made signs with their fingers. Were they warding off Cora's hand-drawn black magic?

The man with the straw hat asked, "This ever happen before? Folks woulda said."

"The last eclipse in this part of the world was in 1869. Nine years ago," said Cora. "The next one in the Colorado region will be in 1889. Eleven years from now."

Straw hat looked to me and asked, "That true?"

Probably he imagined there was a hierarchy of authority and knowledge in the world—and for the most part, there is—white men, followed by white women, and then everyone else in no fixed order. I shrugged my shoulders at his question and said, "She's the one who knows these things."

The little boy who was standing behind the woman with the tattered skirts peeked around her and asked, "Gonna be scary when eclipse come?"

Cora smiled at him. "No. It will be dark only for a couple of minutes. Then the world will light up again."

The woman made another sign with her fingers and said in a nervous voice, "Well, we got a supper here for all who's hungry."

Thank the gods and the stars and the coming eclipse.

I was as hungry as that stewed rabbit probably had been earlier in the day.

She served up two plates of food to the young girl, who then handed them to Cora and me and invited us to sit. For some reason I felt a momentary twinge of guilt at being served first, but then remembered I'd paid over a hundred and fifty dollars in guns for these plates of campfire grub. I dug in. Cora waited until the three men received plates and had taken seats on the benches. It seemed everyone was hungry, and the meal was eaten in silence. The older woman announced there would be coffee soon, and I nodded my thanks to her.

I finished my plate and glanced around at our company. I almost laughed out loud imagining my high-minded, often pretentious mother appearing in this prairie camp to find her oldest son in the company of Negros and a woman who was not his wife. She'd swoon. And how would she react to the news that earlier in the day her son had shot two men and thought to shoot a third man for no particular reason? I had wandered into a life in Colorado she would not have been able to comprehend. Best not ever tell her any of this.

The three men finished their meal. The bearded man looked over at me and said, "That's a fine gun belt there. Have to get me one of those now." He smiled his chewing-tobacco teeth at the idea and said, "Name's John Lincoln, by the by."

"Mr. Lincoln." I nodded, thinking he'd given himself that name about fifteen years ago.

Straw hat introduced himself as George Stevens; the wearer of the bowler hat named himself Williams. Whether Williams was a surname, a given name, or some truncated version of a whole name, he did not say, and I did not ask. The little boy said, "I'm Daniel." In response to his declaration, I reminded him I was Nolan.

"That's a funny name ya got," he said.

The younger woman—Lydia—shushed him.

"It means noble." Though I was feeling and looking far more common than noble.

I turned to Cora and put my hand out for her empty enameled plate. "I'll take that for you." She surrendered the plate and spoon, and I said to the woman by the fire—her name was Magdalene—"I can take these to the spring for washing."

Lydia said, "No, no. Jenny here do that. She know how to clean up the dishes."

I handed Jenny our plates and spoons. The others followed suit. Soon she was struggling with a messy pile of plates in danger of toppling over. Catastrophe loomed. But then she lowered the pile into a weathered wooden bucket.

Before she walked away, I said, "Wait a moment. I have something that will help."

I retrieved my lamp, relit the wick, and then showed her how to hold it so she wouldn't burn her hand on the top vent. Now, bucket in one hand and lamp in the other, she walked by the string of mules and down to the spring.

I looked back at Cora; she was leafing through the pages of my journal. I sought to take it from her, embarrassed at the opinions she might have of my scribblings.

She looked up and said, "You've done quite a bit of writing and sketching here. What is all this writing intended for?"

"Reminders of things," I said. I held out my hand for the book and she surrendered it with a mischievous look about her.

"Am I a reminder among those pages?" she asked.

"Between the shooting and the stampeding and the riding, there hasn't been a quiet moment to do any recording."

I felt awkward under her gaze but was saved from saying anything foolish when Magdalene declared the coffee was almost ready. I walked over to the buckboard with my notebook and pitched my saddle and bags under the wagon. I pulled some half-empty sacks into the shape of a bed on top of the wagon and laid the horse blanket on top of them. If Cora could get a blanket from our hosts, she'd have a decent enough bed for the night. Done with making up Cora's bed, I walked into a batch of stubby grass to check on Barley. He was still working on his dinner and did not seem inclined to wander too far. I gave him a pat on his flank.

I returned to the campfire. Cora was telling our hosts something about the stars. I looked up at the sliver of the Moon. Almost a new Moon. Time was ticking by. Still looking at the night sky, I found myself wishing for an hourglass-shaped constellation to remind all of us of the relentless passage of time. Maybe we'd pay more attention to the details of our lives if we had such a celestial timepiece hanging over our heads every night. I sat down and Magdalene handed me a cup and then poured thick coffee into it.

"Thank you."

"Tain't got no sugah," she said.

"This is fine." I took a cautious sip and was reminded of Mrs. Sullivan's morning jolt back in Pueblo.

Cora stood up and suppressed a yawn. I walked over to her and said, "I made up a bed for you on the

buckboard. It's not much, but it beats the hard ground."
We walked over to the wagon and I showed her what I
had done.

"One other thing." I pulled a pair of low-cut
moccasins out of the saddlebags and handed them to her.
"Bought these from a Navajo woman in New Mexico
Territory. I started sleeping in them on the trail
after…June. It's uncomfortable sleeping in boots you've
been wearing all day and hard on the feet if you have to
get up and move around at night in only your socks."

She took the sheepskin shoes and said, "They're
light. And soft. I have your big, floppy gloves; now I
have your big floppy shoes. Do I get your big, floppy
bandana next?"

Before I could form a clever reply, Lydia appeared
beside me and said, "Got this ol' quilt for your missus.
Got no stuffin' left, but it's warm night."

My missus.

Cora thanked her. I took the quilt and handed it to
Cora. Lydia walked back to the campfire, and I said to
Cora, "Here, let me help you up. It's been a long day,
and it'll be a short night. Best try to get some sleep."

I helped her step up from the back wheel. She settled
herself on the sacks and untied her riding boots. I wanted
to say, 'Let me do that,' but instead I said good night and
walked back to the campfire.

****

I returned to my coffee cup. The women were
settling the two children in the canvas-covered wagon. I
was left with the three men, two of whom were re-
examining their new rifles.

"So, where are you coming from?" I asked.

John Lincoln said, "Come outta Kansas City. Gettin'

crowded there. Too many white men with guns and laws all their own." He looked at me without blinking.

The law, in all its manifestations, was creeping westward. "You staying in Colorado? It's a state now, not a territory."

Lincoln said, "Headin' down New Mexico way. People say lotta red and brown people down there. We'll hardly be noticed." His companions chuckled.

I nodded and said, "Yes, there are a lot of tribes in the New Mexico territories. And a lot of Mexicans. But you'll also find plenty of Texans driving cattle up through the territory and the occasional group of pilgrims—European immigrants mostly—wandering about."

I had come across a family of Ottoman Turks on the other side of the New Mexico line. How they got to New Mexico from the Holy Land, and why, was a mystery, but there they were: settled in the American desert. Maybe it looked like home. Swedes were settled in Colorado and the surrounding territories, and I read Englishmen were buying ranches in Montana and Wyoming. There were so many Germans in Denver that German was now the third most common language after Spanish and English. The West was welcoming people of every stripe and tongue.

This particular group of people had been pushed— more likely they ran—from the old Confederacy. Now they were being pushed west. If they reached California, they'd find more of what they'd been running from in the first place. Driving all the way into Mexico might help. But how welcome would they be among the Indians and Mexicans and the mestizos on the south side of the Rio? Maybe more so than here in the States. There would always be hatred here because no one can abide the constant reminder of one's past crimes when the victims of those crimes are before you every day.

What if Travis the Southern soldier were here with me? How might the conversation go with these men?

I finished my coffee. The last mouthful was still warm but full of grounds. "It's been a very long day, so I'll say good night to all of you. And thanks."

I got a nod and a wave from them and walked back to the buckboard. Cora was on her side, facing away from me. She appeared to be asleep. I stared at her covered back for a second, trying to imagine me lying there beside her.

I found the canteen and rinsed the gritty coffee grounds from my mouth. Then I kneeled down and spread my duster on the ground and pushed the saddlebags into the rough shape of a pillow. I took off my gun belt and covered it and myself with my jacket. I kept my boots on.

****

We were among strangers. Now armed. The prairie's nighttime denizens—coyotes, snakes, and bobcats—would be out tasting the cooler air. The only warning of their presence might be the snort of a nervous horse or mule. My nerves were frayed from the long ride and the gunfight with the drovers, and now my imagination added to my nervous state. I rolled onto my back and checked that my pistol's trigger was buried deep enough in the holster that I might not shoot myself during the night. I closed my eyes, determined to relax and sleep.

For a while, I did. But something jerked me awake. Drovers' leering faces and the sounds of gunfire followed me from a troubled sleep to a fitful waking. I found I had a death grip on my holster. I took a deep breath and relaxed my hands. Lying still, I listened to the sounds of the prairie and the thumping of my heart. An owl hooted in the distance. I caught the sleepy shuffling of the mules beyond the other wagon. I stared up at the cracked framing of the buckboard. Rubbing my eyes, I turned my head to look out from under the wagon.

Cora stood off in the distance.

Chapter 7

She was a shadow against the brilliance of the late-night sky. The Moon was gone, leaving overhead a bright beach of sparkling lights and the wispy white froth of the Milky Way. I watched her raise an arm to the sky. Then she moved her arm a little to the side. After a while, she extended both arms outward to form an angle. It looked like she was talking to the stars with sign language. Curiosity got the better of me, and I rolled out from under the wagon and walked over to her. She turned at the crunch of my boots on the dry grass.

"Isn't it lovely?" she asked.

I stopped and looked up for a long time.

She brought me back to Earth.

"I was practicing some ancient astronomy. The Greeks and the Babylonians didn't have telescopes or slide rules, but they had fingers." She raised her arm, pointing at the Big Dipper, and spread her thumb and pinky to their limits and said, "That's about twenty-five degrees. The distance between Alkaid, the first star on the Dipper's handle, and Dubhe, the top star forming the cup. From Dubhe up to the North Star is about twenty-eight degrees."

I mimicked her pinky and thumb sign and said, "My hand is bigger than yours."

She whispered, "Well, you can calibrate your big fat fingers by remembering the degrees between the Dipper stars or to the North Star."

I laughed at her critique of my fingers and then remembered we weren't alone on the starlit prairie. "What are you doing awake? You shouldn't be out here alone. Some wolf will come along and that will be the end of Professor Cora Harrison."

"Why did you tell them I was a professor?"

"I don't know. Maybe the same reason I let them imagine I was an experienced gun hand. Safety in status? It doesn't matter. We'll be on our way in a few hours. Of course, the point of stopping here was to get some sleep, not watch the night sky."

"The stars woke me." She laughed quietly at her own silly response.

I moved closer, slowly, as if drifting on a warm prairie breeze, and kissed her.

And she kissed me back.

I had a sudden vision of us riding off in the night: to hell with the eclipse and Professor Mitchell and Travis and all the world.

She stepped back, flashed a wide grin, and said, "You were right. A wolf came along and got me."

For a second, I was tempted to toss back my head and howl, but it would wake the camp and beg any number of odd questions from our hosts. Instead, we stared at each other for a moment that seemed eternal, and then she said, "We should get some sleep. Like you said."

"Pay no mind. I give terrible advice." Now, I wanted to stay up with her.

She took my arm and leaned into me. We walked back to the buckboard. I helped her back up. Barley hobbled into the camp. I glanced his way and put an index finger to my lips. He snorted and looked off in the direction of the spring.

Cora pulled up her quilt and rolled away from me. "Good night, Nolan."

"How am I going to get back to sleep?" I asked her covered back. I made a show of straightening her quilt. Reluctantly, I bent down and rolled back under the wagon. I lay on my back, thinking about her lips. Then I wondered what time it was. My watch was in my vest pocket, but I made no effort to retrieve it. The hour didn't matter. I knew it was Friday. Time was slipping away.

****

Somehow, I fell asleep again. The rest of the night was undisturbed by apparitions of Mexican gunmen or Babylonian astronomers. I woke to the sounds and smells of cooking. The sun was still resting on the distant horizon. The early morning sky was a layer cake of red, orange, purple, and darkest blue. I crawled out from under my dusty bed. Cora was still asleep. I stumbled to the campfire, arthritic and tired, and wanting a hot bath.

I sat down on the bench and said good morning to Lydia, who was busy with the coffee pot and a covered pan of biscuits.

She looked over at me. "Mista' Carter, good mornin' to ya. Ya look like the hard ground got the better of ya. Coffee almost done."

"It's early yet. I may recover."

Noises emerged from the covered wagon. The kids got up. The three men crawled out from under the wagon in unison and began sorting themselves out for the day. Lincoln waved my way, and I returned the early morning salute.

Lydia handed me a plate of suppertime beans and

hot brown biscuits, and a short cup of coffee. "That fer your lady now."

I got up—painfully—and stumbled back to Cora's wagon. She stirred at my heavy-footed approach. I put on a cheerful face, held up the plate and cup and said, "Breakfast in bed. What more could you ask for?"

She was wide awake and swung around to prop herself against a small wooden box. Her feet in my oversized moccasins looked like two boneless rabbits dangling over the side of the buckboard.

"Well, this is a treat. A hot breakfast. Could you now, Nolan, arrange a hot bath and a change of clothes?"

"Sadly, no. Not yet. I need the same myself." I handed her the plate and placed the cup beside her. "I'll be back in a while. Don't go wandering off to study the sky or wash your feet or pet a rattlesnake or do anything likely to summon *Eris*."

She turned a mischievous smile on me. "I am too hungry to wander at the moment," she said, and sipped from the battered tin cup.

****

I joined this odd family group of mismatched men, women, and children for breakfast. The beans and biscuits went down quick, and then I lingered over the black coffee—taking a moment to again curse Blue for running off with my little satchel of sugar, among other things.

George Stevens, sitting across from me, asked, "So, you goin' nawth to Denver for that eclipse thing? On one horse?"

"We'll strike the road again and head up to the nearest town. I'd like to get Cora, Professor Harrison, on a train as soon as possible."

"Ain't seen a town in some time now," said Stevens. "Supplies gettin' low." He glanced at the covered wagon.

I looked off in the distance and said, "Those rifles you have now. You might hunt up a pronghorn or a deer. There's plenty about. And if you were to head south a few miles, on those mules, you might scare up a stray longhorn steer. Some drovers got their cows scattered yesterday. Those beeves might still be wandering around the plain."

John Lincoln said, "Them owners might not take too kind t'us turnin' one them cows to steaks and stew."

"True, but it's possible there aren't many of them in fighting shape. And you have maybe half their guns."

He seemed to consider the idea and then picked up the Winchester I gave him and said, "How many bullets in this gun?"

"No idea." I walked over and asked for the rifle which he handed over. I grabbed the lever and said to him, "Catch."

I worked the lever back and forth, popping cartridges out of the breech. The last one ejected. Lincoln picked a few stray bullets off the ground.

"Got ten here," he said.

"It holds fifteen," I said.

I picked a bullet out of his cupped hands and slid it through the gate on the side of the rifle in case he didn't know how to load it. I handed it back and let him load the remaining nine bullets. "Maybe those vaqueros didn't have much ammo."

Cora appeared beside me, said hello to everyone, and then asked, "Can I borrow your things again? To wash up at the spring."

"Of course." I rubbed my bristled face. "I should do

the same."

I sat back down near the fire. The men peppered me with questions about the road south and the towns of Colorado Springs and Pueblo, and beyond, into New Mexico.

After I answered their questions, I said, "Listen, if you're headed that way, you might keep an eye out for a mustang wearing a McClellan saddle. Like the one I'm using. His name is Blue. He's my brother's horse. If you find him, and you're near a town, would you leave him at the livery and send me a telegram?"

Lincoln said, "Got no money for the telegraph."

"I've got enough to pay for a short message."

George asked, "How you know we don't just head out with your horse and money?"

I shrugged. "I don't. But some nosy lawman might want to know why you have a horse with Denver markings and a saddle with my brother's initials on it."

"Fair point," said George.

"If we see this horse along the way, what kinda message would we say?" asked Lincoln.

The little boy asked, "Does he bite?"

"He's usually too scared to bite." I stood up. "I'll get some money and write a note you can give to the telegrapher."

I walked back to the buckboard and picked up my saddlebags. My journal and another book were missing. "Damn that nosy girl." I started for the spring.

I found her sitting on a boulder, leafing through the pages of my notebook. She looked up at my approach, amusement on her face, but not a trace of guilt.

"Ah, the thief is found," I said.

"Nolan, you're quite the writer. These are some

wonderful observations and sketches of Colorado." She gave me a look and said, "There's not much, however, about our current travels or about the eclipse. And nothing at all about me. Do you need a quote, perhaps?"

She was laughing now, and I extended my hand for the notebook. "We need to get going. This isn't the time for games."

She closed the notebook and handed it to me but held on to it with a firm enough grip that I had to tug it from her tight fingers. Then she picked up a small, hard-bound book.

"And what's this? Late-night reading around the campfire? Thoreau's *Walden*. You've marked up a perfectly good book with lots of little notations and penciled lines."

I held out my hand for that book too. She twisted away and read aloud: "'I went to the woods because I wished to live deliberately, to front only the essential facts of life, and see if I could not learn what it had to teach…'"

"Are you living deliberately, Nolan?" she asked with a light laugh.

"Yes, deliberately. Until just a few days ago."

She read another passage I had underscored. "'If a man doesn't keep pace with his companions, perhaps it's because he hears a different drummer. Let him step to the music which he hears, however measured or far away.'"

"What do you hear, Nolan?" She sounded serious.

I moved close enough to ease the book out of her hands and said, "Woman, I hear the ticking of the clock. I hear a train whistle in the distance. And I hear your professor jumping up and down, anxious about her telescopes."

"You have excellent hearing. Now tell me about the drummer you've been listening to."

She had me smiling now. "Later." I offered a hand. She took hold and I helped her off the rock she was sitting on. "We need to get going," I said.

It was fully light now. She stopped by the spring to pick up my soap and towel. Then I guided her back up the path to the campsite. She was kicking up dust, and I looked down to see she still wore my oversized moccasins.

Ahead of us, something moved in a clump of sage. I jerked Cora to a stop.

"Wait." I fumbled my books into my left hand and pulled my pistol.

"What's wrong?" Cora asked. She looked around the ground in front of her.

"Rattlesnake." I pointed my pistol at the sagebrush.

Under the shade of the bush lay a coil of reptilian poison.

"Don't move." I eased back the Colt's hammer and leaned toward the bush. An agitated rattle tried to warn me off. At a distance of five feet, I couldn't miss. I pulled the trigger. The snake jumped at the impact; Cora jumped at the report. The long, fat reptile undulated violently. I went in for another shot and cut it in two with the second round.

"Come on." I pulled Cora to the left, and we hurried away from the dying snake.

"How did you see it?" Cora asked.

"I was looking around. It moved its head. Lucky for us."

Aside from test-firing the Colt after I bought it in Colorado Springs, I had never had a reason to fire it until now. George Stevens and Williams appeared on the track, rifles at the ready. I waved to them and shouted, "Rattlesnake."

The four of us walked back to the buckboard. Cora stopped to put on her boots, and I walked back to the campfire bench to scribble my note about Blue. I handed it to Lincoln, along with a dollar. Another dollar gone.

"Just give this note to the man at the telegraph office. It says, 'To N. Carter 1st Natl Bank Denver. Blue at X.' The 'X' is for whatever town you find yourself in. A dollar should cover the message. If you find him."

John Lincoln looked at my note, folded it in half, and stuck it in his shirt pocket. He didn't say whether he could read it or not. I handed over the dollar, and he dropped it in with the note.

"Okay. If we see this horse needin' a rider. And we come cross a telegraph town."

Cora appeared in her boots, her hat, and my gloves.

"I'll saddle Barley and pack up the bags, and we'll be on our way." I gave her a look and wagged my index finger hoping to convey a silent message: *No lectures, no quizzes, no wandering, no anything. Just sit there and wait for me.*

Barley looked content. Moving around him, I rubbed my hands up and down his legs, feeling for cuts or swelling. Yesterday had been hard on him too. I gave his shoes a quick inspection and then saddled him. I loaded my kit, my lantern and books, and my moccasins, and strapped the bags to the saddle. Sliding the Winchester back into its scabbard, I said to Barley, "A lighter load today. The armory's gone." I gave him a pat and led him over to the campfire.

I found Cora giving a public lecture about the

coming eclipse. Everyone was in attendance and seated on makeshift pews to hear Cora's secular sermon delivered on the morning prairie. Cora held a stick in her hand and had drawn circles in the dirt to represent the Earth, Moon and Sun.

She said to them, "Even if you leave here and move south, even as far as Pueblo, you'll still be in the shadow of the Moon and will be able to see the total eclipse of the Sun. Be sure to stop somewhere on Monday afternoon so you can watch. It will be the most amazing thing you will ever see. For a little more than two-and-a-half minutes, the whole world will change, becoming dark and silent, and a little colder."

She was an enthusiastic preacher of her science, and she held the attention of everyone in the camp. I could have ridden off in their wagon and they wouldn't have noticed. Cora looked over at me and waved her improvised pointer.

"Enjoy the eclipse. But remember, don't look at the Sun until it's completely covered by the passing Moon. It's bad for the eyes."

"Can ya be blinded by the 'clipse?" asked George Stevens.

"No. That would be unusual. But you can damage your eyes permanently. So, only a quick glance now and then and wait for total coverage of the Sun before you take a longer look at the phenomenon," she said. "That will be the best sight: Once the Moon fully blocks the Sun and allows its corona—the fiery crown of the Sun—to appear."

Cora looked to me. "Nolan, can you spare two blank pages from your notebook?"

I tilted my hat back on my head and nodded. "Sure."

We weren't going to get away yet.

I unbuckled the bag and pulled out the notebook. I flipped to the back pages, past Cora's earlier drawing of the eclipse, and teased loose two white pages.

"Does someone have a sharp pin or a small nail?" she asked our prairie hosts.

Lincoln got up and stepped to a wooden pannier on the side of the wagon. He returned with a small carpenter's nail. Cora took the nail and punched a neat little hole in the center of one of the pages. Then she took the second page, placed it on a smooth bit of ground and weighted it down with four little pebbles. She stood up and turned her back to the rising Sun.

"This is a pinhole projector to watch the solar eclipse safely. Turn your back to the approaching eclipse. Hold up this piece of paper with the hole in it so the Sun hits it. An image of the Sun will appear on the paper on the ground. You may have to move it up and down to get a well-focused image on the ground page," said Cora.

She moved the page up and down to demonstrate focusing the pinpoint projector. "As you watch, the circle of light shining on the ground page will turn from a solid circle of light to a crescent shape and then to a thin ring of light."

She picked up the sheet of paper from the ground and handed both pages to Jenny. "Keep these safe and clean until Monday. You don't want to hurt your little eyes."

The girl asked Cora, "How you get ta know about the stars and Sun and such?"

Surprised, Cora hesitated for a moment and then said, "Well, you have to go to a school to learn reading and writing. Then later you go to a bigger school to learn all about numbers."

"It hard?" she asked, still holding the two white pages.

"No. But it takes a long time. And lots of practice."

The show over, I decided it was time to leave. "Cora. We need to ride," I said.

"Yes, of course." She looked at her class and said, "Thank you for everything. I hope you enjoy the eclipse on Monday."

She picked up her riding hat and my gloves and stepped away from the dying campfire. Cora placed her hat on her unbrushed hair, and I helped her up onto Barley. She settled herself behind the saddle and put on the gloves. She wasn't holding any reins this morning, so I wondered for a second why she put the gloves on. I pulled on my jacket and adjusted my holster.

I looked at the group of people before me and said, "Thanks for the camp and the meals. Best of luck down New Mexico way. And remember, keep an eye out for stray cows." Which was my way of saying, 'Keep an eye out for my horse.'

I had a boot in the stirrup but then I stopped. Stepping around Barley, I opened the other saddlebag. Inside was a large bandana protecting a small square of eclipse glass. I unwrapped the blue-tinted glass and handed the bandana to Cora.

"Folks," I said, "Here's something else for the eclipse. You can use this special glass to look at the Sun too."

I handed the blue square to Williams and said, "Some of you can try the pinhole paper while others are looking through the glass."

Williams looked at the small square and then held it up to the morning sun. He closed an eye and squinted through the blue tint. "Still bright," he said.

"Don't look too long, even through the glass," said Cora.

I gave a wave to the group and saddled up, careful not to hit Cora with my boot or the round nob of the spur. Settled in the seat, I pulled Barley around, waved, and rode toward the road. Cora called out a goodbye and we were on our way. Again.

****

The mountains ahead were lit with the cool light of the morning sun. We rode in silence for a while. I thought about the people behind us. The girl, Jenny, who seemed interested in Cora's knowledge of the sky, and for that matter, the very existence of someone like Cora. If that little girl had any dreams at all, they would die out here, far from any university or observatory. She never would have a chance to learn in a proper school and would find only the meanest kinds of employment. It wasn't fair; Cora said as much about herself, and I had gathered similar hints from Professor Mitchell's comments about professional women when we were back in Pueblo. What chance would Jenny have when women like Cora and Mitchell—already educated and with money to study and travel—still struggled for any recognition or opportunities among their male peers and among the larger society?

And did I ever feel a sense of superiority or entitlement because I was white and a man? Or because of where I lived in Chicago and the money my father brought home to that address? I knew there were classes of people in today's society: the idle rich and the desperately poor, busy merchants and day laborers, the Oriental and the European, among others. But I could not remember an occasion when I was acutely aware of being special, of having a special status in society. Maybe having such a status meant you didn't have to think about it. It was an aura, perhaps. Something everyone could see but need not comment on.

In the middle of my self-examination, Cora said, "That was nice of you giving them your eclipse glass. You won't be able to buy another piece in Denver."

"That's okay. I know someone with three telescopes."

She laughed. "We'll be busy with all three telescopes, but I'm sure we'll be able to offer you a quick glance or two."

"Either way, I won't miss seeing the totality part of the eclipse," I said.

We were silent for a while, listening to Barley's hooves strike the broken ground, sending out tremors to warn the smaller creatures of the summertime prairie that something big was coming their way.

Then Cora said, "Did you know Professor Mitchell is great friends with Frederick Douglass? What do you suppose will happen to those people back there?"

Nothing good. "I don't know. It's a hard world in most places. They won't find things as agreeable as Douglass did after he escaped to Philadelphia."

We came to the railroad track again. I looked down its length and then willed a train to appear from out of the distance. But none did. I had no magic, or as the Indians might say, "no medicine." The rails, with their polished tops, remained silent. All around us was a deep silence—as if nature had decided to hold its collective breath for a moment. Even a golden eagle drifting over the tracks declined to announce its passage.

I broke the stillness with a tongue-click aimed at Barley's jackrabbit ears. He took the hint and marched over the two steel rails and then eased into the East Plum Creek. He carried us across and then climbed up onto the roadbed. I reined him to a stop, wondering where we might be. A wooden signpost stood off in the distance. Too far away to read, we rode over to it. Passing the wooden sign, I twisted around to read "Larkspur- 1 mile." So, we had ridden farther in the dark than I had guessed. We must have ridden past the eastern edges of the town and not seen a building or a light and instead spent the night with the homesteaders.

Cora saw the sign and asked, "Should we ride back?"

"I don't know. It would make sense if we knew there'd be a train. But we don't. And money aside, we won't find another horse there for sale or rent either."

"We keep riding?"

I glanced over my shoulder at her. "I'm afraid so. But it's only eleven miles between Larkspur and Castle Rock. Ten miles now."

"Is there anything in between?"

"Just a couple of settlement towns waiting to become ghost towns. Though we might find some soup or chili for a lunch," I said. I glanced at her again and noticed her lips were chapped from the dry air. Her cheeks had taken on a red gloss from the sun despite her hat. I passed her the canteen.

While she sipped the water, I looked north. A dark line sat on the distant horizon. Clouds? The weather at this time of the year is dry, and Monday, eclipse day, was expected to be sunny and clear.

Cora presented me with the canteen, and I took a quick drink. "Okay, on to Castle Rock and…hopefully…the elusive town of Denver," I said.

I turned Barley back to the creek. He waded into the water again and then re-crossed the railroad tracks.

"Are we not staying on the road now?"

"The ground might be easier off to the east here," I said. "This is hard-packed road for a horse having to carry two riders all day." I pointed ahead and said, "The land back this way is more pasture and pine stands. Softer ground. It's easier walking. It may be shorter too by half a mile or so. Castle Rock is on this side of the creek. And so are Huntsville and Douglas. Those are two places we might ride through in search of a lunch."

Cora asked, "Does the town of Castle Rock have a depot or station?"

"Yes. Brand new DRG station. In fact, the whole town is new. There may be more surveyor's stakes and line markers than actual buildings. But people are moving in, including a lot of Swedish immigrants who moved to the Rock to work a quarry near Castle Butte."

"It seems odd along this one road some towns are thriving while others are dying."

"Well, sometimes it's the fault of the railroad and where they decide to lay their track. Bypass a town and it's dead. Now Castle Rock, it's got the DRG railroad, a busy quarry, a good-size creek for water, and a connecting road to the Cherry Creek Road that runs up to Denver and down to Monument. Should be a big busy town in a few years."

"Might we not hope to find Mr. Travis and Elizabeth there? They may wait at the depot?"

"They might. I don't know. It's Friday, and Travis may feel compelled to drive on. We'll have to wait and see. At the least, we can check the telegraph office and send word up to Denver that you're all right. I'm sure Professor Mitchell is worried about you."

"Worried about me being missing or worried I'm with you?" Cora asked.

I heard the amusement in her voice. "Well, Mitchell doesn't know me, so yes, she might be worried about a Pueblo cowboy who's run off with one of her astronomers." I twisted around to look at her and said, "Are you worried too? Worried I might try to kiss you again?"

Her hat was pulled low, so it was hard to see her eyes. "Are you planning to try again?"

"I'm working up the courage. Give me a moment."

She laughed. "Oh, what would Professor Mitchell say to hear this talk."

I noticed Cora did not kill the idea of a future kiss with a definite "no." I took that as active encouragement on her part.

She slid around to catch a glimpse of my face. "Nolan. I'm sorry about snooping into your journal. I just got curious as I was holding it last night."

"It's okay. It's just some notes to remember Colorado and the West, all of it slipping so quickly into the future."

"I thought the West *was* the future," she said.

"No. It's the past. Indians, saber-waving pony soldiers, sod houses, bows and arrows, conquistador hamlets and monasteries. The future is back East with telephones, electricity, phonographs, steam engines, and all the rest of modernity. All those things are headed this way."

"Will you miss it? The West?"

"Yes. I'll miss some of it." I looked to the mountains and the endless plain stretching back to the Mississippi. I thought of coyotes and antelope and riding for days through this sunlit wildness. "But wouldn't it be nice to have a streetcar come along right about now?"

"Perhaps." She wrapped her arms lightly around my waist and leaned her head against the rough-spun cotton of my dusty jacket.

Chapter 8

We rode through a beatdown land of yellowed grasses and gray-green prairie brush. Islands of pine and birch dotted the landscape. Little groups of black-eyed mule deer sometimes burst from the cover of the trees and darted away as we rode by. I had a childish urge to chase after them.

By midmorning, we came upon the fading town of Huntsville; I had stopped here on other trips. On the edge of town, beside an empty barn with half its wall boards missing, I spotted a water pump and a sun-cracked bucket. I helped Cora slide off the horse.

"Think there's water?" Cora asked.

"The way our luck's been going, I'm guessing we get a bucket of sand." But after a little strong-arming of the handle, a gush of rusty water erupted. I pumped the pipe clear and then filled the bucket for Barley. He drank faster than the bucket leaked. I filled our canteen from the pump and passed it to Cora. While she drank, I tossed my jacket across the saddle and looked around.

No one was on the street or around the neglected buildings, but light smoke drifted out of a rough stone-and-mortar chimney at the opposite end of town. I pointed this out to Cora, and we headed up the street, trailing Barley. The chimney was attached to a squat little building that once was a dry goods store—a faded sign stated as much—but now it was part store and part café. We went in through the open double doors. An old black mutt of a dog got up from its corner and barked a greeting at us.

"You the owner?" I asked the dog.

The dog wagged its tail and snapped out a friendly little bark in the affirmative.

"He's a liar," said a voice. "I'm the owner here. And the mayor. And the sheriff. And if we had a post office I'd be the postmaster. And the telegrapher…if we had a wire. Used to do all that hotwire tapping during the war. Probably still can."

The voice belonged to a man standing in a doorway in the back of the room. He was wild-haired and bearded but looked middle-aged. He had the gnarled and scarred hands of a miner and he was busy drying those well-worked hands with a clean white towel. He wasn't armed. Neither did he have on boots or socks. Long, hairy toes were splayed across the well-worn flooring.

"This Huntsville? We're just riding through," I said.

"This is Glade."

"Glade?" I was puzzled because if Larkspur was behind us, then the next town up the road should be Huntsville.

"The Hunts moved out. Now it's Glade," said the man with a note of satisfaction.

"Okay. Well, we stopped in looking for a meal. Is there food to be had, Mister…?"

"Glade."

Behind me, I heard Cora suppress a laugh. "Well, Mr. Glade, is your café open for business?" I asked.

"Indeed, it is. I got a Mexico gal out back workin' up a fine chili verde con venison, and corn tortillas. Smell it?" He tilted his head back and sniffed the air as if to prove his point. All I smelled was prairie and horse.

"Got cash?" he asked.

"We do." I slid a hand into my right pocket and jingled some coins. The jingling was getting harder to hear.

"Then have a seat while I check the functionings in the kitchen," said Glade.

He disappeared to the back, and we found two painted chairs at a corner table. The dog took up station beside us. Sitting down, I wondered what green chili would do to a dog's digestion.

"We'll be on our way again within the hour," I said to Cora.

"Mr. Glade doesn't have much of a town left. Or a wardrobe. Perhaps you could sell him your moccasins."

"You might need them again." I looked around the café-store. "No, not much town or wardrobe or anything else here." I got up from my seat and said, "Be right back. I'm going to ease Barley while we eat."

I stepped outside and made our horse more comfortable. Down the street, a lone woman worked the water pump. But for her, the rest of the town was quiet and seemingly empty. I went back in to find a very tall Mexican woman arranging two black bowls of chili on the table along with a clay platter of steamy tortillas. Cora said something to her and then got up and followed the woman into the kitchen. In the crooked doorway, Cora turned and raised an index finger to signal, 'Back in a minute.'

I sat down again and looked at the dog. "Should I wait or start in?"

The dog was undecided about lunchtime etiquette. I picked up a tortilla, tore off a piece for the dog and a piece for myself, and started eating.

I finished off one tortilla and was thinking about the chili bowl before me when Cora reappeared, drying her hands on a short, frayed towel.

She sat down again and said, "Sorry. Did you start?"

"I was waiting for you." I picked up a large spoon and said, "Let's hope this stuff isn't too potent."

It was mild by Pueblo standards, and the venison was tasty. I watched Cora tear up one of the tortillas. "You're getting good at eating with your hands," I said. "I don't imagine there's a lot of tortilla-tearing to do in New York?"

She seemed to give the question serious consideration and finally said, "I can't think of a single cantina or Mexican restaurant in New York City or Poughkeepsie."

After that we ate in silence, hungry and happy to be off a cramped saddle and out of the sun. I finished first and got up to look for the mayor-owner-sheriff-et-cetera in the kitchen. He wasn't there. I asked the woman where I might find *el jefe*. The boss. She pointed to a staircase and then to the ceiling.

"Oh." Probably at his *siesta*.

I took some coins from my pocket and held them out to her. "For the chili," I said. She looked at my offering, picked two coins, and slipped them into her apron. I asked, "Is there an outhouse or WC available?" She pointed to the back door. "*Gracias*," I said and stepped outside.

Behind the building was a small garden that appeared healthy and well-tended. The outhouse also was well-tended, much to my relief. Exiting it, I scared up two prairie dogs lurking in its shadow.

Cora was standing by the front door. I stepped back into the main room. "Ready?" I asked, knowing we needed to be on the move again. I wanted to reach the Rock before dark. I cinched up Barley, and we rode back out the way we came in. We did not see the mayor again or any of his constituents.

"The next town is Douglas?" Cora asked.

"It is unless the Douglases have moved out and someone's renamed the place." I laughed at the idea and at the self-described mayor of Glade whose town probably had more dogs and prairie dogs than two-legged citizens.

****

An hour later I caught the smell of smoke. Not the clean aroma of a campfire or a cook's fire, but of a mixed burning of wood and paint and leather. Then it was gone. The wind was from the north. Dark clouds were forming on that far horizon. It looked like rain. I half-turned to Cora and pointed to the blue-black line of clouds ahead of us.

She stared at the clouds for a minute or two and said, "It couldn't be rain. Could it? The weather was predicted to be dry and clear. Which is normal here at this time of year. We checked all of the territory reports."

"It may be only a little summertime shower off the mountains. I wouldn't worry about it." But I was wrong.

****

We pressed on across the prairie. The wind picked up, and again I caught the smell of something smoldering. We came upon the town of Douglas.

One minute we were riding through grass and thin stands of trees, and the next we were beside a tight cluster of buildings and houses. Three of the seven structures were blackened and had collapsed in on themselves. Eddies of black smoke swirled about one of the larger buildings like miniature tornadoes. We stopped and stared. No one was on the street or moved among the remaining buildings.

"What happened here?" asked Cora.

"Not sure. Looks recent, though. Smells recent. Let's walk in. Quietly."

I helped her slide down and then I dismounted. I reached back over the saddle and pulled my rifle.

"What's wrong?" asked Cora. She looked around us for some sign of trouble.

I expected to see residents picking through the debris and drowning any lingering embers, but there was no one in sight.

"Not sure. Let's look around."

I led Barley up the street with Cora trailing close behind me. Beside a half-empty water trough, I saw the narrow imprint of carriage wheels in the damp ground. I left Barley to take a drink from the trough. Cora and I walked to the opposite side of the street, to the larger of the burned-out buildings. It appeared to be the remains of the saloon-hotel I remembered from a visit earlier in the year. A pungent odor contaminated the prairie air.

I stepped up on the remnants of the building's porch and looked into the wreckage. Two charred bodies lay on the blackened floor. Distorted by the heat and blackened by the flames, it was impossible to tell if they were men or women, old or young. I stepped away.

"What?" asked Cora.

I took her hand and led her away. "Bodies. Two people. Maybe others."

We hurried back across the street to an intact

building that was once a dry goods store. My eyes darted here and there like a nervous cat sneaking through a dog's back yard. I felt my heart against the fabric of my vest. I let go of Cora's hand and stepped up to the shattered front window of the former store. My boots crunched on bits of broken glass. Glancing inside, I saw a man face down on the floor. Blood from a head wound formed a reddish-black halo on the floor. Flies buzzed about the man's head and the sticky puddle that had been his life-giving blood. I glanced back at Cora, who looked like a startled deer.

She looked around the street and buildings and asked, "What has happened here? Where is everyone?"

I noticed another set of wagon wheel tracks beside a hitching post and said, "There are wheel marks in the street. Someone was alive here…and left. In a hurry, I imagine."

I looked around the hardpacked street and squinted at the glare it reflected from the overhead sun. Shiny points of light lay scattered on the main street—the only street. I stepped over and picked one up. It was a brass casing from a Spencer carbine. I picked up two more. Then I found several fresh casings from a Winchester.

Looking around the desolate town, I said to Cora, "We need to go. There's no one here but the dead."

"What's happened?" she asked. I heard a growing fear in her voice.

"Something bad. That's all we need to know right now."

I led her back to the horse. We mounted, and I kept the rifle ready in my right hand. I pointed Barley around, and we trotted back the way we came. Then we rode north again.

Cora grabbed my shoulders, and not in a tender or comforting way. "My God. Is it so easy to die out here? Where is the law?" she demanded.

"We're on the frontier...between the wild, natural world and that big blundering civilization back East. The law is still catching up out here. Just behind the settlers and homesteaders. It's always a town or a train away from trouble." I knew that first-hand.

It was an imperfect answer, but more or less true. Now, my only concern was to get clear of the town and whoever shot it up and burned it down. Castle Rock was a few miles up the road. There would be law there and the reassuring accoutrements of civilization.

I pushed Barley to reach a narrow stand of trees. We slipped in among the trunks and brush and stopped. I dropped the rifle back in its scabbard and asked Cora for the binoculars.

I scanned the area, looking for riders or more smoke. The prairie was still and silent. I held the glasses up and asked Cora if she wanted a look.

She declined with a simple, "No." Maybe she'd had enough of the Colorado vistas.

Or maybe she'd had enough. Period. She was lost on the frontier with a stranger. Her friends and colleagues were gone. People were killed. Towns burned. Denver and safety were a long way off. There was only me to guide and protect her, and I did not feel adequate to the task. I wasn't a soldier or a sheriff. I hauled freight and scribbled in a notebook.

Twisting around to look at Cora, I forced a smile meant to be reassuring and said, "Castle Rock isn't much farther. We'll be there soon and then put you on a train."

I got a return smile for my efforts. She exhaled; it

seemed like a shout in the stillness. "I hope next week's eclipse will be as memorable as this journey to the eclipse."

"Yes. I'm sorry about all this. It's been…"

"You told me it wasn't my fault. Now I want you to know it's not your fault either. We are, I would say, the victims of…circumstance."

I turned away from her again and said, "Well, whatever the circumstances have been, I'm glad to have been through them with you."

That didn't sound quite right, but I wanted her to know I was glad to be traveling with her, whatever the circumstances or consequences of our journey.

****

The sun slipped behind a layer of thin white clouds. The wind shifted and the colors of the surrounding landscape grew richer and darker under the diffused sunlight. The terrain sloped downward, and we entered a large stand of cottonwoods and stony outcrops. I let the horse pick his way among the trees and stones as we continued following the gentle slope of the land.

Barley lifted his head and stopped. Horses snorted in the distance. I sat there for several seconds trying to imagine how the noise ahead might not be more trouble for us. But I was not that imaginative.

Cora asked in a quiet voice, "Do you hear horses?"

I nodded. "Yeah, I hear them." I pushed my hat back on my head. "We need to look ahead. Quietly."

Cora slid to the soft ground. I hopped down and said, "I'll be right back."

I dropped my hat on a knee-high outcrop and started moving forward from tree to tree, trying to keep to cover and careful not to step on deadfall and patches of sun-dried leaves. The trees thinned out ahead. Looking down the slope, I counted seven horses. Four of the horses sported blankets, but no saddles. The other three animals were on guide ropes.

Off to the left were four Indians. Their narrow bronze faces were streaked with white and yellow paint. They wore their long black hair tied back with wide bandanas or twisted into thick snakelike braids. Silver necklaces and earrings flashed in the sun. They had on cotton leggings, dyed wool breechcloths, and striped red-and-blue Mexican shirts. Long knives hung from knotted leather belts. I counted four rifles.

But for the northerly breeze, they would have heard us before we heard them. Blind chance was at work again; no wonder so many people were superstitious.

The four men were gathered in a knot and sat on the grassy meadow. Their heads were bowed for a minute or two, and then one of them stood up, raised his rifle with both hands, and did some kind of ritual dance. Then he sat again. A second man repeated the same little dance and sat down again. Faint murmurs from the men, chanting I supposed, caught my ear.

Their horses were relaxed and feeding on the grasses and bushes. A noise from me or another shift in the wind might alert them to our presence. That could not happen.

I inched away from my tree. On the way back up the slope, I saw Cora. She was standing by a big cottonwood looking down at the Indian horses. I put a finger to my lips, took her hand, and we hurried back to the horse.

Cora had tied Barley's reins to another tree. I could have kissed her for that single act.

"What's wrong?" she asked with a nervous look on her tired face. A thin film of dust had settled on her cheeks.

Today, Friday, had become as harrowing as Thursday. "Indians," I whispered.

"Oh, dear God…" she said.

I whispered. "There's four of them. They've got guns. And they've got seven horses. Probably taken from Douglas."

"They burned the town?"

"That's my guess. It would explain where they got the extra horses." I looked back through the trees to make sure they weren't coming our way.

Cora asked, "Who are they? Is there an Indian war in Colorado?"

We still had not been detected by them. But that wouldn't last. The wind might change, or Barley might start stomping around.

"They may be Utes. From out of Utah or northern Colorado," I said.

"Is there an Indian war?" she asked again.

"Not yet, but maybe soon. Come on."

I took her hand and led Barley away from the four mysterious men. We glided through the trees, looking back every few seconds. Clearing the stand, I jumped into the saddle and then pulled Cora up behind me. I took the Winchester, levered a round into the breech, and slid it back into the scabbard. I pointed Barley south again, and we started off at a brisk trot.

Cora leaned around me to ask, "Can you hold off four Indians if it comes to a fight? Like the Mexicans?"

I shook my head. "No." I twisted around to look behind us again—half expecting to hear the mad gallop of horses pounding through the trees—and said to Cora, "If they spot us, if they come after us, I'm getting down with the rifle. You're gonna ride like hell to the road. Flag down a train if you see one. Otherwise, keep moving toward Denver."

She was silent for a few seconds. I hoped her silence would last, but then she asked, "What about you?"

Yes, what about me? The end of my luck?

There was no way I was going to best four men who spent their lives riding, hunting, tracking, and fighting. For them, the situation was always: miss a shot and your family goes hungry; miss a shot and your enemy kills you. No, I had no chance against them. They were Indians living on the plains. This was their world. I was a *faux* cowboy from Chicago. I looked over my shoulder again.

We had hurried away from possible danger around the burned and abandoned town of Douglas only to ride into the very source of that danger. We were saved now by little more than a gentle breeze flowing toward us. I could not imagine being luckier. We cleared the cottonwood stand, and I put the spurs to my horse.

We were moving fast, covering ground we'd already been over, and getting farther from Denver with every punch of Barley's hooves on the dusty plain. Cora and I made up a loose and uneven load atop the horse, and it was hard to judge who was having the worse time of it, Barley or us. We couldn't keep up such a pace. The road was up ahead. I reined him to a walk.

Cora twisted around my left side to say something. I heard a sudden whine in my right ear. Barley jerked his head as if to shy away from an unwelcome presence.

A bullet zipped past my head.

Barley shied to the left, and I looked over my shoulder to see what appeared to be a single horseman coming at us. I heard another whine. A puff of smoke and a rifle report erupted from the rider.

I reined the horse. Cora fell against my back. I jumped down.

She shouted at me, "What's happening?"

"Indians." I pulled the Winchester free and shouted to her, "Stay low."

I looked back at the shooter. What appeared to be a single man on horseback became four. They had been riding close, in single file, with their best shooter out front. Now they were spread out in a line and pounding toward us in an unworldly silence.

I pushed the horse around and yelled to Cora, "Go. Ride for the road."

Before she could say anything, I yelled, "Ride," and smacked Barley's flank.

I didn't watch her gallop off. Instead, I fired a single wild shot at the approaching Indians. I didn't except to hit anyone. Instead, I was hoping to keep their focus on me and not on Cora as she galloped away. I ran toward an arroyo that meandered from the road onto the plain. My boots kicked up dust and fine pebbles as I scrambled between clumps of dry sage. I heard a high-pitched whine. Another bullet passed very close. A second later, another invisible chunk of lead snapped by me. Then something tugged at my shirt.

I reached the arroyo and jumped in. Sliding down the steep gully wall, I landed in fast-moving water at the bottom. I climbed out of the knee-deep water and lay against the sandy side of the gully. I was shaking and gasping for breath. And swearing in between those needed breaths.

Shit all, this is it. This is it. There's no rescue.

I clutched my rifle with both hands, afraid to lose it and afraid to see my shaking hands if I let go of it. I looked down at my feet. Water raced through the gully floor.

I felt something wet flowing down my left side. I twisted around on the sandy slope to look at a furrow of torn fabric a couple of inches below my armpit. A bullet had plowed through my vest, shirt and some quantity of flesh, maybe grazing a rib. Now that I knew I'd been hit, I felt a searing pain. My left side began to burn from my armpit to my hip.

But there was no time to worry about my wound or Cora or the rushing water at my feet. There was only the next few seconds. I rolled over and scrambled up to the top of the arroyo. The four horsemen were closer now. My own personal apocalypse.

Two of the riders let off shots that kicked up dirt near my head. I slid back down and looked at the flotsam the last spring flood had deposited here. There was a small tree stump, its trunk sheared off by the violence of the last flood. I scrambled down and pried it loose from the rocks and muck. I crawled back to the edge of the trench. With my right arm I flung it up on the edge of the arroyo to protect my face and head. Tossing my hat aside, I snuggled up to the stump and laid my rifle on the dry ground. More bullets zipped around me like angry bees. One bullet slammed into the tree stump. I wasn't going to last long behind this rotting shield. I slid the Winchester forward and looked down the sights.

But what to aim at? I couldn't hit a man on a galloping horse. I would waste all of my cartridges trying to hit one of them. And then what?

Instead, I found a larger target. A horse. One of the

153

prairie ponies came straight toward me. I tracked the creature down the sights of the barrel. I held my breath and pulled the trigger.

The mustang collapsed in a roiling cloud of dust. Its rider catapulted through the air, still holding his rifle. He hit the ground and rolled for a few yards before coming to rest on his back. He made no move to get up.

Two more bullets plowed up the sand around me. I dropped back down into the rushing water. I waded downstream through the churning brown water and its grasping debris. Those warriors were still up there, and I imagined they would press me from upstream, downstream, and directly above. They'd have the high ground, closing from three sides, and I'd be dead quick and neat. I scrambled up the side again and peeked over the edge, hoping a bit of dry grass and cactus might conceal me for a second.

The other three men had stopped and gathered around the fallen rider. He was on his feet now, holding his right arm. One of his companions held up his rifle. The stock was snapped off from the fall. The other two stared along the edge of the ditch looking for me. I slid back below the edge. I wasn't going to help them spot me.

After a minute, I heard the sounds of their horses close by. I crawled back up and took a prairie dog peek at the terrain. The man with the injured arm sat on a horse. Then one of his companions jumped up behind him carrying two rifles, including the busted one. Angry, alien words rolled toward me. The other two mounted up and after a lingering glance at the arroyo, they all turned away and rode off. I watched them until they disappeared into a brown haze of dust and sunlight.

Perhaps they thought they had pushed their luck after burning Douglas, tarrying too long with their stolen horses, and then pursuing Cora and me. Someone on the road might have come upon the smoldering town and raised the alarm. The Army or a posse might be on the move now. So they rode off to collect their other horses and head for home.

I lay sprawled against the gully wall, listening to the rush of the water below. It seemed to be louder and faster now. This in a place that did not have water at this time of the year. Some tiny bit of my mind was puzzled by the water. Is it raining to the north?

Maybe a flash flood will drown me before I bleed to death.

Grabbing hold of the grass at the top of the slope, I pulled myself up and lay in the dust to rest, to calm down, to feel the blood still leaking from my side, and to thank the God I didn't believe in that I was alive. My face sideways in the grass, I watched a finger-long grasshopper jump from one grassy stem to the next, oblivious to my presence. My eyes must have closed because I had to open them again. Had I slept? It seemed impossible.

Chapter 9

I was still lying there. I yelled out loud, "Christ Almighty. All this for a three-minute eclipse. Damn it all to hell."

Get up, I told myself. But I didn't.

Instead, the ground began to shake with the steady hammering of a fast-moving horse. I dragged my head around to see Barley's hooves come to a skidding stop a few feet away. Cora's boots appeared, and then she was kneeling beside me, clutching a Mexican pistol.

"Nolan! Nolan, are you hurt?" She helped me roll over on my side. Her face was pale and beaded with tiny droplets of sweat. Her eyes were owl-wide, taking in all of me in an instant.

I looked up at her and said, "Good God, woman. Don't you ever listen? You're supposed to be flying up the road."

"You're bleeding," she said. Her gloved hand brushed the torn fabric of my vest.

I surrendered my anger. I was glad to see her here again. I needed help. "I don't think it's serious." It throbbed; I felt like I'd been branded.

I let go of my rifle and sat up. Cora helped hold me in place. She said, "I was hiding among the trees on the other side of the tracks. Then they rode off."

We were almost nose to nose looking at each other. I laughed. It sounded—to me—like someone on the edge of hysterics. "Hiding, were you? It would have taken them five seconds to find you."

I eased the pistol from her unsteady hand. I'd already been shot once. Rolling onto my knees, I stood up, swaying as I did so. I pointed at the saddle. "The canteen. Please."

I unbuttoned my vest and pulled it off to examine my bloody shirt and wounded flank. My shirt was a sticky red mess. Blood ran down my left side into my pants. I unbuttoned the shirt and peeled it away from my side. The bullet had cut a ragged trench along my left side about two inches long. It looked like some flat-faced carnivore took a bite out of me. Much deeper and the passing projectile might have struck a rib and caused serious damage. I didn't see any shiny white bone, but then I didn't look too long. The sight made me ill, and I already had plenty of other things to worry about.

Cora handed me the canteen and I took a long drink. I set it on the ground and dug out my pocketknife.

I turned my back to Cora and asked, "Can you help me pull this shirt off?"

She shook the leather gloves from her hands. Then I felt her fingers on my collar and shoulder. With a little tugging, we got my shirt off.

Turning back to her, I asked, "Well, how is this Chicago boy looking this fine day?" I was sweating, bleeding, covered in dust and mud, and smelled like a cattle car at the end of a cross-country trek.

Cora gave me a serious look. She shook her head and said, "You are a mess, Mr. Carter. And you're bleeding still. We must stop that."

"Fear not. I have a plan. I always have a plan. How do ya like my plans so far?" I think I was grinning at her like a lunatic.

But then I got hold of myself again and said, "Hold the sleeve out. Please."

She took hold of the cuff end of the shirtsleeve. With my knife, I cut the sleeve loose at the shoulder. Then I took the amputated sleeve and split it lengthwise twice, from the cuff up to the ragged shoulder. Now I had a strip of cloth long enough to reach around my chest. I handed it to Cora.

"You're making a bandage," Cora said.

Removing my blue bandana, I nodded to her, and folded it into a convenient hand-size patch. I picked up the canteen and soaked the bandana. Then I pressed the wet bundle against my wound and winced. "Cora, I hate to ask, but would you reach around and tie the sleeve, so it covers this little nick on my side?"

She stepped closer, wrapped her arms around me, and pulled the shirtsleeve into place.

"Okay," I said.

She tied the ends in a tight, flat knot. Cora stepped back and looked at me. "All of this." She spread her arms to encompass the whole of the prairie and the Rocky Mountains. "This wasn't some elaborate plan to get me alone with you, was it? It seems an awfully complicated scheme, when you simply might have asked me to lunch or to the evening theater."

I straightened up as best I could and looked at her. "Now, you tell me. And here I was paying extra for the Indians."

We both stood there laughing, not so much for any clever remarks, but for the sheer tension of the last few minutes. And for the last day. It was a welcome release of pent-up anxiety and real sour-tasting fear. My battered frame wasn't shaking anymore. My breathing returned to normal. Cora's cheeks colored up, and her owlish pupils contracted in the calm aftermath of another violent encounter on the Colorado frontier.

I slipped on the remains of my shirt and then my damaged vest. I pulled my pistol and banged and blew dirt from around the cylinder and hammer. Cora picked up the canteen and started for the arroyo, but I stopped her.

"Don't go down there. It's filling fast. It may be raining up north and flashing through this creek bed. It should be dry this time of year. We'll get water up near the road." I looked northwest and spotted a line of darkness dragging across the gray peaks.

Something moved on the edge of my sight. I looked back at the horse I had shot. Three buzzards dropped out of the sky. The scaly-faced scavengers landed with surprising grace and folded up their serrated black wings. They bird-hopped around the dead horse, debating where best to begin their meal. It could have been me on the noonday menu.

I got hold of Barley and untied my jacket from the saddle. The jacket hid my bloody, one-armed shirt. Cora found my hat a few yards back. Now I looked as good as I was going to until Denver. With the canteen, Cora's pistol, and my rifle tucked away, I climbed into the saddle. A sharp pain radiated up and down my side. I reached my right arm down to help Cora up. Another hot stab of pain ran through me.

She settled herself behind me and I said, "Let's try this again. This time, no Indians."

I tapped Barley with a wet boot tip, and we started back to the road.

****

We climbed onto the roadbed and down the other side to splash through the creek. On the opposite bank, I reined Barley.

"We can stop here a bit," I said. I needed to rest. I felt dizzy. I closed my eyes. My mind flooded with riotous images of painted Indians, smiling Mexicans, rifles in the dark, and the mosquito-like whine of bullets all around me. I wanted a place to hide. Then Cora said something, and I was back on a horse in summertime Colorado.

I reached back and she slid off the horse, using my arm for a guide and brake. It hurt. I climbed down and looked back the way we came. No one was in sight, though with Indians that meant nothing. I passed the canteen to Cora and led Barley back to the creek.

Long blue dragonflies with fishnet wings hovered over the sparkling water. Vibrant purple and red flowers dotted the grassy bank. I didn't know what they were called. I had a silly urge to pluck a few and present them to Cora, but then reason presented itself. What would she do with them? Clutch them in one hand while trying to stay on the back of a horse?

The flowers' bright colors darkened as I stared at them. I glanced up at the sky. Clouds formed overhead, and more hurried down from the mountains. I felt the temperature drop.

Cora stepped over to the creek bank and handed me the almost empty canteen.

"Thanks." I drank the last of the water and stepped down to the creek bed to refill it.

From behind me Cora said, "Professor Peters over at Hamilton College didn't want to observe the eclipse in

Montana. He was worried about the Indians."

I scrambled back up. "Sounds like a smart man. The Lakota are still itching for another fight. You must have read how they wiped out Yellow-Hair Custer and his men two years back. Gave them all Lakota haircuts. I don't know what they'd do with a fancy Eastern professor and his telescope."

"On the train out here, someone said it might be dangerous to observe from the Wyoming-Colorado border because of Ute Indians. Is that who attacked us? Utes?" asked Cora.

I looked off to the empty plain to our right and shook my head. "Maybe. I don't know. I can't tell one tribe from another. But a lot of Utes live in Colorado. And all of them are furious about whites moving in and soldiers pushing them around, taking their land and their horses. There could be trouble here too. Like Montana."

I tied the canteen on the saddle again and glanced over at Cora.

She stood there, studying the endless stretch of the high plains. She seemed calm. Perhaps she was waiting for some new catastrophe to occur. Dressed in her riding clothes and hat, she might have been on a Sunday afternoon ride through the countryside, but for the dirt smears on her skirt and jacket and the disheveled hair that crept from under her hat. She'd been through a lot in a short period of time: almost raped by drovers, sheltering on the prairie with former slaves, and now dodging Indians. I knew she was smart—certainly the smartest person I knew—and now it was clear she also was tough. There had been no hysterics. No damsel-in-distress escapades. No handwringing or pacing or whining. She wasn't blaming me for any of our problems. She had not galloped off and left me to the Indians. Even knowing it wasn't going to end well, she stayed. You had to admire that in anyone.

She turned to me. "Do you think they're gone? For good?"

"Yeah. I think we're okay." I untied the duster lashed to the back of the saddle and handed it to Cora.

"What's this?" she asked.

I pointed up and said, "I think it's going to rain soon. You should put this on, and then we'll get moving again."

She glanced up. The clouds were dark and thick. The wind picked up. "Oh, it can't rain," she insisted. "We've come so far." She stared at me. "We've been through so much to have it all end in rain and clouds."

Now she sounded distressed. Vaqueros, Indians, and rattlesnakes didn't bother her as much as a summer shower.

I must have been grinning because she looked at me and asked, "Why is this funny?"

I tried to lose my smile and said, "It's not. I don't want to get wet either." But then for no good reason I started to laugh again. Barley swiveled his long hairy head around, wondering at my abrupt change in mood.

I walked up to Cora and said, "Come on. We need to keep moving."

She gave me a suspicious look, thinking perhaps I might start laughing again. She pulled on the long brown duster. It dragged on the ground and hid her hands. "Well, now I have your big floppy coat too."

"Let me help you." I stepped closer, rolled up the cuffs, and straightened the duster's split back. I took hold of the collar points to raise the high collar, but then I pulled her to me. I kissed her. She kissed me back, and we stood for a long while in a tight embrace. At some point, I lifted her off her feet and spun the two of us in a slow circle. I brought our brief revolution to an end and she said simply, "Mr. Carter."

"Professor Harrison." I hid a grimace. Picking her up had sent another sharp pain radiating up and down my side.

"What are we to do?" she asked my tired gray eyes.

I didn't know whether she meant the immediate or the eventual. So I said, "Time and weather…and restless neighbors"—I glanced east—"suggest we ride on. But I wish we could stay right here for a long while."

I pulled away, reluctantly, and helped her button up the front of my voluminous duster. In my saddlebags, I found the spare bandana that had protected my blue eclipse glass. I shook it open and wrapped it twice around her neck. "This'll help keep the rain out."

She spread her arms and asked, "Well, I seem to have half of your wardrobe now. What will you wear in the coming weather?"

"I'll be all right." I buttoned my jacket and pulled the collar up, and pushed my hat down on my matted, messy hair. "Come on."

I led her to a flat-topped boulder on which she could step. After I pulled myself up on Barley, I reached a hand over to help her up. But she made no move to take my hand.

Instead, she said, "You must be a cat."

"What?"

"They have nine lives. And you've used up four lives already with your friend Davey, the cattle drive, the drovers, and now the Indians. No. Wait. Five lives. The rattlesnake too."

I leaned toward her. "Take my paw. We need to go. Besides, Colorado's thrown everything she has at us and we're still standing. Some of us on all fours." Clever me.

"You're running out of lives, Nolan." She took my hand, swung up behind me, and wrapped her arms around my waist.

Resettled, we started again, keeping the creek and the road between us and the four Indians out on the prairie. I hoped they would stay out there, away from the main road and the rails. Yet I was certain they would head north too. That meant we would be separated by little more than a mile or so of intervening trees and exposed plain.

The creek, the train tracks, and the road meandered toward Castle Rock. We needed to ride back and forth between them as they crisscrossed one another. Parallel lines never meet on paper, but the north-south contortions of the creek, the road and the rails obeyed a different geometry on the narrow space between the flat brown prairie and the jagged gray mountains.

We had not been riding for five minutes when I felt the first rain drops. Barley made a noisy protest about the rain. I patted his neck and said, "Yes, you're going to get wet. That's the least of your troubles."

Cora leaned around and asked, "Is he all right? Two riders over two days cannot be good for him."

"He likes to complain. He should give Blue a good two-legged kick if we ever find him again. He wouldn't be in this mess if only Blue had stayed calm for a minute or two."

Of course, none of us would be in this mess if I had left my brother's horse behind in Pueblo. With one horse,

Cora and I would not have had a chance to ride around and get separated from the wagon. Somehow a skittish horse and the mathematical movements of the solar system had taken hold of my destiny. I had lost control of my life. Or did I ever have any such control?

****

A hard, cold rain came down from the mountains. The surrounding countryside was dark under a layer of saturated clouds that cast everything in dreary gray and shadowy black. We were on the road, plodding along over rough-cut bridges and railroad crossings. The roadbed turned to mud and loose stone.

Cora pressed against my back, which was a warm but soggy support. A steady trickle of water ran down my neck, into my shirt, and down into my cotton drawers. I wondered if some of that trickle might be blood, but there was no way to stop and check.

Barley trudged along with his head down as low as it would go. I felt Cora shiver now and then.

Without turning around, I said, "After the Philly Expo, my parents, Brian, and I took a steamship down the river to Cape May, New Jersey. It was the first time I ever saw the ocean. Lake Michigan always seemed boundless until I stood on the shore of the Atlantic. Have you been to Cape May?"

Cora didn't respond. She was asleep. On a horse. In a heavy rain.

We had been riding in the deluge long enough to be thoroughly wet and miserable. I imagined our next travail might involve blizzards and howling wolves—we'd experienced almost everything else worth writing about.

Cora shook me. "There's a sign off to the right," she

said over the noise of rain tapping on her once-stylish riding hat.

We were at a junction of the creek and the railbed. We rode up to the sign, which read, "Castle Rock 2 Miles."

"Two miles. We're almost out of this."

"Wonderful," she said to my back. "Shall we gallop?" She wasn't serious.

"I wish we could," I said.

We plodded on, feeling the rain and the enveloping darkness. A steady wind shook the telegraph wires. I had no idea what time it was; my watch—if it was still running—was buried under my wet jacket. Ahead, a coyote bolted across the road, looking as unhappy as us. A few minutes later, we rounded a slight bend in the roadway. Ahead, a one-horse buckboard pulled out of a side trail to the right. The driver, covered up in a heavy canvas, did not see us and soon disappeared into another curtain of pelting rain.

I tapped Cora on the leg and said, "I just saw a wagon pull onto the road and head up. We must be close."

"Oh, thank God. This rain will be the death of us."

The rails ran close to the road. Up ahead, a pinpoint of light shined like a beacon in the dark. We came upon a large wooden sign painted in yellow letters that read, "Castle Rock, CO. Pop. 197. Welcome."

Excited by the sign, I announced to Cora, "We're here."

Beyond the sign were two lighted windows and the dark outlines of a building. We rode toward it, and in another minute a train station emerged from the gloom. To the right, we found a freight ramp that led up to a covered platform. Barley tiptoed up the wooden ramp and stopped under the shelter of the platform roof. We were out of the rain and in town. Not the right town, but this was close enough for the time being. I felt relief and not a little satisfaction, considering the long delays and the near-deadly dramas in which we had been forced to participate. This was more adventure than I ever anticipated.

I helped Cora dismount, and then I slid clumsily to the wooden floor.

Cora clung to a post and said, "Oh, my God, what a nightmare this day has been."

We were both as wet as two people could be and splattered with mud kicked up by Barley's heavy-hooved plodding along the road. A door banged open behind us, and then a voice said, "There's no livestock to be on the platform."

I looked around to see the DRG station agent framed in the backlit doorway. I pulled my Winchester from the saddle and left Barley untied. He wasn't going to walk off in the rain. Taking Cora's hand, I guided her toward the door. The station man yielded the doorway—I don't think he wanted to get too close to two wet, muddy strangers—and we stepped into the warm, well-lighted station. It still smelled of fresh-cut lumber and new paint.

"We've had a helluva time with Mexicans, Indians, snakes, horses and railroads." I placed the rifle on the counter with enough force to emphasize my lack of patience with any additional problems.

The manager closed the platform door and hurried behind the counter. He adjusted his round railroad cap and asked, "Well, what can I...?"

"When's the next train to Denver?" I demanded.

Water still ran off the limp brim of my once-stiff gambler's hat. I suppressed a shiver.

He looked up at the wall clock. "About three minutes."

I turned to Cora. She looked like a rag doll rescued from a mud puddle. My soaked and spotted duster hung on her like an oversized bedsheet. Her arms were crossed against the chill of the rain. Her hat was snugged to her head by the chin cord.

We stared at each other for a second or two— shocked, I suppose at the idea of a train coming along at any moment. We had made it. Not to Denver, but to a town with a train and a telegraph and a warm building with a roof overhead.

"You need to get on that train," I said.

"Yes, oh God, yes," she said and laughed. Then she asked, "What about you?"

"Don't worry about me. You need to get to Denver. I'll…I'll be along. I need to find Travis. Check the Western Union for any messages."

A steam whistle blew in the distance.

The station manager interrupted us to say, "Train's comin' in. You want a ticket for it?"

"Yes. One ticket. One way," I said. "What's that cost?"

"First class, second class, or emigrant?"

I said, "First," at the same time Cora said, "Second will do."

"We don't have any money to spare," she said.

True enough.

I nodded and asked the manager, "What's that cost from here, one way?"

"Be seventy-five cents for second-class." The

manager dropped a pad of yellow tickets on the counter, tore off the top one, and signed his name to it. He pulled a brass punch across the counter, punched a crescent-shaped hole in the ticket, and handed it to Cora. She took it and clutched it in her two hands like it was a thousand-dollar bill.

I unbuttoned my soggy jacket and dug a silver dollar from a vest pocket—my last one. Everything else was a couple of nickels and some two-cent coppers. I slid the dollar across the counter, noticing at the same time a second pad of yellow-colored tickets. Employee passes for the DRG Railroad. The manager stepped away to a desk drawer to get my change and I had a brief fantasy—steal one of those rail passes, forge a signature, and hop the train with Cora. But the reality of what to do about Barley, and the whereabouts of Travis and Elizabeth intruded, and the fantasy dissipated like desert dew.

The manager handed me the change. I was about to ask him a question when he was silhouetted by a bright yellow light. The train's brakes hissed on hot steel. The manager said, "Train's here."

He came around the counter, pushed his cap down on his head, and hurried to the platform door. I scooped up my Winchester, took hold of Cora's gloved hand, and followed the station man. On the platform, a dozen people appeared out of the darkness and the rain. None of them looked as disheveled as Cora and me. I tucked my rifle away and led Barley around to the front of the station office and tied him to a post. I didn't want him to get spooked by the train's noises or the milling passengers.

The black-and-green engine—almost hidden in clouds of steam—crept by, followed by the tender and a baggage car. The passenger carriages rolled up and stopped beside the platform. Doors popped open, and the handful of people on the platform surged forward, eager to get aboard, find a seat and relax in the dry, lighted cars. A conductor directed people to one car or another. Arriving passengers stepped onto the platform and then hesitated about getting down into the rain and the mud. There was a rumble of shouted greetings and stumbling about with luggage from the people on the platform and those disappearing into the railcars.

I said to Cora, "You should get to your car. They'll be leaving in a moment."

She spread her arms and said, "I'm dressed for travel…in the stock car."

"Maybe we should have got you the emigrant-class ticket after all?"

She stepped closer and took my hands. She was still wearing my gloves. "I'm sorry. It's not enough to say for all you've done these last two days…but thank you."

I hesitated to reply, thinking everything was somehow my fault. My infatuation led me to let her ride off on Blue. Everything that happened up to now was chained to that one carefree decision to ride onto the prairie. From that point, I'd led her through a Colorado hell she would never forget. Travis was certain to blame me for ignoring the business of getting up the road and instead riding off with this fancy Eastern girl. And he'd be right.

I managed only an inadequate reply. "Well, let's not do this again."

I took her arm and guided her to an open carriage door. The conductor looked at us with unconcealed distaste.

"Better get aboard now. I've got to find Travis. And your telescopes."

Where was Travis? Still driving the wagon and telescopes north? Or did they get a train along the way?

"But you'll come to Denver won't you?" she asked.

Did I see an imploring look on her tired but still attractive face? Maybe I was letting fantasy get the better of me. Again.

"Yes. I'll come. By train or horse or something. That was the job—to get to Denver. We're not there yet."

"You won't be either. Less'n you get on the train, miss," said the conductor. He hesitated, then offered a reluctant hand to help Cora step through the carriage doorway.

She looked back. "Nolan, I'll see you in Denver. You don't want to miss the eclipse. You gave away your glass, so now you'll need one of our telescopes."

She waved, and the train lurched forward. The conductor jumped into the doorway, and I lost sight of Cora.

I shouted past the conductor, "I'll be there."

The pulsing engine, wreathed in clouds of steam brought on by the rain, pulled the train away. The cars slid by, and I searched the passing windows to catch a last glimpse of her. I couldn't spot her. The cupola caboose rolled by. Two men stood on its covered back platform determined to have a smoke in the rain. I leaned against a roof post to watch the twin lights of the caboose disappear into the rainy night.

Cora was gone. I should have kissed her. Now I felt her absence as a sudden wave of melancholy that made me clutch the roof post. Some time passed and the banging of a station door distracted me. I found the will to step away from my support.

Cora was gone. The fate of Travis, Elizabeth, and the telescopes was still a mystery. They might be anywhere. Maybe I could track them down with a few telegrams, but I didn't have enough money to do so. I needed food and a dry place to sleep. I might have stood there half the night thinking about my problems, but then someone said, "Hey, there's a horse on the platform."

****

Back in the station house, I asked the manager if he had seen our green freight wagon come through town or charged any freight up to Denver today.

"I haven't," he said. "But then I just come on from Denver. Walsh, Mark Walsh, he's been here all day, so he's the best one to ask about the day's ticketing."

"Okay. Where's he in town?" I leaned on the counter, half listening, thinking about dry clothes and a bed.

"Probably up the street at the Quarry Café. Likes to take his supper there. Maybe 'cause of the big Swede girls." He winked at me.

At the moment, a welcoming tribe of naked Amazons would not arouse my interests, never mind the harried daughters of Swedish quarrymen. I thanked him for the information and left to retrieve Barley. He was content under the platform roof, but he could not stay there. I led him around to the ramp and down to the muddy street. It was still raining, and we walked up the deserted main thoroughfare. Storefronts were shuttered. I found the café with its bright front windows and smoking chimney. It was a big brick-and-board building, and next to it was a half-built structure covered over with canvas awnings. I pulled Barley under the canvas and out of the rain and tied him to an exposed wall support. I retrieved my rifle and saddlebags—in the dark town, they might go missing—and hurried to the café.

The café was almost empty, but the aromas of coffee and baked goods lingered in the damp air. Behind a lattice partition, an iron oven door slammed shut. A chalkboard menu, hung high on the back wall, announced all of the day's foods I could not afford. I found Walsh in his blue-black railroad suit sitting at a corner table. His short-billed cap hung from a wall peg near his head. A square leather travel case sat on the floor by his chair.

"Mr. Walsh? The station manager said you'd be here," I said.

He looked up at me, glanced at the wall clock, and said, "Son, you missed the northbound. Stay outta the rain and the last southbound will be along in ninety minutes, and the northbound again at seven-thirty a.m."

Time was everything to these railroad people. They were forever glancing at clocks or winding their own timepieces and advising everyone to be mindful of time's hurried passing.

Pulling out the ladderback chair opposite him, I asked, "Do you mind?" I leaned my rifle against the wall and dropped my saddlebags beside the chair. I sat down and rubbed my face with the palms of my hands.

"Sorry to intrude, but I've been on the road, in the rain, and I'm trying to find some people who may have taken a train to Denver from here."

"You the law?" He raised a skeptical eyebrow.

"No, nothing like that. I'm Nolan Carter. I work for the Front Range Freight Company in Pueblo. We were taking two passengers and some telescopes up the road these past days. We got separated, and I'm trying to find one of them and the freight. I'm hoping they got here ahead of me and then were able to catch a train the rest of the way to Denver."

"Telescopes?"

"Yes, for Monday's eclipse. They belong to a party of young women from Vassar College in New York."

"I put a young woman and three lacquered cases on the Denver-bound train earlier today," he said. "She had tickets and baggage receipts through to Denver, and even though they were AT&SF issue, I couldn't see my way to not honor them. Rail lawyers be damned. She seemed desperate to get to Denver."

"I'm sure she was. That's great news. Thanks." I spotted the coffeepot on the table and pointed at it. "Could I have a bit of that coffee?"

He looked down at the pot, and I took a moment to reach over to an empty table and grab a china cup from the table settings. Walsh nodded and poured some coffee into my borrowed cup. I spooned in some sugar and gulped down the hot, sweet liquid.

"You look like a saddle tramp who's all tramped out, Mr. Carter."

"I had a hard ride up the road with another of those Vassar girls looking to get up to Denver. I got her on the train a couple of minutes ago."

I glanced at a biscuit on a serving plate by his elbow. He caught my stare and pushed the plate my way. "I'm full," he said.

"Thanks again." I sliced open the biscuit, smeared both halves with butter and started chewing. Walsh poured the last of the coffee in my cup.

I'd reached a new level in society—that of beggar.

In truth, I was embarrassed for myself. My mother would have fainted at the sight of me—wet, muddy, and hungry and begging food from another man's table. There was little I would ever be able to tell her about my time in Colorado that would not send her into some kind of fit. Her oldest son turned saddle tramp, gunman, and beggar. And what would Cora think of this scene? From hero to vagabond in but a minute.

I said, "We had a freight driver with the telescopes. Travis Sullivan. Would you know where he went after Elizabeth and the telescopes were transferred to the train?"

"Fella with a limp. Yes, he said he was going back down to Larkspur," said Walsh. He tilted back in his chair and added, "Said he had to go looking for a damn Yankee kid on a damn Yankee saddle riding a damn Yankee horse. He was quite emphatic about the damn Yankee description."

I nodded. I watched a young girl deliver a bowl of stew to a table across the room. "Yeah, that would be Travis…and me."

"You got any money, Mr. Carter?" asked Walsh. I guess I still looked hungry.

"Not enough. Not until I get to my bank in Denver. I've been paying for unexpected food and tickets and telegrams the last few days."

Mr. Walsh stood up, took his cap off the wall hook, and settled it on his neatly combed black hair. He reached in his pants pocket, extracted a handful of coins and sorted through them. Then he slid two dollars in my direction and asked, "You good for it?"

"I am. Soon as I ride down from Denver next week. Thank you." I left the coins lying on the table.

"Well, then, I'll say good night. I've a little poker game over with sheriff."

He picked up his rail case and left for the door, but I jumped up. "Wait. I almost forgot what with everything else... There's been some trouble down at Douglas. Indians, it looks like." I gave him a fast account of what Cora and I had found in the smoldering little town and our own violent encounter with the four painted Indians.

"That's a harrowing piece of news. The whole town...burnt." He looked me over again and said, "You did well against them, coming away with but a scratch. I'll tell the sheriff straight away. If he has questions, where should he find you this night?"

I shrugged and then said, "A loft in the public livery, I suppose. Is there an army detachment about? They might scout for them east of here."

He shook his head. "No. They've gone down to the Pike for the eclipse. There's the sutler and a couple of privates to mind the stock, but that's it. I guess we'll have to make do with the sheriff. Maybe a posse."

"Speaking of my scratch, I don't suppose there's a doctor in town. I'd like him to take a look at this." I moved my left arm for emphasis.

Walsh shook his head. "Gone off to the Pike with the Army. Won't be back for some time. You think you'll be okay till Denver?"

"Just a scratch. It'll keep." I sat back down and waved to the serving girl.

Walsh looked at me again and said, "You know the DRG is going to put you freight haulers out of business."

"It's okay. I'm thinking I need a change in careers."

****

After Mr. Walsh left, I bought a bowl of stew and

lingered over another cup of coffee. I looked at the wall clock. Cora should be pulling into Denver soon. Minutes from here to there. Was there ever a starker difference between a horse and a train?

Somewhat revived by the food and coffee, I gathered up my gear and then walked Barley around the corner to the livery. I saw no lights inside, but I pushed through the main door into the dry, quiet barn. Three other horses were stabled for the night. I relieved Barley of the saddle and tack. A door creaked open behind me. Lantern light spilled from the doorway, and I turned to find a sleepy-eyed colored kid of twelve or fourteen years.

"Two bits for the horse overnight," he said. "Have to pay first."

"I have money," I said, and handed over the coinage. "You'll feed him?"

"Yes, sah."

"Seen a Southern fellow with a limp and a green freight wagon around town?"

"No, sah."

"I need a place to sleep too."

"Mistah Olmsted says this not a hotel." The kid raised the lantern for a better look at me.

"I told the sheriff I'd be here if he needed any more information about an Indian attack down the road." I handed him a few pennies. "We don't want the sheriff looking all over town for me."

He pocketed the pennies and agreed the sheriff didn't want to get wet wandering the streets in search of me.

I hung the saddle and tack on a railing. The kid led Barley to a stall off to the right. He poured some oats in a trough and placed a bucket of water in a corner of the stall. Barley was set for the night.

The loft ladder was near the stalls, and I tottered over to it. I tossed my bags up, followed by the saddle blanket and my rifle. Then I climbed the ladder with all the confidence of an old man. In the loft, a few feet above the lodged horses, I pulled off my muddy boots and peeled off clothes made heavy and sticky by so much rain. I hung my threadbare jacket from the rafters to dry and spread my shirt and pants on a mound of loose hay.

My improvised bandage was still in place. I eased it down, but it was too dark in the loft to tell how the wound looked. I didn't want to risk a match up there, with so much loose hay about. The bandage was damp. But from blood or rain or both, it was hard to tell. The skin around that ugly gash felt hot and throbbed with a steady pulse of pain. I pulled my shirtsleeve bandage back in place.

I lay down in the straw and fell asleep to the pelting of hard rain on the tin-sheet roof. But sleep didn't last. I jerked awake with kaleidoscope images of Indians and vaqueros, muzzle flashes in the night, Davey falling over dead, and the echo of loud screams. I sat up breathing hard and looked around.

Nightmares. That's all I needed.

I didn't remember any screaming with the Mexicans or the Indians or even the foothills ambush. Why were there screams? Below me, the horses shuffled in their stalls, and then it occurred to me I might have been the one screaming. Did I wake myself up with my own terrors and startle the horses?

I flopped back in the hay. "Jesus, Nolan, get hold of yourself."

Chapter 10

In the morning, I felt feverish. But there was nothing to be done about it. I dressed in my damp clothes and climbed down to the floor of the barn. The double doors were open to a morning breeze full of drizzle. I did not see the kid from last night. I fed Barley more oats and some hay while I saddled him for the day's travels. I was ready—but reluctant—to ride. Instead, I left the livery, dodging from eaves to overhangs to porches, trying to stay dry—or less wet, at this point—and worked my way to the Western Union office.

Inside, I found an equally damp telegrapher keying off a message. While waiting for him to finish, I looked around for a coffeepot. He had no coffee, but there was a clock on the wall. I found my pocket watch, set its thin black arms to the time, and wound it for the coming day. The clerk ended his tapping with a smile meant for the telegrapher on the receiving end. He turned to me with a raised eyebrow.

"Any messages pass through for Nolan Carter?" I asked.

The clerk stood and picked up a wire basket from a desk littered with newspapers and telegram forms. He sorted through the half-sheets. "Nope."

"Anything regarding telescopes? Our freight company transferred three telescopes to the DRG for delivery to Denver."

179

"Telescopes," he muttered as he picked through the sheets again. "Nope."

"Anything to or from a Travis Sullivan with the Front Range Freight Company?"

He didn't bother looking and said, "Nope."

Like a telegram, the man was an economy of words. But then he managed to form a complete sentence.

"Seems you're not too popular." He waved a blank telegram form at me. "Want to send something?" he asked.

I did. I wanted to fire telegrams up and down the lines demanding to know where everyone was. Had the telescopes arrived in Denver? Where had Travis and the wagon rolled away to? What did Thaddeus back in Pueblo know about any of this? And was Cora safe? But I didn't have the money for that kind of telegraphic mania. I shook my head and left.

The rain picked up, and I hurried across the muddy street to the café. I found an empty chair and table at the back of the now-busy establishment. The place smelled of steam and smoke and fresh-brewed coffee. A thin man with a heavy tray of steaks and flapjacks sailed past me. I ordered coffee and toast. A sleepy girl in a stained apron brought me a heavy mug of coffee and two pieces of thick-cut toast. I lathered the toast with jam and butter. Chewing slowly, I considered my options. I needed to get to Denver. I had money in a bank there, and I needed it for clothes and food, and to pay Mr. Walsh for his charity last night. I wanted to see the eclipse. Of course, I could watch it here just as well as in Denver—assuming it didn't rain on Monday. But mostly I wanted to see Cora. We had…what?

We'd made a connection on the prairie these last two

days. Like two telegraphers tapping out a coded message to each other, I felt the electrical energy of her every movement. Every glance. Every kiss. So, yes, I was going to Denver. I was going to Denver for a girl who owned a slide rule and measured the late-night stars with the angles of her delicate fingers.

How to get there now? It was raining. Castle Rock to Sedalia was eight miles. Another sixteen to Littleton. Eleven more to Denver. Cora covered that distance in about ninety minutes. Thirty-five miles…in the rain. Barley's going to be an unhappy horse. And I an unhappy rider.

Breakfast was finished all too soon. I left some money on my table and stepped out into the drizzly, half-built town of Castle Rock. I walked back to the livery and found the kid from last night sleeping in the tack room. I woke him with a persistent knock on the doorframe.

He opened his eyes but made no move to leave his bunk and blanket.

"I'm leaving," I said.

"Sheriff find you?" he asked.

"No. Was he here this morning?"

"No, sah. Just wonderin' since you mention him las' night."

It occurred to me I should have asked the telegram clerk if the sheriff had stopped in to send out alerts about the Indians at Douglas. But I had my own problems to solve, and the sheriff would get around to making the necessary inquiries in his own time.

I glanced around the tack room and asked the kid, "Hey, any chance there's some old dusters or rainproofs here I could borrow?"

"Borrow?"

"Rent. I can give you a few pennies now and some more money next week when I come back down from Denver. I already owe the station man two dollars."

This got him out of bed. He walked over to a leather trunk, pulled up the heavy lid, and produced a roll of shiny black cloth. He held it up with one skinny arm and said, "This it. Man left it while back."

I took it from him and unrolled it. It was an old army gum blanket of canvas and vulcanized rubber. "Thank you, Mr. Goodyear," I said to the room.

"I don't know the man's name, but he never come back for it," said the kid.

"This'll do." I took four pennies from my vest pocket and handed them to the kid. "I'll give you a little more next week. Thanks."

I tucked the blanket—poncho really—under my arm and got Barley. I led him out of his stall, cinched him up, and pulled the poncho over my head. A little twisting here and there and pulling the collar up and fitting my hat back on, and I was ready to ride.

"Ready for a long, wet ride?" I asked Barley. His ears tilted back, and he glanced at the stall. "Yeah, I don't like the idea either."

I rode up the main street, passed the train station, and rode by some staked-out properties awaiting carpenters and bricklayers. The horse stepped over the shiny wet rails and wooden ties, and we were back on the road, riding toward Denver. Again.

My thoughts again turned to Cora. If she was riding with me now, she might point out, in her mathematical way, our approach to Denver was *asymptotic* in that we might appear to be getting closer with each passing hour, but we never would reach the city. Always approaching. Never reaching. It had felt that way the last two days. I was amused at this dim schoolboy memory of lines that approached one another but did not merge, and I wished I could share it with Cora. And then I wondered about the everyday geometry of our separate lives.

Had she and I been like two separate lines curving toward each other over the last few years? Philadelphia. Mitchell. The astronomy column. Now we'd met. Intersected. Crossed paths. The trick would be not running off on new tangents. On separate trajectories. Could we find some common…what? A common arc? A common orbit? Orbit seemed the appropriate metaphor, given the pending eclipse.

****

I plodded on through lonely miles of rain and ground-hugging fogs that seeped from stands of trees along the road. I passed a couple of wet riders heading to the Rock and gave them a wave. Later, I surprised a lone mule deer standing in the creek. It retreated into the woods at a leisurely pace, never once looking back.

For much of the day, the world—my little part of it—was empty and quiet but for the fall of rain and the rush of the creek. I wondered about the four Indians somewhere off to my right, maybe working their way north like me. The vulcanized army poncho was keeping my right hand dry and my jacket was unbuttoned for easy access to my Colt.

****

The rain was a constant companion. Heavy black clouds skimmed the treetops, dumped their contents, and moved on. Higher up, gray cotton ball clouds released a steady drizzle of fine droplets. My horse tramped through it all while I wondered about all the astronomers stationed around Colorado and Wyoming waiting for the Monday afternoon eclipse. Their collective nerves must be on edge wondering if the weather would break in time. All that time and money and planning for an event that might be masked by a passing shower or a slow-moving cloud. Later, I read in the newspapers hour-by-hour reports had flickered up and down the telegraph wires from Montana to Texas, giving the local weather conditions and making predictions about what Monday afternoon would look like in their respective locations.

I passed by Sedalia. A southbound train idled at the station, taking on passengers and water. I didn't stop. I did not have the time or the money to spend on a midday meal or the proper care of my horse. A mile north of Sedalia, I passed over a wooden bridge and rode down to the creek bank. I climbed down and let Barley drink from the fast-moving water.

"Water, water everywhere, and more than a drop to drink," I misquoted to Barley. I looked up at the gray sky. For some reason, I thought of Ishmael floating on a coffin in the middle of the ocean, hoping for rescue.

Cora came out here for the eclipse. She must hate this unexpected weather. Maybe she hated all of Colorado and the West by now. Indians. Lecherous drovers. Rattlesnakes. Burned towns. Hot, dusty roads to nowhere. She'd be glad to get away from all of it. *And when she does get away, will she come to hate me for having dragged her through all of it?* Chance brought us together. Now chance seemed to be driving us apart.

****

It was dark when I reached Littleton. The road crossed Plum Creek to the south of town, so I avoided having to cross the South Platte River. Still, there were any number of tributaries, creeks and gulches to contend with, all of them swollen with two days' worth of rainwater. Coming down the main street of the town, I saw a lighted cantina and a bar, and off to the right, a general store. A shopkeeper out front, under the protection of the overhung porch, was packing up display goods for the day. I hurried over and bought four apples for ten cents. I rode back to the cantina, tied up Barley, and fed him two of the apples.

Littleton is not a town bursting with residents. There might be seventy or so living here on a regular basis. Tonight, they all appeared to be in the cantina. I made myself unwelcome by adding to the crush of people inside and then made a few enemies when I pulled off my wet poncho in their vicinity. There were no free tables or chairs, so I made my way over to a serving bar. Behind the bar, a busy, middle-aged woman was pouring coffee and setting plates. She looked up at my wet presence.

"Cup of coffee. And maybe a couple of biscuits or rolls you might have on hand?"

She poured some coffee in a mug and placed it on the counter. She looked at me again and asked, "You come off the road just now?"

I nodded and took in a mouthful of sweet coffee.

She glanced down at the cutting board counter and said, "I got a lone egg here. Put a fried egg with those biscuits for five cents more?"

After a quick mental inventory of my pockets, I nodded at the idea of an egg.

Despite the noise of the cantina, or maybe because of it, the woman was inclined to talk, and I was willing

185

to keep up my end of the conversation with an occasional nod of agreement or acknowledgement of her comments.

"You a ranch hand?" she asked.

"Freight company. Pueblo. Got separated from the wagon. I've been spending time and money trying to find them again."

The woman said, "Heard of freight getting misplaced. Never heard of freighters themselves getting lost, though. Not good for business, I'd imagine."

She slid a small plate containing two biscuits and one fried egg in front of me and then disappeared on another errand. I'd finished eating by the time she got back.

"Mam, do you know if the boardinghouse has room tonight?"

"I very much doubt it, mister. People been coming to town for the eclipse the last day or so. Coming down from Denver because it's cheaper here. Couple of local ranch families come in from the prairie, too. Even the livery's full up now. Least till Monday."

She poured me half a mug of coffee, and I asked her, "Any idea where I might get out of the rain for the night?" Standing upright in a closet had a certain appeal right now.

"Well..." She wiped her hands with a dirty apron and pointed behind her. "Up the road on the left is a half-built store. It's roofed over now, so you'll be dry enough sleeping on the floor, if that appeals to you."

"It does. Thanks." I counted out twenty cents and maneuvered toward the door.

Too stiff to get back in the saddle, I led Barley up the street and found the black shadow of the construction site. Two broad steps were in place, and I eased Barley up the steps and into the open store front. Stacks of cut lumber were piled to one side. I smelled damp sawdust and fresh tar. Otherwise, the front room was open and empty, and most importantly, dry. I groped around in my saddlebag and found the lantern. A match flared in my hand, and I lit the lantern to cast a comforting spread of yellow light around me. I set the light on a keg of nails and propped some long boards across the doorway to keep Barley in and discourage any late-night intruders. Then I took off the saddle and bridle and cut up the remaining two apples to feed my damp horse. Looking around, I said to him, "Be nice to have a fire in here, but burning down the building tonight isn't going to help matters."

The planked floor smelled of newly sawed wood. I made a bed of the poncho—rubber-side down, the blanket and bags, and my soggy coat. Searching the saddlebags again for lost coinage, and finding none, I picked up my journal. Cora was right—I hadn't written anything in days. Who had time? I leafed through the pages.

At the back of the notebook, I found a folded sheet. It was Cora's drawing of the transit of Mercury. I unfolded the paper and looked at her diagram again. I remembered her thin fingers moving above the page and the curve of her serious, attractive face while she drew this little astronomical lesson.

I hope she's warm and dry in Avery's Denver house.

I replaced the drawing and studied my temporary bedroom again. There was a four-legged stool. I placed it near my bedding and laid a plank from the stool to the stack of lumber. My makeshift desk needed a chair. So I rolled the nail keg closer to the horizontal plank and sat on the keg to scribble a few notes about my recent adventures.

****

I pulled out my watch to wind it and was surprised to see more than two hours had passed since I sat down. I should be sleeping. Barley seemed to be, with his head nodding closer and closer to the floor. Instead, I had penciled in a number of solid descriptions of the people we came across since losing track of Travis and Elizabeth. Sitting here alone, in the quiet of this half-finished building, I also formed a clearer memory of the first vaquero I shot.

The fully-remembered image of him emerged like a photograph in its chemical bath. His eyes were as cold and clear as the water in which Cora had soaked her feet. He was not scared of me and my Winchester. When he stepped in front of his friend, hiding the other man's draw, it was something he'd done before. They'd done before. The two of them, smiling their sly smiles, knowing they were going to kill me and take Cora. It was a relief to me to remember those eyes now. I needn't feel bad about shooting the two of them. Instead, I found myself wishing I'd shot all three of them.

I considered the Indians, and my mind went blank. A sudden rush of raw panic swept through me. My stomach heaved. I stood up, breathing hard. The four Indians on horseback. That was the closest I had come to dying. Ever. Even during the ambush with Brian and Davey. That had been flashes of light and noise in the black woods. Invisible assailants. Somehow, four men with guns, in the open, and under a bright sun, had been a far more real and terrifying encounter. Yet I survived. With one very lucky shot.

I sat down again and rested my head in my hands. After a minute or two, calm again, I picked up my pencil and wrote down more pleasant remembrances of the homesteader family who gave us supper and a prairie bed. And I made a quick sketch of Cora standing on the empty plain, her arms out, signaling the pencil-dot stars above her slender graphite shape.

Not bad. I should show it to Brian someday.

I stood up and stretched as far as my wounded flank would let me. The constant pain had given way to a periodic ache. I left the lantern burning on the plank and walked over to an unfinished window. Looking out, a soft rain fell. Off to the east and above the treetops, I spotted a few stars between the drifting clouds.

East. Maybe I should go...where? Home to Chicago? Follow Cora to Boston? Would she even want me to? She can't stay out here, of course. What would she do here? A girl with a slide rule and a telescope. And what am I doing chasing after such a girl?

On Monday, the Newtonian forces of Nature would align the three most important bodies in the solar system. Many people would see some meaning in this spectacular arrangement. Weather permitting. The astronomers no doubt would seek a greater understanding of those natural forces during the event. Cora had told me there was no more special meaning in the coming eclipse than there would be in Tuesday's sunrise or the setting of the Moon on Friday. Eclipses happened all the time.

Yet it was hard not to see some message in Monday's spectacle. It had brought Cora to Denver. It had brought me to Denver—I was almost there. It seemed like a shared destiny, though I did not believe in fate, or omens, or any gypsy prophecies.

I might be lovesick. Or I might just be sick of hard living, rough sleeping, and scrounging for coins. Maybe Cora was but another symptom of my own need to find a place in the world and get on with the business of living. Or maybe she was the cure, the thing I told Brian back in Pueblo I was staying on to search for. And if she was that sought-after thing, I should do all I could to hold on to her. Wherever she went. If she'd let me.

Drifting clouds shrouded the few stars. Stepping back to my plank desk, I picked up the lantern. Looking around again, I found a white piece of cloth on top of a half-finished cabinet. It was a clean, dry dishrag. I set the lantern on the cabinet and peeled off my shirt. The wound still hurt, but the morning's feverish spell had passed. I pulled away the messy bandana and aimed the lantern light at the spot where the bullet had plowed up my skin. It was raw and ugly, leaking brown blood and yellow serum in spots. Crusty scabs were forming along the edges. I pressed the dish rag to the wound and pulled up the tied shirtsleeve to hold it in place.

Setting the lantern on the floor by my bedding, I lay down. I hoped filling the pages of my journal with the bloody details of the week might exorcise my nighttime demons. I needed a peaceful night.

The lantern burned itself out, and I fell asleep to the heavy breathing of my horse.

****

Cool, gray light seeped in through the empty window frame. Barley moved about the room, careful not to step on me. It was early enough that the town was not yet stirring. I rolled over and got to my feet. I wanted to be gone before anyone came in the building to start another day's work. Barley had made a mess on one side of the room, but it wasn't anything water and shovel wouldn't take care of. I just didn't want to be the one tasked with doing it. I pulled the boards away from the front entrance. It had stopped raining, but the roiling overhead cloud cover hinted at more to come.

I got my weary horse saddled and scooped up my lantern. Journal packed, jacket on, and poncho at the ready, I led him through the doorway and down onto a wide main street of clinging mud and pond-size puddles. There was no money for breakfast. Instead, I rode out of town intending to push hard while the rain held off. It was eleven miles to Denver. I could cover that distance without much trouble.

And then? Find Cora? *God, what must I look like after these last days in the saddle? I've got no money for a bath or hotel until the bank opens on Monday.*

A train roared by, and I cursed the owners of all railroads. It started to rain again, and I slipped back under the protection of the vulcanized poncho. I stopped every few miles to water Barley and let him nibble at some grass. Ranches and farms began to appear closer to the road and the rails, and Barley raised his head now and then at the scent of cattle and other horses. I didn't stop at any of these dwellings. I had nothing to offer in the way of news or cash, and I was tired of begging for handouts.

Approaching Denver, hand-painted signs appeared along the road and tracks, advertising hotels and boardinghouses for eclipse watchers, and prime viewing points from atop various Denver buildings. A few Lutheran churches were advertising space in their steeples and bell towers. "Watch the heavens from church," declared one sign.

By noon, the sky grew darker and a northwest wind brought down hail from the mountains. The pea-sized bits of ice began to hurt. I pushed Barley into a thicket of pine trees where we found good cover from the sharp sting of the summertime ice.

"What next, my good horse? Thunder maybe? Snow? Locusts?" I asked him.

The answer turned out to be Indians.

We were not a minute under the trees when four Indians burst into the open from the woods ahead of me. I recognized them—not by their rain-washed faces, but by their horses' markings and blankets. The first three riders stopped and searched up and down the visible parts of the road. The fourth man—his arm in a rope sling—led two other horses on long tethers. He trotted across the road, splashed through the creek, and disappeared into the opposite woods.

I stopped breathing. I put a hand on Barley's neck to keep him still. The darkened sky and the shadows of the trees made for weak camouflage. If they saw me, I would pull my pistol and charge straight at them, firing as I came on. They might not expect that kind of suicidal lunacy. If I could get clear of them without being hit, the rain and fog might provide cover enough to throw off their shots and let me gallop away. Denver was so close.

The three men, indifferent to the weather, sat in the road, watching for travelers, rifles in hand. Finally, they moved into the woods, heading west, perhaps toward the Ute White River settlement. I waited. How long, I don't remember. But eventually, I forced us out of hiding and onto the road. I put the spurs to Barley, and we pounded through the puddles and gravel until we were both tired of the flight. The hail moved off onto the prairie, and I continued up the road, feeling an unusual chill.

White River was a long ride. Those Indians would still be picking their way through the Front Range foothills when the eclipse arrived tomorrow afternoon. What would they think was happening, I wondered? Angry deities? Some trick of the white man? I was curious to know, but not curious enough to ask the next passing Indian.

Crossing the DRG track line again, I rode over a small stone bridge that spanned the Merchant's Mill Ditch. On the other side of this little waterway, I was greeted with a stone-cut sign that read, "Denver City, Incorporated 1861."

I reached up and gave Barley's broad neck a pat. "Good job, horse. We're here at last. And still alive." Perhaps I should have felt triumphant at having arrived, but now I only felt tired of the ride. Of the road. Of the West. And of my place in it.

****

I rode up South Street in a light rain. The usual mountain vista was obscured by the mass of dark rain clouds. Big brick buildings with their doorway awnings extended against the rain lined the red mud street. Wagons, gigs, and buckboards maneuvered slowly through the mud, careful not to throw up any more muck than was necessary. A surprising number of residents were out, scurrying between shops and homes, jumping over puddles, and wielding black umbrellas against the erratic weather.

No one took any notice of me. I was just another wet cowboy riding into town for the eclipse. At Colfax Avenue, I crossed the bridge over Cherry Creek and entered East Denver. I zigzagged up through the neighborhood blocks looking for the corner of 20th Street and Champa Street. I followed the streetcar tracks laid down in the middle of Champa and soon stopped in front of an imposing two-story house surrounded by a low, wrought-iron fence and tall trees planted along the sidewalk.

I rode up to the front gate. "Well, the doctor has done herself well," I announced to Barley and the passing streetcar. "And now she has a beggar at her front door." I had no money until the morning and no place to sleep tonight. Once again, I was a charity case looking for bed and board in a town now crowded with moneyed tourists.

I tied Barley to the iron fence and proceeded up the brick walkway. I wondered what kind of greeting I might receive from Cora and the rest of her party. I wasn't expecting compliments or congratulations from Professor Mitchell. Quite the opposite, in fact. I had no idea if she had her telescopes or not. That they were put on a train with Elizabeth back in Castle Rock did not mean Mitchell received them here in Denver. They may not have been unloaded and instead been shipped back down to Pueblo. Or they might be sitting in a freight depot a block from the passenger station.

I stepped to the front door. Under the protection of an overhead balcony, I pulled off the bulky, wet poncho. Taking a deep breath—I was nervous—I pulled the doorbell. The bell chimed on the other side of the glass-fronted door. A shadow appeared behind the opaque glass and turned the doorknob.

The shadow became a young maid who stepped back at the sight of me on the stoop. Had I been her, I might have run. What she found on the doorstep was a wet, muddy stranger, unshaved and unbathed, with, I imagined, a gaunt look about him.

Before she slammed the door, I asked, "Is this the house of Alida Avery, a friend of Professor Mitchell's?"

"It is. And who might you be, sir?" she asked in a light German accent. Or maybe it was a Swedish accent; she had bright blonde hair, the likes of which you usually had to travel to Wisconsin to see.

"I'm Nolan Carter from the freight company in Pueblo. I was helping to move the telescopes…"

"You're the one was with Miss Cora. Saved her from the bandits." She was all smiles now and threw open the door to me.

"Yes. Is Cora…Miss Harrison here? And Professor Mitchell? Did the telescopes arrive?"

"No. And yes…about the telescopes. They are here."

"And where are the professor and her students?" I looked back toward the street, wishing them to appear out of the drizzle.

"They have gone out to the viewing site. It is down Park Avenue, near the St. Joseph's Home. I should think the rain will not keep them," she said.

I was disappointed to hear this news. I had hoped for smiles and greetings, and a joyful reunion with Cora. Despite my current state and status. Instead, I was met with an empty house and an immigrant maid. "Oh," was all I thought to say.

"Would you come in, please," she asked and stepped aside.

"Ah…" I looked down at myself and then glanced back at my wet horse. I said, "Perhaps I should come in through the kitchen. I'm a bit of a mess, what with the weather and all. I don't want to despoil the doctor's home with muddy boots and wet clothes."

She nodded at my appearance and leaned out the door to look at my horse. "Well, yes, best to come around back through the gate. There is the carriage house you can put your horse to. I shall meet you around the back door."

"Thank you," I said and stepped back into the rain to get Barley.

I walked him around to the back of the house where I found an expansive garden of flowers and a small grove of apple trees. A bright red, double-door carriage house sat farther back on the property. I tied Barley to a post under the long slope of the carriage house roof.

I hurried over to the kitchen door. The maid opened the door, and I stepped into a warm, dry kitchen that smelled of bread, blueberry pie, and baked ham. The mingled aromas stopped me on the spot. I must have looked like a dog with a compelling scent in its nose, because the maid smiled and asked, "Have you eaten something today?"

Now in a kind of daze, I shook my head.

She pointed to the kitchen table and said, "Please, sit here. Let me get the hero cowboy something to eat. You can tell of your adventures. Ya?"

She worked on a loaf of bread and the still-warm ham. I watched the formation of a ham sandwich with great interest. She wanted to hear my story, but Cora already had provided details of our travails off the Pueblo-Denver road. Instead of repeating a known narrative, or worse perhaps, adding some detail Cora had decided to leave out, I asked her about the situation in

Denver—specifically, where I might find a bed for the night and a bath in the morning.

"Everything is filled to the attics with tourists and professional persons come to watch the eclipse. You could not find a hotel room for less than the Crown's jewels. Even the German gymnasium on Arapahoe Street has become a boardinghouse for all manner of persons."

That was depressing news. Not unexpected, but depressing, nonetheless. I asked, "The banks. Will they be open tomorrow? I need to get to my money."

"Most of them shall be for an hour or two, to accommodate travelers and us locals needing cash and wire transfers," she said.

She set a dish with the sandwich in front of me and then placed a glass of milk beside it. "Eat now," she said.

I took her invitation to be a holy commandment.

"I'll make up some coffee to go with slice of the doctor's pie."

Biting into the sandwich, I nodded in agreement.

****

Later, having finished what I hoped would be my last beggar's meal—and remembering to ask the maid's name—I asked Anna about a place in the house where I might wash up. It felt like I was wearing much of the Denver road and all of the recent weather. Standing by the kitchen stove, she stared at me for several silent seconds, reminding me of an earlier scrutiny by Professor Mitchell.

"You are…" she said and stopped. Then she said, "Wait here a moment, please," and she left the room.

I heard her booted feet on the stairs. Then an upstairs door slammed, and I heard her rapid footsteps on the staircase again. She came back through the kitchen door

197

with a large towel and a larger flannel robe of green and black striping.

She handed both items to me and said, "This should fit well enough. Go out to the carriage house, put this on, and I will bring you some soap and hot water. I think your clothes can be washed out and iron-dried quick enough. You will not mind the carriage house? The upstairs here is full now of the professor's students."

I shook my head, smiling, and said, "No. It'll be two steps up from where I've been sleeping these last days."

I pulled open the back door and she said, "Mind the doctor's horse. She's a fat old mare for the shay."

At the carriage house, I opened one of the doors and stepped inside to check the accommodations. Two windows in the back wall let in the day's gray light. The mare was in her stall. The doctor's red-and-black shay was parked in the middle of the space.

Behind the two-wheeler were three long narrow boxes shut tight with brass latches. The telescopes. I squatted down and gave one of the wooden cases a pat on its lacquered top. "Here you are. Now the skies must clear."

On the opposite side of the carriage, I found room enough to tie Barley away from the mare. I brought him in and got him a bag of oats from a bin and pumped him a bucket of water from the garden well.

With Barley secured, I took care of myself. I emptied my pockets of eleven cents, a small folding knife, and my watch. My muddy boots and wet socks put up a fight, and I came away from that struggle even dirtier than before. I peeled off my coat, vest, and mangled shirt, all made damp by days of sweat and rain dribbling down the back of my neck.

My bandaged side around the bullet wound was stiff. The wound was beginning to itch.

That might be a good sign. I hoped Dr. Avery might examine it, so I resisted the urge to poke and pry at the wound or the wet bandage.

I dropped my gun belt, unbuckled my pants belt, and then pulled off my wet, muddy pants. Off came the drawers, and I slipped on the flannel robe. Looking down at my pile of vile clothing, I felt sorry for Anna. If I'd had anything else to wear, I would have told her to burn the whole pile and be done with it. But I wouldn't have other clothes until I had money again, and that wasn't going to happen until the banks opened on Monday, now a semi-holiday for the eclipse.

There was a knock on the front of the carriage house, and then Anna pulled open one of the doors. "Hello again. I brought the water and soap. You are comfortable?" she asked.

"Yes, thanks." I came around the shay in the flannel robe and bare feet, stepping carefully on the splintered floorboards.

Steam wafted from a bucket in her hand. She held a tin basin in the other hand. I took both of them from her and set them on the feed bin. She handed me a bar of white soap smelling of lilacs.

"I should take your clothes, please," she said.

I retrieved the wet, odorous pile and apologized for their sorry state. "The shirt's not worth the bother."

But she waved off the apology and any embarrassment I felt, saying she had two younger brothers and sometimes played nurse to some of Dr. Avery's patients. Then she took up my clothes and left the carriage house.

I spent the next half hour soaping, rinsing, and drying myself to a healthier and happier state of being. I retrieved a comb and toothbrush from the bags and combed my hair and brushed my teeth with the remains of the still-warm water.

Padding around in my moccasins, I hummed a few bars of "I'll Take You Home Again, Kathleen." I found a blanket under the seat in the shay and then pulled four bales of hay together to make a comfortable bed off the floor. I lay down intending to wait for what I imagined would be the noisy return of Cora and the rest of the Mitchell party. But I failed in that too.

Chapter 11

It was early morning. Still dressed in the borrowed robe and my moccasins, I replaced the blanket and bales, and fed the horses. Someone knocked on the double doors. Anna stuck her head in through the partially opened doorway.

"Ah, you are up with the roosters," she said.

"What's happened? Are Professor Mitchell and her students here?"

"Yes, yes. Everyone is getting up. Breakfast shortly." She handed me a neat bundle of clean clothes and said, "There is a different shirt here for you. The doctor's patients sometimes leave behind some things. It will fit, I think. Dress now and come in for the breakfast."

"Thank you." I accepted the bundle of pressed clothes and asked, "What time is it?"

Stepping through the doorway, she said, "Half-past the six."

I set and wound my watch and got dressed. My boots were mostly dry—I scraped some caked mud off—and pulled them on. Presentable now, I stepped outside in search of Cora.

Bright morning light filled the verdant backyard. Monday had arrived, and with it was a blue, cloudless sky. Astronomers across the state and the territories must be giddy with relief at the end of the rains and the clearing of the western skies.

I was halfway to the house when the back door opened and Cora stepped out.

I hurried to her, grinning, and thinking to take her in my arms. But I saw several unfamiliar faces looking out from the second-story windows and restrained myself. I didn't want to embarrass her with my desires. Instead, I sought to catch her hands in mine, but she brushed my offered hands aside. She threw her arms around me and hugged me close. And I did the same to her, the onlookers be damned.

"I'm so happy to see you. Safe! And dry," I said. I kissed her.

She wore a dress I had not seen before. A dark blue silk affair that seemed to flow around her like an airy cocoon. Her hair was done up with a silver comb, and I caught a hint of an expensive perfume.

She took hold of my upper arms and said, "I've been so worried for you. Did you have any other problems on the road? I wanted to wake you last night, but Anna insisted you were sleeping like the dead. Dr. Avery and Professor Mitchell said I should let you sleep until the morning."

"Yes, I missed your return." Dead to the world and untroubled by nightmares. "Did you have any trouble getting here from the train?"

She said, "I looked like the most forlorn of passengers arriving in Denver. Then I could not find a carriage to take me down the street. So, I walked through the rain to the house. When I arrived at the front door, Anna gave me such a look! She must have taken me for a beggar woman, dressed in your big wet duster." She laughed at the memory.

I laughed with her and said, "I know that look. I got the same disapproving scrutiny yesterday." I looked to the kitchen and said, "Come on. I don't want you to miss your breakfast. The eclipse won't wait."

We stepped into a whirlwind of people, foods, and aromas in the now cramped kitchen. Anna, with a teapot in one hand and a coffeepot in the other, pivoted and banged her way through a swinging door to what I guessed was a dining room. A girl of Cora's age was prying blueberry muffins from a tin tray and keeping a close eye on a skillet of German sausages.

Cora pulled my sleeve and said, "Nolan, this is Emma Culbertson. She graduated with me, class of 1876."

I said, "Good morning," and she gave me a friendly morning grin.

An older woman with a stack of china plates came toward us.

"And this is Dr. Alida Avery. Dr. Avery, Nolan Carter of Chicago," said Cora.

Doctor Avery was a short woman with ginger-brown hair tied up in the back and parted down the middle. She had a narrow nose and thoughtful, olive-green eyes. My first impression was of a serious woman in a serious business and doing very well for herself. Cora told me later Avery earned more than ten thousand dollars a year from her medical practice and suffragette speaking engagements.

Dr. Avery pushed the stack of plates into my hands and said, "Mr. Carter of Chicago. I understand you were to deliver two former students and three telescopes to Denver in time for today's event. You have succeeded, yet with an extraordinary degree of drama wrapped up in that simple task."

"The drama was unintended…"

"Yes, yes," she said.

With a gentle tug, she urged me toward the swinging door and said, "Please deliver the plates to the dining room without getting lost or shooting anyone."

Now I felt more like a suspect than a hero. I pushed aside the door, finding a dining room on the other side along with four women, three of whom I recognized. They were scattered about the ornate room, setting out china pieces and moving chairs to accommodate what I guessed would be a large party for breakfast. Elizabeth Abbot called my name and hurried over to me. She took the plates, set them on the table, and gave me a welcoming hug.

"It's so good to see you again. We were so worried, and then Cora showed up," she said.

"I'm glad you and the telescopes caught a train. And Travis, he drove back to Larkspur?"

"That was his intention, yes."

"Well, you'll have to tell me all that transpired after we parted company, but first…"

"Oh, and this is Cornelia Marsh from Illinois. Vassar class of '73," said Elizabeth.

I nodded and said, "A pleasure, Miss Marsh."

Class of this. Class of that. I was truly "outclassed" here. I hoped no one would ask about when and where I went to college. Cattle drives and freight companies did not issue diplomas.

"And you remember Phebe Kendall from Pueblo, and of course, Professor Mitchell," Elizabeth said.

The professor and her younger sister were at the far end of the room. I gave a quick nod to Phebe and said,

"Miss Kendall. Very nice to see you again."

Professor Mitchell was giving me another of her quiet, stern-faced inspections. This one seemed to go on longer than necessary, since she had seen me in Pueblo and done a thorough enough examination there. Admittedly, I was still looking travel-worn and in need of a shave, but then she said, "Mr. Carter, you said you would deliver our colleagues and our equipment to Denver before the eclipse. And you and your colleague have done so with surprising ingenuity and determination in the face of great adversity. We thank you for delivering everyone safely to Denver, along with our equipment."

I didn't think the word "surprising" was necessary to the compliment, but this was the best I likely was to get from this stern-faced Yankee Quaker.

"I'm sorry it took so long and led to so much suspense about our location." I tried to get the upper hand in this conversation by asking, "I hope you didn't misplace the optics on the train from Pueblo."

"We have everything we need for this afternoon's viewing," she said. She sat in a chair on the other side of the dining table and reached for the teapot.

****

Professor Mitchell and her sister had arrived in Denver on Wednesday. At Dr. Avery's house, they were met by Emma Culbertson, who had traveled from California, and Cornelia Marsh, who came from Illinois. Together, they began a regular search of the Denver train depots looking for their telescopes and waiting around the telegraph offices trying to locate Cora and Elizabeth. They even had stopped freight wagons on the Denver streets to see if their equipment might be aboard.

The professor, I learned, had a curious fear of lightning. Maybe because she spent so much time out of doors holding onto a large brass telescope. But she suppressed her fear during Friday's rainy search of the depots and telegraph rooms. Most of her anxieties ended with the arrival of Elizabeth and the telescopes on the train from Castle Rock. After that, only Cora's situation—and the rain—continued to trouble her and the Vassar contingent.

****

Cora came through the swinging door with a wheel-size platter of scrambled eggs and said, "Everything is ready. Everyone find a seat." She looked at me and said, "Nolan, please sit. We'll bring everything out."

She set the platter down and disappeared back into the kitchen. In a moment, Cora and Emma and Dr. Avery returned with the rest of the food. I sat down, Cora slid onto the chair next to mine, and I surveyed the morning's feast thinking no one would need lunch today.

Dr. Avery took a seat, looked about the table, and said, "Well, my dear colleagues, science and medicine aside, there is nothing to beat a generous breakfast. Let us eat."

And with the end of that secular benediction, we took our measure of the waiting spread.

I glanced at Cora and then eased my booted foot in her direction—moving with caution lest I contact another's wayward foot or snag mine against the carpet—until I contacted hers. From the corner of my eye, I saw her glance at me. She didn't move her foot.

****

I ate my breakfast in between questions. The other Vassar girls were consumed by the story of Cora and me riding through the wild prairie. For them, it smacked of a Wild West story come to life, and with all the expected terrors of dangerous outlaws and hostile Indians, and all the unexpected twists of lost horses, friendly homesteaders, and burned-out towns. I felt like a cliché; I tried to play down the encounter with the vaqueros and the brief fight with the Indians, but they were having none of it. I had become their adventure. Never mind the eclipse, at least until this afternoon.

Professor Mitchell surprised me by asking, "What was it like, Mr. Carter, to confront the Indian in his natural element?"

"Well, I confess I was lucky to kill one of their horses. It seemed to scramble their plans for a quick attack and a quick retreat to wherever they were going. Otherwise, things might have turned out very different."

"You must have been relieved to see Cora come galloping back after the Indians left." Emma said with a hint of mischief. "Lying out there all alone, you might have fallen prey to more savages or hungry buzzards and wolves."

"A western heroine," Phebe said of Cora.

I stole a quick look at Cora and said, "She was supposed to be galloping off to Denver, but I'm glad she decided to stay nearby. I…needed help. And a horse."

"You were a mess. And wounded," Cora said.

Still staring at her, I said, "I saw them again. The same Indians. Just outside of Denver. They just appeared on the road in front of me…but they didn't see me."

Wide-eyed, Cora said, "Oh, my God… What…?"

"I was under a thicket of trees and hidden by the hail and rain. They rode west, and I galloped away."

My audience was silent, impressed by the proximity

of such dangers. In the quiet, Cora grabbed my arm with her hands. Her grip was firm, but her face was soft. She said, "You are a nine-lived cat and shedding those lives willy-nilly."

I placed my hand over her clutching hands. "How many left?" I asked with a smile.

"Three now, with this last encounter." She released my arm and picked up her teacup.

"What happened to the earlier five?" asked Emma.

I changed the subject by asking Elizabeth what happened after Cora and I failed to rejoin the wagon.

****

When Cora and I didn't reappear along the road, Travis had let loose with a steady barrage of colorful complaints about me, about the failure of the best-laid plans, and about the foolishness of passengers on a freight wagon. His petulant monologue and his increasingly harsh vocabulary reached such a pitch Elizabeth began to feel uncomfortable seated next to the volatile Southerner. But then Travis either came to his senses or ran out of vitriolic steam. In either case, he apologized to Elizabeth, assured her all would turn out well, and pressed on to the town of Monument.

In Monument, he sent Elizabeth to a café to get sandwiches and apples for the road. Then he limped over to the DRG station to check on the train situation and to leave word with the station manager should I and Cora show up there. He left a similar message at the Western Union. But Cora and I never made it to Monument, so we never found those messages. From Monument, they pressed on up the road. They reached Castle Rock, where he got Elizabeth and the telescopes on a Denver-bound train, and where Travis had vented his frustrations to Mr.

Walsh, the station manager.

****

Except for her one question about the Indians, Mitchell said little about my recital or her students' questions and comments. Now she declared, "Our journey here has been fraught with all manner of obstacle and danger, and all of it driven by the greed of devious men, be they presidents of railroads or foreign bandits. But we are here now, and but a few hours from participating in this important scientific endeavor."

She glanced at Dr. Avery and then at a clock sitting on the sideboard. "Our transportation shall arrive soon. We must get our equipment and supplies in order."

Everyone got to their feet. Emma, Anna, and Dr. Avery piled the dishes and carried them back into the kitchen. Phebe, Elizabeth, and Cornelia hurried through the parlor to the staircase at the front of the house.

I turned to Cora and said, "I have to ride to town. To the bank."

"You'll come to our viewing site, won't you?" she asked.

"Of course. I'll be in town and back out before you know it. I doubt the bankers will want to linger either."

Hearing this, Professor Mitchell said, "Since you need to saddle your horse, might you take a minute to help us rig Dr. Avery's shay and assist with carrying the telescope cases to the front of the house? We have contracted a wagon to take them out to our viewing site at the McCullough's Addition."

"Yes. Happy to help out. I'll be out at the carriage house." I slid by Cora, letting my hand brush her shoulder.

"That can wait a moment," said Dr. Avery. "Come

into my office and let me look at this bullet wound of yours. There's little merit in dying so soon after getting the girls and the telescopes up here. This way."

I followed her into a front room fitted out with a desk, bookcases, glass-fronted cabinets, and a small examination table.

"Let me see your side," she said.

She busied herself with clean cotton patches and tape, and a bottle of iodine, while I pulled off my brushed jacket, torn vest, and borrowed shirt.

Avery stared at my shirtsleeve-dishrag bandage. "I've seen worse." Then she cut it away with a pair of scissors. She eased the dishrag from the drying wound and leaned in to look more closely at it.

"Hmm. Yes, this is coming along." She probed the red-tinted skin around the bullet's furrow with a firm index finger. "You were lucky, indeed. Any trouble breathing? Not coughing up any blood?"

"No." I shook my head. "I'm fine."

"No, you're not. You've been shot. You'll be fine later."

She dropped a little iodine solution onto a square cotton patch and pressed it to the wound. I winced at the sting.

"Hold this in place while I get the tapes," she said.

She cut three sticky strips and applied them across the patch and my skin. "That should hold well enough."

"Maybe not for long," I said. "I'm going to try to find a bathhouse this morning. The bandage may not survive the scrubbing."

Dr. Avery looked me in the eye and said, "Yes, please do some scrubbing. But not around the wound. And be sure to pay for clean, hot water." She walked over to one of the glass cabinets again and retrieved another cotton patch and tape. "Take these. If the first bandage comes loose, you can make a clean, dry one with this. I'll check it again later."

****

Patched up by a real doctor, I felt better about my long-term prospects and went out back to help get things ready for the eclipse. I led Barley out of the carriage house and let him wander within the fenced confines of the property. Then I grabbed the shafts of the doctor's shay and pulled it into the yard and collected the traces and bridle.

Cora appeared behind me. I turned around, and she gave me a quick kiss on my stubbled cheek. "I'm so glad you made it to Denver. I'm sorry we've had so little time to talk. Everyone's here, and now we're all so busy today. And all my colleagues want to talk to you. What did Dr. Avery say about your side?"

I waved off her question about the doctor. "She said I'll live." Stepping closer to her, I said, "As for your friends…well, I only want to talk to you anyway. There'll be time enough after the eclipse. Right? When are you leaving?"

There it was: the question that needed asking. When are you leaving? I had no expectation but that she would leave. She had a life and a compelling job back East. Friends and family in New York and Boston. There was nothing for her here on the narrow strip of frontier towns between the vertical mass of the Rockies and the numbing flatness of the plains. It would be a wasted life and a wasted education to remain in Colorado.

"I'm not sure. Professor Mitchell may stay over another day or so to give a lecture. But sometime this week. Summer will be over soon."

Please, let the railroad war continue, and the conductors and engineers strike.

I nodded, not knowing what else to say and knowing that now was not the time for any long or emotional conversation. I didn't know what to say anyway.

"Well, then, maybe before everyone…packs up, can I take you to dinner in town? I know one or two interesting places."

"That would be wonderful," she said. "We'll not have much time to take a proper tour of Denver. Dr. Avery says the city is growing fast. There are even plans for a telephone exchange next year."

Dr. Avery stepped into the carriage house to get her horse. I followed her outside and helped set the mare in the traces. Cora walked Barley back to the carriage house, and I saddled him. I left my guns and saddlebags on a bale of hay. After that, I picked up the smaller of the three telescope cases and followed Cora around to the front of the house. Cora said this particular telescope was the same one Mitchell used to observe the 1869 eclipse in Iowa. I placed the lucky instrument on the grass beside the front gate. We walked back to the carriage house, passing Professor Mitchell and some of her former students as they carried the other two telescope cases.

Dr. Avery's carriage was ready. I pulled Barley away from a tempting bed of flowers and climbed up. Cora stepped away from the horse, and I said, "Back as fast as bankers' hours will allow."

"Do you know our viewing site?" she asked. "Down Park Avenue. Right across the road from a Catholic hospital."

"I'll find you. How hard will it be to spot half a

dozen women with three telescopes?"

She called to my back, "It begins at 2:19."

****

Denver's residents were up and about. The streets were crowded with wagons and carriages splashing through vast interconnected puddles left by three days of unwanted rain. Pedestrians hurried across the wide muddy intersections and marched down the sidewalks, everyone in a hurry to finish last-minute business and errands before the afternoon's astronomical event began. Temporary signs and banners were up to advertise private homes for rent and rooftop space for viewing the eclipse. On one street corner, a man selling smoked eyeglasses for the eclipse was surrounded by a compact mob of eager buyers.

Across the street, two men in bowler hats and badges guarded the Clark and Gruber Mint. Would an eclipse be a good time to stage a robbery? Or did the mayor think some of the residents might panic and do something rash when the sky blackened this afternoon? Again, I wondered about the ignorant, the superstitious, and the just plain crazy. What might such people do in the face of the spectacular? Well, the mint looked safe enough.

I rode on but kept thinking about the mint and the banks. A robbery during a total eclipse. Sudden darkness. Everyone out of doors and preoccupied with the event. If I could imagine such a robbery, then maybe someone else could imagine the same thing and actually carry it off. I reminded myself to write to my father and ask if his newspaper knew of any rumors or actual reports of such robberies during this eclipse. If not fact, it still might make a fine story for a dime novel: *The*

Eclipse Robbers.

I rode the few blocks over to the corner of 16th and Larimer where the big brick building of the First National Bank sat like a citadel. But it was closed. Eclipse or not, the bank seemed determined to keep to its usual opening time. It was eight o'clock. I had an hour to kill. I rode up the street and passed by the Western Union office. I should send a telegram to Thaddeus to let him know I was alive in Denver. A block up, on Holliday Street, I stopped at the Denver Dry Goods Company.

The store was open, and I went in looking for some additions to my limited wardrobe. The floorwalker gave me a disapproving look, but I told him I was here to buy and described for him what I needed. I followed him about the main floor like an eager tourist, calling out for socks, denim pants, cotton drawers, a white linen shirt, a canvas vest, another packet of Bromo Paper, and a jar of minty Colgate toothpaste. At the counter, I asked him to wrap everything up and then said I'd be back after the bank opened.

"Well, hurry back. We'll be closing before noon," he said.

I retrieved Barley and rode over to the DRG passenger depot. Often the first things train travelers want upon escaping from their sooty, shaking rail cars is a bath or a bed or both. This part of town had plenty of cheap hotels and boardinghouses, and a half dozen bathhouses. I found one next to a German laundry that promised clean, hot water for fifty cents. Soap and a towel for twenty cents more. And a shave for another fifty cents. I ordered the works from an attendant and said I'd return within the hour.

Back at the bank, I found a short line of cash-seeking

citizens beside the door. I joined them. A minute later, the heavy front door was unlocked and we all hurried in, looking for enough money to get us through the day. At the grilled window, I signed a bank slip for twenty-five of the thirty-eight dollars in the account.

The mustached man on the other side of the bars asked, "Keeping a few dollars aside in case the world doesn't end today?"

I laughed and said, "Yeah, I may need breakfast tomorrow…if there is a tomorrow." Then, on an impulse, I asked, "Does it take long to close an account? I may be leaving town permanently."

He shook his head. "No. You just withdraw everything from the account as cash or a bank check; we'll stamp it closed forthwith."

I wasn't sure why I asked. If I wasn't coming back to Denver, then I wasn't going back to Pueblo either.

Where did I think I was going?

Where indeed? One person who was entitled to know where I was and where I might be going was Thaddeus. I rode back over to the Western Union. There was a stand-up table in the center of the office, littered with stubby pencils and message drafts. I picked up a half-sheet and a pencil and considered what to write. After some hesitation, I wrote, "Arrived Denver w/ passenger July 28. All well. Travis? Return soon. N.C." That was enough to tell him I was alive, as was Cora, our wayward passenger. From Travis he would have learned the telescopes had arrived here along with Elizabeth. Anything else he wanted to know he could send another telegram with questions or orders.

****

I took a long, hot soak at the bathhouse and then had

a shave from a man who knew how to wield a razor. Dressed in my new clothes, I rode back down to Dr. Avery's home. Anna was in the back yard.

"All cleaned up you are," she said. "Well, you've missed their leaving, but you know the way, yes?"

"I do, thanks." I hefted my paper package of old clothes and said, "I'll leave this in the carriage house and head down to the site. Are you staying here for the eclipse?"

"Oh, sure. The house should be looked after. My sister will come soon, and we watch it from the upstairs."

"Okay. Enjoy the spectacle," I said and slipped into the carriage house to drop my clothes and retrieve my saddlebags. I emptied the bags except for my journal and a pencil borrowed from Avery's house. I rolled up my gun belt and stuck it in the other bag, and then tied them to the saddle. Outside, I waved to Anna, who was standing in the garden, and I rode off.

Even without directions to the Vassar site it would have been easy to find it. The streets now contained a steady stream of people on foot, on horseback, in wagons and carriages, all heading toward the edge of the city, away from the buildings and smokestacks that might obstruct a view of the Sun. A photographer's panel wagon rolled by, and I noticed a number of men carrying binoculars and brass spyglasses. Children ran along the edges of the streets, chasing or being chased by pet dogs. Many adults were dressed in what looked like their best Sunday suits and dresses. Among the crowd, not a few carried umbrellas against the Sun or the return of the rain or perhaps as a shield against some unexpected manifestation of the eclipsed Sun. Looking up, though, the sky was a vivid blue with not a puff or a streak of whiteness to be seen from one horizon to the next.

It was late-morning, and the Sun was still rising on its long arc across the state. Of course, I knew it was the Earth rotating and not the Sun trekking across the dome of the sky. Yet it seemed more poetic and—at the same time—more conventional to describe the Sun moving over a stationary Earth. Still, that astronomical reality conflicted with the daily "common sense" observations of endless generations of people who plotted their lives and their travels against the rising and setting of that Sun. But the Earth did rotate. And it revolved around the Sun. The Moon revolved around the Earth. The planets—even Monsieur Le Verrier's distant Neptune—revolved around the Sun. It was the Sun that was a stationary presence in this vast and ancient ballet of moons and planets. Or was it? Did the Sun rotate too? Was it also revolving around some structure larger even than the solar system? Perhaps everything was in motion, impelled by the still mysterious forces of Nature. I would have to ask Cora.

Coming down East 18th Street, I reached another bend in the serpentine irrigation canal that wandered through the eastern part of Denver. I followed the canal north for a block and found the three-story brick building called the St. Joseph's Home. The large cross atop the peaked roof marked it as a Catholic hospital. This was the edge of Denver. A few steps farther out and I was back on the sharp dry grass of a plain that reached all the way back to Missouri.

I spotted Mitchell and her party a little farther out. They were hard to miss. Their three brass telescopes were mounted on tripods and shining in the late morning light like swivel guns. A new stepladder stood beside one of the telescopes. Beyond the trinity of telescopes, a boxy canvas tent was up, surrounded by a number of folding chairs and a stool. Dr. Avery's shay and horse were off to the side of the Vassar encampment. All of the women wore light dresses, and their heads were covered with bonnets, leghorn hats, and one lone Spanish riding hat. I rode over and dismounted a safe distance from the telescopes. I let Barley wander and walked over to pay my respects to the professor. She was sitting on a chair beside her five-inch Clark telescope.

She looked up from under her white leghorn when I approached. "Mr. Carter, you have returned," she said.

"Good day, Professor. I see the weather is going to cooperate for the eclipse." I looked up and saw the full moon, a soft white orb suspended in a clear blue sky.

"Indeed. Three days of rain had me worried. There were only two days of awful, rainy weather back in '69 in Iowa. So now, will you stay in our company through the afternoon?"

"If I won't be in the way, yes. If you don't mind."

"Not at all. In fact, you may be of some…earthly assistance to us."

"How so?" I asked.

She stared out at the vast openness. Behind us was the red brick city and the high gray peaks of the Rockies. People were arriving from downtown and the surrounding neighborhoods, gathering in little groups, and staking out temporary plots from which to set a picnic and await the event.

She looked up at me and said, "It has been my experience from previous observations of astronomical phenomenon that some small number of local residents will wish to insert themselves into our work and our property. Some are merely curious. Others are driven by internal compulsions. Whatever the motive, it is a distraction. And there must be no distractions during an event which will last but minutes."

"I see. And you would like me to discourage curious visitors and the like from interfering in your observations."

"If you would be so kind," she said with a firm nod that shook her big iron-gray curls. "Alida tells me the mayor has loaned a policeman to Elias Colbert for a similar purpose. Perhaps you know of Dr. Colbert? From the Dearborn Observatory in Chicago."

"I know the Observatory, yes," I said. "I'm not the police, but I'll do my best to discourage bothersome intruders."

She turned again to stare at the endless lawn stretching from this high Denver field. Looking off to the distant horizon, she said, "It must be centuries before the unpeopled lands of western Kansas and Colorado can be crowded."

I wasn't sure if she was expecting a comment from me. But after a second or two of silence on my part, I said, "Well, the railroad might speed up the populating of these lands. There are about a hundred new people arriving every day at the Denver depots. So I've been told."

"That is tragic." She turned back with a wistful look.

"Excuse me." I tipped my hat to her and walked over to talk with Cora. She stood beside the larger telescope.

"Well, Nolan, look at you. New clothes," she said.

"And a shave, a bath, and money in my pocket. I'm ready to face the day, however dark it may become."

Cora spread her arms and said in a dramatic voice,

" 'Nothing can be surprising any more or impossible or miraculous, now that Zeus, father of the Olympians, has made night out of noonday, hiding the bright sunlight, and fear has come upon mankind.' "

I clapped my hands. "Some Greek writer I've never heard of?"

"Archilochus, a Greek poet, who must have been around to see the total solar eclipse that spread over the Aegean in 648 B.C."

"I wonder if it frightened him?" I asked in all seriousness.

"Very likely," she said. "It left enough of an impression that he wrote about it, and other people bothered to preserve his words over the centuries."

The other Vassar students—former students, in fact—joined us. Most of them had graduated in '76 or earlier. Dr. Avery took a chair over to sit with the professor. There seemed little to do now but wait. I asked the group what each of them would do during the eclipse, who would be staring through the telescopes, and what they expected to find.

Emma Culbertson said, "At the approach of first contact, I'll be counting out the time with the chronometer."

Mitchell's younger sister, Phebe, said, "I'll sketch the period of totality and try to capture the corona as fast as I can move my pencils." She glanced up at the empty sky. Then she hefted her sketch pad and said, "Excuse me, I'll be back," and went to join her sister and Dr. Avery.

Elizabeth said, "Well, Professor Mitchell, Cora, and I will observe with the telescopes. Cornelia will keep an eye on everyone and everything to make sure all goes as planned, and then take a turn at one of the telescopes."

Cornelia said, "During totality, we'll try to spot Mercury, Venus, and Mars. And then any anomalous features—a comet perhaps or this theoretical Vulcan."

"Will you make a sketch or two, Nolan?" Cora asked me.

"No. Not when you have an accomplished artist among you." I glanced back at Phebe. "Besides, your professor has given me the more important job of bouncer."

The three women seemed unfamiliar with the term. "I'm to keep the riff-raff away from this site."

"Oh, yes, the overly curious and the local busybodies," said Emma. "Though to be fair, perhaps we are an unusual sight: a group of women with telescopes on the edge of the plains."

"That reminds me," I said. "I need a few things from my wandering horse. Excuse me."

I walked over to where Barley was inspecting a leafy bush. I took him back to the site and tied him to the back of Dr. Avery's shay. From my saddlebags, I retrieved my notebook and gun belt. I placed the pistol on a small wooden box next to one of the telescopes, covered it with my coat, and left the notebook on top of both. Rejoining Cora and her friends, I spotted four women in black robes and cowls—nuns from the Catholic hospital— crossing the road.

In a low voice, I said to Cora and the others, "Here comes the riff-raff. Shall I throw them off or first see what they have to offer?"

One of the nuns carried a large enamel pot by its wire handle. Another carried a tray of mugs and a loaf of bread. The bread's aroma proceeded them.

Elizabeth giggled, and Cora said, "Oh, how interesting. Ladies of faith come to meet with ladies of science. What fun. Perhaps there'll be thunder and lightning when they meet Professor Mitchell."

We walked over to where the professor, her sister, and Dr. Avery stood to greet the nuns. Their black habits were speckled with the red dust of the sun-dried road. All four nuns wore belted rosaries and had thin gold rings on their left hands. Three of the nuns looked about the same age as Avery and Mitchell. The fourth one was as young as Cora, and I wondered what might have driven her into the nunnery. We reached the gathering, and Mitchell introduced the rest of us to these Sisters of Charity.

She seemed to hesitate in introducing me. I was an outlier, an anomaly among the Vassar women. Mitchell finally said, "And this is Mr. Carter of Chicago, who has been so helpful in getting our equipment and persons to Denver in a timely fashion."

I nodded to the nuns and smiled at the younger one holding the tray.

The sisters had brought out a pot of hot tea, sugar, a short bottle of milk, and a warm loaf of sliced bread. I declined the offer of a cup, thinking they should have brought wine. And then I wondered if they would offer a prayer or a blessing for the Vassar expedition. Cora said Mitchell had no use for hierarchal religions. Maybe there would be thunder and lightning.

One of the older nuns wore a tight coif and a heavy silver crucifix that hung almost to her waist. She glanced at Mitchell's array of telescopes. "Three of our brethren from the Society of Jesus have just arrived to observe the eclipse from our grounds." She pointed back toward the hospital. "They have set up a large telescope on the far side of the building."

Professor Mitchell nodded, sending her gray curls into a brief convulsion. "I visited the Jesuit observatory at the Church of St. Ignatius in Rome long ago."

Professor Mitchell did not smile while she recalled the visit.

The youngest nun distributed the sliced bread. She offered a piece to me, but I waved her off with a light hand and a polite, "No, thank you." Wisps of blond hair escaped from under her veil. She continued over to Phebe and Cornelia with her offerings.

Watching the young nun, I thought of having rescued Cora from the vaqueros days ago, and she in turn rescuing me at the arroyo. We all need rescuing sometimes. From others. From events. Sometimes from ourselves. Did this novice sister need rescuing? Or was she already saved? Either way, her immediate future seemed set in the black-and-white forms of the older sisters. Would that my own future should be so clear.

"It's all very exciting to have this grand occurrence play out in the skies above Denver. Such an extraordinary vista for observing God's creation. His Excellency Bishop Machebeuf is expected to attend the viewing with our visiting Jesuit fathers," said the older nun.

At the mention of the bishop, Dr. Avery's eyes narrowed. Her face darkened. She sipped her tea, masking the look she presented.

Was there some personal history at play here? I was curious about what encounter there might have been between a Catholic bishop and a suffragette doctor. Likely, the bishop objected to women doctors and to women professionals in general. I never heard of any priest or pastor who advocated for change or progress of any kind for any person.

Avery's sour expression hinted at the philosophical gulf presented here on the high plain of Denver. On one side of the road was the medieval church with its ancient rituals and mythologies, and the men—the priests and bishops—who ruled it. On the opposite side was the modern, scientific world represented by half a dozen educated women. The actual distance between the two parties was but three hundred yards of dusty road and brittle prairie grass. Yet they were separated by an immeasurable, invisible chasm of history, culture, tradition, power, and of course, gender. Avery must have looked deep into that chasm. I supposed Mitchell had too.

The professor asked for the time and Emma said, "It's 1:35."

Mitchell stood up and handed her teacup to one of the nuns. "Thank you so very much for taking time out of your day to bring us tea. But now the celestial bodies are beginning to align, and we must attend to our work."

The nuns collected their cups and things. Wishing Mitchell and Avery success in viewing the eclipse, they retreated back across the invisible chasm. The younger nun glanced back at us as she crossed the road.

Cora came alongside me as we walked back to the telescopes. She whispered, "In Rome, the Jesuits would not allow Professor Mitchell to remain at night for any astronomical observations."

"I see. I imagine she was furious?" I wanted to ask her more about Mitchell, but I noticed a group of boys making their way toward the Vassar encampment.

"Excuse me. Bouncer duties." I walked over to the

boys and blocked their path. "Gentlemen, the famous professor and her students need the area clear of noise and distractions." They stared at me. "There's a telescope set up on the other side of the hospital. Maybe the priests over there will let you have a look."

One of the older kids said, "We ain't papists."

Still, they moved away and cut across the road toward the back of the brick-faced hospital. I did not see them again: a gaggle of kids out for fun and adventure and to see something they'd remember well into the next century.

I walked back to check on Barley and then over to where I'd left my things. I slipped my jacket on, buckled on the gun belt, and slid the holster well under my left side to conceal it. Picking up my notebook, I strolled over to Cora, who stood beside one of the four-inch telescopes.

"I have something for you," she said.

Before I could ask what it might be, she handed over the small brass telescope she and Elizabeth had used around Colorado Springs and Pikes Peak.

"Since you gave your piece of eclipse glass to those Kansas homesteaders, and we will be using up most of the telescope time, I thought you would like to use this," said Cora.

"Thank you." I took the hand-size telescope and unscrewed the end cap. Putting it to my eye, I twisted the side-screw to refine the image. The photographer's wagon I saw earlier came into sharp focus. I scanned the distant horizon.

Cora said, "Remember not to look at the Sun with it. You have to wait for totality."

"Can I take a quick peek beforehand? Without using

this?"

"We'll have about seventy minutes from first contact—when the edge of the Moon first touches the edge of the Sun—until totality. You can peek through one of the telescopes then."

"Won't that still be too much light?"

"It's filtered," she said. "Come, look at this."

I followed her to the viewing end of one of the large telescopes. She pointed to the angled eyepiece and said, "There's an inclined glass plate in here to reflect only about half the sunlight to the observer's eye. Then there are three shade-glasses we can insert—one at a time—to reduce the amount of light even more. We'll add and then remove the various shade-glasses depending on the stage of the eclipse and the amount of sunlight falling on us. The other big scope uses similar filters set in a rotating plate so you can quickly change from one filter to another without losing too much time."

I studied the eyepiece arrangement for a moment and said, "That's very clever, being able to observe the Sun without going blind."

She said, "Yes, it's a wonderful arrangement. Otherwise, we would have to look indirectly, with a whiteboard to collect the image so we could watch some of the partial eclipse without being blinded by the intense light from the Sun."

"Like you showed the homesteaders with the two pieces of white paper," I said.

"Exactly." She looked at me for a second and said, "Oh, I forgot to tell them they might notice crescent-shaped spots of light from the partial eclipse when they use the pinhole.

"I wouldn't worry. They'll see plenty one way or

another."

"Yes, I suppose. Still…"

Mitchell approached the telescopes and announced, "Dear colleagues, we have now twenty-five minutes to get ready for first contact. Let us make certain everything is aligned, that we have our notebooks and sketch pads at hand, and Emma, you do have the chronometer?"

Emma said, "I do."

The party of women took up their things and scattered to the telescopes and to three chairs set off to the side for Dr. Avery, Cornelia, and Phebe. I stepped out of the way while they prepared to make the first observation of the event. I placed Cora's handheld telescope and my notebook on the wooden box.

Behind me a voice announced, "It is a most sacred occasion which they will observe."

I spun around expecting to find a priest from across the street, but it was a man in an ill-fitting suit of frayed cuffs and collar. He needed a shave. This odd man stared with wide open eyes, as if to take in the vast prairie and all of its temporary occupants at a glance, but his gaze was unfocused. He settled red-rimmed eyes on me and edged closer to whisper, "The gods have gathered above us. We shall witness them this day."

He was touched by some madness. I nodded to him, put a finger to my lips, and then said, "We must be quiet now." Gently, I took him by the arm and guided him back onto the road, away from the Vassar group. He did not resist. I stopped and handed him a nickel after we had put some distance between us and Mitchell's site.

"Enjoy the day," I said and watched him shuffle off to where dozens of groups of picnickers and local residents had gathered for the show. Turning back to the

Vassar group, I saw Mitchell glance in my direction. Then she returned to her work, satisfied perhaps that I had managed to keep her site clear of distractions without resorting to any frontier drama.

Chapter 12

2:19 p.m.

Silence fell over the Vassar group. The first visible contact between the Sun and the Moon was but a moment away. The telescopes were manned... Well, maybe that's the wrong word. The telescopes were attended by those who knew how to use them.

Emma sat in a chair behind the observers at the telescopes. She held the wooden case that housed the chronometer. I stepped behind her to get a better look at the instrument. Its glass face was tilted up so she could read it. Brass knobs set in the box allowed for winding and locking the tilt of the clock. Two thin brass arms on the clock face gave the time. A single black arm ticked off the seconds on a smaller dial face set near the bottom. At the top of the clock face was a third dial marked off in eights whose purpose was a mystery to me.

Mitchell had braved the Denver storms on two occasions over the weekend to bring the chronometer to the Western Union offices. There they received a daily time signal telegraphed from the Washington Naval Observatory. The minute-long signal allowed a proper calibration of their chronometer against Washington time.

Emma called out the time and began to count out loud. I moved away, aware now of how quiet the countryside had been until she began her count. The

229

afternoon wind fell off. The people grouped about the fields seemed to have stopped talking all at once. I glanced over at Barley, whose ears were erect and twisting about to catch some hint of the normal, noisy world. But there was only Emma's steady count.

Emma's counting of the passing seconds against the predicted time of first contact sounded more breathless with every second. Very soon she was at the point of gasping out the numbers. She looked like she might fall off her chair in a faint. I took a step in her direction, but then Professor Mitchell began to count too.

Mitchell kept her focus on the telescope eyepiece as she took up the count. Emma stopped and tried to regain her composure. Someone had propped an antiquated water bottle beside the wooden box, and I handed it to her. She pulled the cork and took a long drink. Holding her throat with one hand, she whispered, "Thank you."

The three observers pulled away from their telescopes and began writing in their notebooks. Everyone relaxed now, discussing the apparent time of the initial Sun-Moon contact and glancing at the chronometer. Later, they would compare contact times with other observers when they got back to Vassar. No one commented on Emma's loss of breath in the middle of the first-contact count.

Cora found me and I said to her, "I was tempted to look up at that first kiss of the Moon on the fiery cheek of the Sun, but I resisted the urge."

She smiled—at my flowery description of first contact, I supposed. "A kiss is supposed to be private. No peeking, Nolan. Besides, that kiss is bad for your vision."

"Honestly, I was more worried about being scolded by half-a-dozen astronomers and the doctor than any possible eye damage."

She touched my arm and said, "I should tell the professor about my observed contact time." I watched her walk over to where Mitchell sat with her sister.

The actual eclipse began with first contact; the main event—totality—was still more than an hour away. It surprised me, and probably amateur observers everywhere, that it should take so long for the Moon to transit across the half-dollar-size face of the Sun above us. In the back of my mind, I knew there were astronomical distances to be traversed; we were watching that lunar trek across the face of the Sun from a deceptive vantage point.

I looked around the encampment but saw no wayward boys or madmen to threaten the quiet work of Mitchell's party. Down the road, I saw the photographer's wagon coming back toward us. I walked over to the dusty lane. When he drew near, I waved him to a stop.

I said, "A fine day for photographs."

The photographer was a middle-aged man with a cropped brown beard and a black vest buttoned over a starched white shirt of fine cotton. "I'm looking to catch a good image of the full eclipse. Gotta set up pretty quick."

Extending an arm to encompass Mitchell and company, I asked, "How about a photo of the Vassar College Expedition? Six women astronomers from New York. With telescopes. An unusual sight, don't you think? Might be something to sell to the newspapers."

He stared at the group of women and the line of brass telescopes pointing at the Sun. "Yes, it is an interesting scene. Do you think they would mind sitting for a picture? Take but a minute or two," he said.

I stepped back from his wagon. "I'm sure they'd be happy to cooperate. Why don't you pull over here, and I'll go ask them?"

Mitchell was seated beside her telescope in conversation with Dr. Avery. When I approached, she looked up and said, "Mr. Carter, I watched you move off one distraction with finesse, yet now you have gone out of your way to bring in another. Why is that?"

I glanced back at the photographer unloading equipment from the back of his wagon. "You wanted to be 'seen' studying the eclipse in Denver. Well, he's a photographer. What better way to be seen than in a permanent rendering? Something for the newspapers and perhaps the history books."

Avery jumped up and clapped her hands. "This is a marvelous opportunity for women in science. Well done, Mr. Carter." Looking at the photographer's wagon, she said, "I believe I know of this gentleman's establishment in town. Excuse me."

She walked over to the wagon. Mitchell rose from her chair and said, "Yes, yes. Very good. I shall inform the others. Perhaps, as you point out, a larger audience shall see us." She nodded. "This is most helpful to our cause. And perhaps to history."

Dr. Avery returned with the photographer, who was gripping a box-and-bellows camera mounted on a tripod and a wooden case of photographic plates. The man stopped, looked about, stepped a few feet to the right, and stopped again.

"This should do," he said and began to set up the tripod and camera directly across from the triad of telescopes pointed skyward.

Dr. Avery introduced him to me as Hans Baur.

He nodded in my direction and I returned the nod, thinking that like Mitchell he probably didn't want any distractions as he set up his camera. He checked the lens, then slid a glass plate from the case into the back of the camera.

"We are ready. Ladies, if you please. Take a seat. Anywhere around the telescopes. And then...please remain still."

Everyone moved to a chair; Mitchell, in her leghorn hat, sat near her lucky telescope. Cora sat to her left. I stood off to the side of the photographer. Dr. Avery joined me, wanting perhaps to make this a photograph of only the Vassar astronomers. But then I noticed the delivery wagon Mitchell had hired this morning. It pulled up to the site again and two men climbed down. They saw the photographer and had the good sense to stop moving. The two of them, along with the horse and wagon, were in the background now. It wasn't going to be a perfect image with them standing back there, but it still would immortalize this unusual group of astronomers.

After many long seconds, Baur straightened up and pulled out the exposed plate. "Okay, ladies. You may continue as before. Thank you." He slid the exposed plate back in the case and began to pack up. I stopped him.

"Herr Baur. Can you move in closer for one more picture? I'll pay for this one."

He looked at me. Then he turned to look at the group of women scattered among the chairs and telescopes. "Which one you want to stand with?" he asked with a friendly grin.

"Follow me." I led him closer to the group. He stopped, and I walked over to where Cora stood with her telescope.

"Well, that was fun. Perhaps we'll be in the newspapers," she said.

I whispered, "Look back at the camera and don't move. He's taking another photograph." I turned and stood as close to her as I could get without starting up a gabfest among her colleagues.

She started to turn to me, but I said, "Shhh. No moving. No talking. Smile at the nice man with the camera."

She did. The process seemed to take even longer than before, and I began to feel the warmth of the still visible Sun and the imagined gaze of a dozen eyes upon me. I hoped the picture would be worth the discomfort.

Finally, Baur waved and said, "That's it." He placed the second exposed plate in the case and grabbed up his tripod.

"I'll stop by your shop later this week," I said.

He gave a running nod to Avery and hurried back to his wagon.

Cora looked at me with a wide grin, bright eyes, and cheeks darkened by the prairie weather. "And what will you do with that picture?"

"Why send it to you, of course. I'm sure you'll want a little reminder of the eclipse and your adventures in the West."

"Perhaps you should—"

Professor Mitchell called out to gather her flock about her, and Cora begged off to join them. I stood there for a moment and wondered what it was she thought I should do. I'd been wondering the same thing too.

I watched the photographer drive off toward the northern edge of the field, his wheels and horse kicking up a swirl of dust that quickly settled back to Earth. Watching the wagon and the dust, it seemed to me the air was unusually clear. The view was…what, crisper? Or perhaps my eyesight had become more acute. Looking about the high field we were on, everything appeared to be more sharply focused. Even the shadows looked as if they had been drawn on the ground with cleaner, crisper lines. My own long shadow seemed darker now and its normally fuzzy black edges were instead well-defined borders between shade and light.

What was happening? I glanced up at the sky, which had taken on a deeper blue color. To the west, it was darkening to a violet tint.

****

3:21 p.m.

I took a quick look at the Sun. A black orb—the now lightless Moon—had eaten away at the white disk of the Sun, leaving in its advance a bright crescent of sunlight. To the right of the defaced Sun, I caught a glimpse of a single bright star. This was the planet Venus shining through the darkening afternoon sky.

I heard Mitchell's voice and looked back at the cluster of telescopes and the women gathered around them. Cora waved me over, and I stepped around the equipment and chairs to come up behind her.

She pointed to the telescope eyepiece and said, "The filters are still in place. Take a look. It's safe."

I took my hat off and bent down to the angled eyepiece. There in the center of the circular view were the remains of the Sun. A halo of soft light surrounded it. Seen through the lens, the angled glass plate, and the

235

shade-glass filters, the Sun was bright orange and shaped like a thin crescent of wavery light. In a few more minutes the black sphere of the Moon would block out the Sun, yet the black Moon would remain outlined by the corona—the long, fiery fingers of the hidden Sun.

I looked up at Cora, who was watching me. "It's beautiful. Thank you." I stepped aside to let her get back to her work.

3:22 p.m.

I noticed the surrounding landscape appeared to have lost its natural colors. Everything was looking bluer or maybe a lighter shade of gray. I looked at the shadows, which were still sharp and angular.

"Cora, the colors are changing," I said. "Everything looks so clean and sharp."

"The Moon blocks most of the Sun's light. What light that still reaches us is now more and more parallel light rays." She held her index fingers out, side by side. "Parallel rays of light. There's less light coming from all possible angles and less reflected light, so everything looks more defined. It's almost magical."

She returned to her telescope and removed the shade-glass. I slipped away and walked over to Barley. He seemed edgy, and I patted him a few times. It was getting noticeably darker now. The shadows faded into the dim ground. I made my way back to the box in the center of the encampment where I had left my notebook and Cora's handheld telescope. I picked up my notebook, jotted down the time, and scribbled quick impressions about the quality of the light and the crescent Sun. Then Mitchell called out, "Five minutes." Everyone seemed to tense. I did. Avery's mare let out a long snort. Barley replied in kind.

Professor Mitchell shouted, "To the northwest. There is the shadow of the Moon."

Off on the horizon, I saw a large blackness hanging in the sky, like a storm thick with black clouds. But it was a narrow-looking storm with clear edges tinged with bright red and orange hues.

It was darker now. And cooler. I looked over at Cora staring through her telescope and clutching her notebook. I walked over, shucking my jacket. It would be cold only for as long as the Moon's shadow lasted.

"Cora," I said and stepped behind her to drape the worn garment over her shoulders. Then, not wanting to distract her further, I hurried back to my spot to await the total eclipse.

Time seemed to speed up now. I felt a chill and pulled at my vest. An unnatural silence swept across the prairie. Even movement seemed to be discouraged. We were all held in the power of these peculiar lights, the deviant colors, and the chilly, gathering gloom on what had been a hot, sunny afternoon but a moment ago. The vast silence was broken by—of all things—the chirping of crickets in the grass. Then, off to the east, a lone dog began to bark.

3:28 p.m.

I turned at the barking of the dog and saw the ground shimmer with alternating waves of light and shadow. All around us these ripples of light raced across the broken ground. For a moment, I had the absurd urge to reach down and touch them.

I risked a quick sideways glance at the Sun. There was but a sliver of sunlight the Moon had not yet blotted out. I looked to the northwest where the black shadow of the Moon appeared. It had grown in size. It was coming our way. I couldn't see its edges now, and staring at the menacing shadow, it appeared like a giant black mouth about to devour us.

And then it did.

We were thrown into sudden darkness as the shadow swept over the plain. I think I fell back a step, as if hit with something solid. But it was the emotional shock of being engulfed, of having a giant black bag thrown over one's head, one's body, one's world. It happened in a second, like a candle snuffed out. Looking up, the full black Moon now was encircled by the thinnest perimeter of sunlight and with a single bulge of bright light on its southwest edge. Then the bulge of last light winked out.

3:29:10 p.m.

Totality arrived.

Seconds later, an enormous roar of voices rolled out of the city onto the prairie. Denver's people, unable to contain themselves, let loose a collective shout when the Sun vanished. It wasn't clear to me at the time whether the city-wide shout was from excitement or fear or both. Then the sounds of gunfire drifted out after the roaring of thousands of excited throats. Celebratory gunfire. Or maybe the mint was under attack. Near the tent, tiny moving lights appeared and began to flash. Fireflies were emerging from the grass in response to the false night of the eclipse.

The city noise did not deter Mitchell's party. The telescopes were locked on the eclipse. The three women at the telescopes pulled out the dark shade-glasses and replaced them with white glass.

The stars and Venus appeared again, all shining in a strange, dark slate sky.

"There's Mercury," said Cornelia.

Opposite Venus, on the other side of the Sun, was the twinkling yellow-orange light of Mercury. Was there another planet lurking near this winged messenger?

Phebe, seated in a chair near her sister, drew on a large sketch pad. It was not so dark as to prevent her seeing well enough to draw. She alternately stared at the astronomical spectacle and then worked her pencil against the page. Cornelia sat in another chair and sketched her own vision of what was occurring. Emma and Dr. Avery stared, transfixed, at the merging of the Sun and the Moon, and the fingers of light surrounding both.

I think I stood there for a few seconds trying to understand what I was seeing. The eclipsed Sun. The vast shadow of the Moon. This total solar eclipse, hanging in the sky above us, was a presence, a literal force of Nature, and it was a shock to behold. Even when I knew, or thought I knew, what was coming, still it shook me to the core.

I finally picked up Cora's little telescope and put it to my eye. The view was of a perfect black circle surrounded by a pulsating halo of pearly white light. The Sun's corona. Great tendrils of flickering silvery beams radiated out into space from behind the shield of the Moon. Alternating bands of light and dark appeared at the top and the bottom of the eclipsed Sun. To the right and left of the black Moon, huge wings of brilliant light extended out beyond the narrow view of the telescope. I lowered the spyglass and watched the Sun with my unaided eyes.

The corona's spokes were less distinct now and did not appear as substantive as through the telescope's lens. Still, this was a new and startling view of the Sun. The enormous halo of pulsating light stretching out beyond the Sun's surface was always there. We just couldn't see it in the normal glare of the day.

Dr. Avery stood alone staring at the once familiar Sun, now transformed into something extraordinary. Emma appeared at my side, and I handed the telescope to her. She put it to her eye, and I heard her sharp intake of breath. I glanced around the encampment; everyone was feverishly busy yet largely immobile, and no doubt counting down the fleeting seconds.

Seconds. I had never been so aware of time as I was with Mitchell and Cora and the others. Time was the overriding issue when first I met them. Time gnawed at me across every mile of road between Pueblo and Denver. Time kept me anxious and awake, and exhausted and slumbering. Time pushed me to kill two men but linger over coffee with homesteaders and railroad agents. Time kept the trains running and me chasing after them. Now time was hastening this stunning spectacle, forcing me to memorize details and feelings that I might carry them into old age. Two minutes and forty seconds were flying by in the blink of an eye and the silent passage of the unstoppable Moon. And time would end Cora's stay here in Colorado. A train, fixed to a timetable, would take her away to another life in the East. Time. The eclipse and I did not have enough of that precious ethereal stuff.

I glanced around the field. I was chilled—as much from the emotional jolt of the eclipse as from the cooling shadow of the Moon. Far off on the horizon, I saw lines of yellow and orange denoting the edges of the 119-mile-wide swath of this dark and chilly canopy. Emma still had the telescope, and I shook myself into movement.

I picked up my notebook and scribbled words onto the page with a shaky hand: 'Cold. Black shadow w/ yellow/orange edges moving east. Solar wings, bands of light/dark above and below Sun. Halo-corona. Shimmering light/shadows on ground. From Denver roars and firing guns. Perfect black Moon. Gray/blue darkness all around. Animals, people silent. Mercury and Venus opposite sides of Sun. Fireflies about, and crickets. One barking dog now, restless horses.'

Emma handed me the telescope and said, "Hurry."

I focused on the eclipse again, seeing the Sun's pulsating corona highlight the blackened Moon. The northwest sky grew brighter. A vivid line of red appeared around the western edge of the Moon. Then a flare of steady white light.

Behind me, someone called out, "Time."

3:31:50 p.m.

Totality ended.

****

I put down the telescope and resisted the urge to look up again. Instead, I watched Mitchell and Cora and Elizabeth insert shade-glasses back into the telescopes. Then they continued to observe the waning of the eclipse. The mysterious shimmering bands of light-and-shade reappeared and raced along the ground as before.

The massive shadow of the Moon sped eastward, across the plains, to darken parts of Oklahoma and Texas. Daylight returned in a rush, like a dawn completing its everyday course in three or four seconds. I blinked in the wash of new daylight. The crickets stopped chirping. I felt the warmth of the air and shivered again at the memory of the earlier cold and the astonishing eclipse that had brought it. In the distance, people moved about in excited little groups. A brief laugh reached my ear. A handful of riders trotted back to town, passing between the hospital and Mitchell's site.

I wanted to talk to someone about what I had just witnessed. Truth be told, I wanted to jump up and down and shout with joy. I was thrilled to have seen this, thrilled to have stood still and taken it in when in reality a part of me—some ancient piece of the human nervous system—had urged me to run and hide. Instead, I stood. I watched. I took notes. Cora, Mitchell, and the others were still at work, peering into the telescopes, jotting down hurried records, and touching up drawings. I would have to wait, contain my questions and my urge to jump up and down. Mitchell was not jumping. So how could I?

A few minutes later, Dr. Avery detached herself from Mitchell's side and walked toward me. I tipped my hat back and grinned at her approach. "Well, Doctor, that was so remarkable I may need morphine to calm down. Or perhaps a little rye and ice."

"Oh, it was so amazing to witness. I can hardly believe it happened," she said. Then she touched my arm and added, "I can supply the morphine, but perhaps we should try the rye first."

Emma and Cornelia joined us. They were smiling, on the verge of laughing out loud, physically energized by the lingering effects of totality. I searched for Cora, but she was still at her telescope, so I resisted the urge to approach her. Mitchell and her sister were looking over pages from the sketch pad.

Emma brushed back her hair and took a deep breath. To Avery she said, "We're off to the hospital to see what facilities might be available."

I thought of this long day and my own needs and said, "I'll escort you. Let's see what this fine establishment has to offer wandering astronomers."

I followed Emma and Cornelia across the road and onto the broad brick steps of the hospital's front entrance. I pulled open the large glass-and-wood door and we stepped into a high-ceilinged lobby with a marble floor of brown and white squares. Off to the left, a nun of indeterminant age stood behind a small reception counter. A gold cross was set on the countertop. The nun looked up at our approach, and Emma explained the purpose of our visit.

The nun asked about the eclipse.

Did she not step outside to see it? What new level of self-denial was this?

Cornelia said, "It was such an amazing sight to have witnessed. Breathtaking!"

The nun smiled, and then she directed them to a hallway off to the right of the lobby. Emma and Cornelia headed down the hall. The nun turned to me with an inquisitive look.

I asked, "Would there be a gent's facility available?"

"Yes, of course. We've a very modern hospital here at St. Joseph's." She pointed to a narrow hall behind the front staircase and said, "Down the hall and on the left."

I followed her guiding index finger and found a well-appointed wash-out water closet with a glazed window for light and a cold-water pipe for washing. All the conveniences, indeed.

I returned to the lobby, waved a "thank you" to the nun, and stepped back outside to wait for Emma and Cornelia. They emerged from the building, and we started back across the street. We were almost back to the site when I heard a voice. I turned. A priest strode toward us.

I said to the two women, "Looks like another distraction. I'll see what he wants."

They walked on, and I waited for the priest. He was old, wearing steel-rimmed glasses, a black cassock, a heavy gold cross on a chain, and a squarish purple hat with too many pointy peaks. His thin lips and angular face held no hint of a jocular nature.

Without preamble, he said, "I only now was informed of the presence of this party." He pointed to Mitchell's group. "They must move off. I am Bishop Machebeuf, and our Order makes use of that field."

He had a French accent, which was odd. In a town full of Germans and Mexicans, he must have stood alone with that inflection. I said, "The eclipse is over. They'll be packed up shortly."

I started to turn away, but then he said, "Their presence is an affront…"

"To what?" I demanded.

I took a step closer and said, "*Un affront? À qui? À toi?*"

I took another step in his direction. He stepped back. I leaned into him and whispered, "*Retourne dans ton temple.*" Go back to your temple.

Wanting to emphasize my point, I swung my hand over his head, knocking his little hat into the road.

He hurried away, calling over his shoulder, "I shall summon the authorities."

"Aren't *you* the authority?" I asked his retreating back.

I watched him climb the hospital steps and disappear. His pointy hat lay in the road, and I bent down to pick it up. I dusted off its fuzzy center pom and marched back to Mitchell's site. Only Dr. Avery seemed to have noticed my assault on God's representative in Colorado. Approaching her, I placed the bishop's crown in her hands. "A souvenir of the eclipse." She looked at the hat, turned it in her hands, but said nothing to me.

I wasn't sure why I treated the bishop the way I did. The pent-up tension of the last days? The excitement of the eclipse? Maybe it was out of sympathy for the things I knew Professor Mitchell and Dr. Avery had had to put up with in their lives, and what Cora and her colleagues would face in their own lives. But for his black dress and his silly hat, the bishop might have been just another crabby old man who could be placated or ignored. But it was his costume and cross which gave him a power that could not be placated or ignored, and instead had to be confronted by someone. So I took up the task of confrontation. And after the hard week I had had, I really needed to knock someone's hat into the street.

****

Professor Mitchell's camp was full of jubilant smiles and congratulatory comments. Everyone took a quick look at the sketches made by Phebe and Cornelia and one by Emma. Mercury, Venus and Mars had been spotted, but no one claimed to have sighted the Sun-blistered planet of Vulcan. They congratulated me again for finding the photographer and for easing off the afternoon's few intruders.

The two men from the hired wagon collected the chairs and pulled down the tent. I helped Cora and Elizabeth box the telescopes again, and very soon we were on our way back to town. The 9th Cavalry could not have decamped so quickly and cleanly.

I followed the wagon and Dr. Avery's shay, glancing back as we passed St. Joseph's to see if the bishop would reappear to send some last-minute damnation in our direction. But he did not. Perhaps he was looking for his hat.

****

Anna had not been blinded by the eclipse, and so she had laid out a cold supper of leftover ham, pie, bread, eggs, and garden vegetables when we arrived at the house. Coffee and tea were brewing. All of us gathered again in Avery's dining room. Phebe passed around her sketches of the eclipse. While I waited to take a look at them, Dr. Avery came up behind me and placed a glass of rye whiskey by my plate.

"There's no ice. I've not had the time to go by the icehouse for an order."

I leaned around in my chair to thank her. She held a glass of her own and took a sip of the amber liquid. Turning back to the table, I did the same, resisting the urge to swallow it all in one anesthetizing gulp. I settled back and let out a quiet sigh. I had not been so content in weeks.

Professor Mitchell said to no one in particular, "The corona is the great glory of the Sun. Phebe has done a fine job of capturing that radiance in her drawings."

Emma asked the gathering, "Did anyone see the strange orange light that bathed the landscape to the northeast?"

A few of the women had; I did not.

"Did everyone see the bands of shimmering lights and shadows racing across the ground?" I asked.

Everyone did, and Professor Mitchell told me it was caused by the moving air of the Earth refracting the last rays of light from the Sun. I didn't tell her I almost reached down to touch those bewildering shimmers.

Cora handed me Phebe's large drawing of the eclipse. She had sketched the dual crown of light and dark bands I saw above and below the eclipsed Sun, along with the two broad wings of light that radiated out from the sides. Mitchell said these streams of light extended millions of miles out into the void of space. It was difficult to imagine something millions of miles in length. Might these solar tentacles stretch all the way to the Earth at times?

Elizabeth mentioned a string of beaded lights called Baily's Beads. Mitchell saw a brief flash of this phenomenon, but Cora did not. I didn't either. Dr. Avery asked what the beads were, and Mitchell said, "In the last second or two before and after totality one may catch a glimpse of what looks like a necklace of lights. This is in fact the very last of the Sun's rays shining through the valleys of the Moon's rough and mountainous surface. The last rays sneak through these low regions of the surface; the other rays are blocked by the Moon's mountains. The effect is a string of separated rays of light reaching our eyes. Like a string of pearls. It also is evidence of the varied topography of the Moon."

Caught up in this scientific discussion, I forgot for a moment where I was and started to raise my hand to make a comment. I jerked my arm back to the table and said, "I saw no such beads, but I did see a flash of bright red along the edge of the black Moon."

Mitchell sat down in a chair across from me and said, "We all observed the same eclipse, but all of us may have taken note of different sights and colors. In the end, an eclipse is an individual experience. Depending on where you are, the quality of your eyes, the clarity of the sky in your location. All affect what you observe. This is why we make notes and compare observations among different individuals in different locations. Only then are we able to piece together all of the many—and fleeting—characteristics of the eclipse and so come to truly know it and appreciate its majesty."

Elizabeth said, "We shall have to consult the Princeton group. They are here in Denver too, are they not?"

"Yes, Charles Young and his group are down at Cherry Creek, which I am told is two miles or so south of where we sited." Mitchell looked to Avery for conformation, and the doctor nodded her head.

"Professor, how does today's eclipse compare to the one you saw in '69?" I asked.

Mitchell looked around the table at her young colleagues. "Well, I think perhaps today's event lacked the overall beauty of the Iowa eclipse. Then, there was an immense, dynamic corona of such extraordinary color and luminosity."

She stopped speaking and reached into a leather portfolio by her elbow. Rifling through some papers, she extracted a small print on cardstock. "I obtained a copy of this from the printers, Bien and Gedley."

She handed me a lithograph of the eclipse at totality. The blackened Sun was surrounded by a white halo tinged at its outer edges with spots of orange, yellow, and red light. Radiating from the Sun's perimeter were alternating bands of white and dark. The narrow dark bands brought to mind porcupine quills stuck in a ball.

I passed the lithograph to Cora, who had not been in Iowa, and said to Mitchell, "It's beautiful. Did you see all of those colors?"

"I did have the good fortune to witness this marvelous display in all of its glory. If you are interested, Mr. Carter, I wrote about this eclipse in *Hours at Home*. The October issue."

"I'll check the library when I have a chance."

We talked through Anna's supper and then through her fortified coffee and crusty pie. Moving plates and dishes about, I pulled out my notebook and jotted down comments from Mitchell and questions from Avery and Phebe, adding to my earlier notes about a phenomenon I was unlikely to see ever again.

Cora sat beside me and periodically tilted her head in the direction of my notebook as I wrote. Catching her eye at one point, I whispered, "I need a quote." Instead, I got a smile and a whispered, "Later."

****

The Sun set in a mundane manner, and the stars began to materialize as they are wont to do on most nights. I stood in the garden, absentmindedly poking at a cluster of yellow and red blanket flowers in Avery's garden.

Cora appeared and asked me, "What did you think? Could you have imagined such a thing?"

I looked at her smiling face. "To be honest, it almost knocked me back. The Moon's vast shadow. The colors and the lights. The eclipse...it was a presence. One that demanded attention. So much so, I had to remind myself to move, to pick up the spyglass, to write in my journal. How did you all stay so calm and focused?"

"I think we were as awestruck as anyone. But we did have a practiced routine to fall back on. And a keen awareness of the fleeting seconds. Professor Mitchell kept us going."

I stepped closer to her. "Thank you for coming to Colorado. Thank you for getting stranded in Pueblo. Thank you for the telescope."

She settled a hand on my arm. "Do you think you'll be here for the next one, in '89?"

"No." I wasn't sure where I would be, but I was certain it would not be on the Colorado prairie. I didn't want to talk about where I might be or where I wanted to be, so instead I asked her when she would leave Denver.

"In the morning, Doctor Avery and Professor Mitchell will drive into town to check on our train tickets and the eastbound schedule. So, Wednesday perhaps? I don't know. But soon. The summer is wearing on, and…well, I have to pack up at Vassar. I can't stay a resident-graduate forever."

"Time to leave the nest." *Stay with me*, I wanted to shout, beg, plead.

She took my hand in her two soft hands. "Yes. Time to get out into the world. Well, the Boston part of the world, anyway. It's a good opportunity at Harvard."

"And you shouldn't miss it. Not for anything." In my mind, I let go of her. "Well, perhaps while Avery and Mitchell haggle over tickets, maybe I can take you up the street for lunch. I know a nice little cantina the likes of which you'll not find in New York or Boston."

In the gathering darkness, Avery's bright flowers faded to shades of gray. I pulled Cora to me and gave her a lingering kiss. Pulling back, I whispered, "I'm grateful for…for all the time we've been together."

Cora hugged me. Silently. And for the longest time. Then she turned away and walked back into the house. I thought she might be crying.

****

I was getting used to hay bales for beds and the early morning company of horses. How would I ever go back to sleeping in a real bed in a proper house?

The sparkling sunlight on the rain-washed windows and the neighing and snorting of the horses had forced me awake. Now I lay there remembering yesterday's solar marvel and all that had happened since leaving Pueblo. I seemed to have lived an entire year in the span of a week. I was exhausted from it. And depressed about the coming days. So, I lay there thinking about the things I needed to do.

Check Western Union for messages from Travis and Thaddeus, and any telegraphed news of my brother's wayward horse. Check with the bank about my account. Buy a train ticket down to Castle Rock to repay Mr. Walsh for his two-dollar loan. Pay the stable boy a few more pennies for the rent of the poncho. There was a photograph in town I needed to pay for. I should write to my parents and Brian to let them know I was alive and had witnessed the eclipse in Denver.

And I needed to clear off Dr. Avery's property. She couldn't have me living in her carriage house. How long could I stay? How long did I need to stay? What was my excuse for staying beyond breakfast? I had made my delivery. The eclipse was over. So, probably, was my welcome here.

I fed the horses. Then I washed up with a tin basin of cold water and got dressed. I let Barley and the mare into the yard and made a quick visit to the outhouse. Anna greeted me at the kitchen door, and I helped her carry some dishes to the dining room again. Cora was already at the table, and I slid into the empty chair beside her. This seating arrangement had become our habit; I wondered if anyone had noticed.

Halfway through breakfast, Dr. Avery asked me if I'd help rig her shay for a morning ride to town.

"Yes, of course. I'm going in too."

Mitchell spoke up from across the room. "Excellent. Perhaps, Mr. Carter, you would be so good as to purchase as many different newspapers as you come across? I should like to read whatever reports have been made of the eclipse here in Denver and around the territories."

"Certainly," I said. "I'd like to see some of those reports myself. If you're going up to the depot, you might check the trains for early editions from the Eastern newspapers."

"Yes, they'll drop copies at the station office," said Avery. "We'll look."

****

We started late. Cora and I walked down Champa Street ignoring the temptation of a passing streetcar. She wore a light blue summer dress and a small blue hat pinned to her piled-up hair. I wore my new clothes and my old jacket, which again concealed my Colt.

I was halfway out of the carriage house when I stopped to consider taking my gun. There was no rational or legal reason for doing so, yet I hesitated. In the end, I stripped the loop holster off the gun belt and threaded it through my pants belt. Now it rested on my left hip, hidden by my coat. Cora walked on my right.

We turned up 14th Street, heading into East Denver. The normal everyday bustle had resumed on Denver's streets. Carriages and pedestrians hurried by. School-aged kids ran around in summertime randomness. And pushcart merchants staked out corners and announced their wares in declarative German and panting Mexican. We stopped at the occasional store or newsstand to buy the morning editions. The eclipse was frontpage news for all the local papers. 'Complete Success in Colorado of the Great Event,' read the *Denver Tribune*. 'The Great Solar Eclipse,' blared the *Colorado Transcript*.

At the corner of 14th and Larimer, I pointed out Cherry Creek and the footbridge over it.

"How many times did we cross over that little creek to get here?" she asked. "Were we following it or was it following us?"

I smiled at the notion. "It was a useful guide."

Cora looked at me and said, "It's so nice to be with you without the worry of some mortal danger."

I laughed. "It is indeed. Perhaps we should take a deep breath, let it out, and relax. Finally. We're here. The eclipse is over. There's no worry but lunch." I pointed across the street and said, "That low brick building with the tall windows is a fine little cantina. I know the owner and his daughter. Sort of."

"How do you know them 'sort of'?"

I tucked the newspapers under my left arm and said, "Well, I was in there a year ago waiting for my brother and a friend. A drunken trail hand grabbed a young girl as she walked by the bar and wouldn't let go. So I slid up behind him and kicked him in the back of the knee." I mimicked a quick little side kick for Cora while we stood on the bricked corner.

"He let her go and fell to his hands and knees. I reached over and pulled the pistol from his holster and slid it down the length of the bar. Then I grabbed him up and pushed him through the doors onto the sidewalk. He didn't come back in. Evidently he was too drunk to notice his gun was missing."

"Nolan to the rescue." She grinned. "Careful. They'll be writing songs about you."

I took her arm and led her across the busy street. "And it's a good thing he didn't come back in. When I slid his gun down the counter, the man behind the bar picked it up and stood waiting to see if he came back through the doors. Turns out that man was the owner, and the girl was his daughter. So now, whenever I come in, I get a nod from him and after I eat, he comes by with a cup of coffee and a shot of tequila. Never says anything to me; just a nod, the coffee, and the tequila."

"Such a strange place this is. So many…unusual characters here in the West. I keep thinking about Mr. Glade. His dog. His tiny little town."

I pushed the doors open and said, "Lunch awaits."

We stepped inside. The cantina was a long, low-ceilinged building with a bar and kitchen to the right and tall street windows to the left. Whitewashed walls and gas-lit lanterns hanging from ceiling beams gave the place a light and airy feel. Two potbelly stoves provided heat against the winter. In the back, an old man sat tuning a guitar.

I did not see the owner. His daughter greeted us as we entered. She started up a smiley, rapid-fire monologue—none of which I understood—as she tugged at my jacket and led us to a table by a window.

Seated now, she stopped talking, glanced at a puzzled-looking Cora and then whispered to me, *"¿Su novia?"*

I didn't know what this meant but, I took a chance and said, *"Sí."*

I was rewarded with a sly smile that might have been a smirk. Before she started up again, I said, "*Sangria y comida*. The works." I waved my hands over the table for emphasis.

She said something else about food and I said, "*Todos*." Everything.

Giggling, she left, hopefully to return with food and the requested wine.

And she did. She came back to the table with two short glasses and a straw-covered jug of sangría. She set them on the table, and I poured. I lifted my glass of dark red wine and said, "To the eclipse."

Cora took a tentative sip and declared the wine good. She sat back in her chair and asked, "What do the papers say?"

I handed her the *Rocky Mountain News* and the *Denver Mirror* while I searched through the other papers. The *Colorado Journal* had printed long columns of technical information about the eclipse and a fair amount of quoted commentary from local residents about what they saw and how they reacted. No one quoted in the newspaper admitted to being frightened. Or to firing off their guns.

Cora startled me with an unexpected cheer and a rustling of the newspaper. "They mentioned us here. In the *Rocky Mountain News*. Oh, this is wonderful."

I peeked over the top of the newspaper.

"It reads, 'Here in our midst, a conspicuous example of the power and grasp of the feminine intellect has been exhibited.' It goes on, 'The success of this party is one more and pointed arrow in the quiver of woman suffrage argument and logic.'"

"Congratulations. You've been 'seen.'" Then I

said, "One more and pointed arrow? Odd phrasing, but I guess the sentiment is what's important."

I went back to my paper to read that local churches had charged fifty cents to view the eclipse from their steeple windows. Evidently, Christian charity did not extend to astronomical phenomena. I put the *Journal* aside and picked up *The Democrat*. It carried a short story out of Wyoming about the planet Vulcan.

Cora was still reading through the *News*. I asked her, "Do you know a Professor James Watson?"

She looked up. "Yes. University of Michigan."

"According to this account, he claims to have spotted Vulcan during the eclipse."

I passed her the paper and she snatched it up to read through the brief news item. Her lips moved and she mumbled, "…a reddish, intra-mercurial object near *Theta Canceri*." She folded the newspaper and said, "Well, that is exciting news, but none of us saw any new or unusual object in that region of the sky."

Cora scanned the paper again and then read aloud, "'He is the Edison of astronomy.' Well, I don't know if Professor Mitchell will believe this about finding Vulcan, but I'm quite certain she won't believe Watson is the Edison of astronomy."

The Colorado Journal had reprinted a map from the *Chicago Times*. It showed the trek of the eclipse across the West. Underneath the map was a telegraphed report from the Dakota Territory. I mentioned this report to Cora because it involved the Cheyenne Indians, who had not been aware of the approaching eclipse.

"It says an Army officer told the Cheyenne about the coming eclipse, but they didn't believe him. When it started, though, the Indians fell into a panic. They fired their guns, made loud noises, lit fires, et cetera, trying to drive off the 'bad medicine' eating the Sun."

I remembered the gunfire in Denver. Maybe there had been a little fear here too.

"You saved those homesteaders on the prairie from a similar fright. Your drawings and pinhole papers gave them something valuable: knowledge. Or at least forewarning."

Cora said, "I suppose for most of human history, an eclipse was a time of sheer terror for everyone. Now we know. We can calculate eclipses far into the past and the future. Forewarned is forearmed. There's nothing to fear now. Of course, some primitive peoples imagined eclipses were a...romantic encounter between the Sun and Moon. Maybe with that image there was less to fear from an eclipse."

I smiled at the notion. Heavenly fornication. "That's not the image I had."

Lunch arrived and we put aside the newspapers.

The owner's daughter and a small boy from the kitchen laid out plates and bowls of fat enchiladas, red pozole soup, steamy tortillas, and lumpy green guacamole.

Cora stared at the display of colorful dishes and asked, "Where do we begin?"

"With the soup." I handed her a spoon. Then I tore up a tortilla and dipped a piece of it in the guacamole.

"Cora, try some of this too. It's mashed up avocado, garlic, tomatoes, onion, and a few other mysterious ingredients."

We ate. I served as the culinary guide, and Cora sampled everything with her usual curiosity and determination. She dipped into the guacamole and took an exploratory bite of one of the chiles swimming in the soup. I poured more wine for her.

I glanced over to the bar to find the owner standing behind it polishing a large glass. He was a tall man with brown leather skin, a graying moustache, and coal black hair beginning to thin in front. I gave him a short wave of my free hand and received the usual reply: a slight nod of his head as if he was sending a covert signal.

Halfway through lunch, I looked up to the jingle-jangle of loose spurs and the bang of high-heeled boots on the wooden sidewalk. The double-doors swung open and three Mexican vaqueros strolled in.

They must have thought it was Saturday night. Or maybe they just got paid. Their boots were polished, and their leather leggings were brushed. They all wore ruffled cotton shirts and short charro jackets decorated with silver thread embroidery. Out of doors, their expansive sombreros would have blotted out the sky from horizon to horizon. I was surprised to see they openly carried polished holsters and shiny silver pistols.

The three cowboys headed to the back of the room, but then one of them spotted Cora and stopped. He walked over to us and planted his fists on the tabletop. He smiled at Cora and said something in Spanish. I heard *gringa*. I took that moment to drop my right hand into my lap. Then he tilted his head in my direction and said something with a gap-toothed grin that stretched out his graphite moustache.

Did he expect me just to sit there and smile in return? I sat back in my chair and asked him, "Is the circus in town?"

I didn't know if he understood English, but he stopped leaning on the table and stood up to stare at me with narrowed eyes. Cora moved in her chair. She looked alarmed. I got ready to stand too, but then someone shouted, "¡*Oye!*"

The three Mexicans turned at the shout from the man behind the bar. He was shaking his head slowly. He said something to them. Inclining his head in our direction, I heard him say *amigos*. While he spoke, he made a show of dropping his right hand below the bar. I took the opportunity to wrap my fingers around the handle of my Colt.

But then the vaquero nearest us threw up his hands in an elaborate gesture of surrender, let out a short laugh, and said something to the owner. One of the other Mexicans pointed to the back of the long room, and all three of them walked away. I watched them settle themselves around a table against the back wall.

Cora leaned across the table and said, "Perhaps we should leave now?" She looked pale.

"It was nothing." I reached for her hand. "We'll head out in a minute."

I glanced to the bar, but the man was gone. A moment later he came through a kitchen doorway carrying a small silver tray. He set a tiny cup of coffee before Cora and then a delicate glass of sherry.

"Thank you," she said.

He gave her a slight bow and then put a larger cup of coffee in front of me, along with a shot glass brimming with yellow tequila.

"*Gracias, Señor*," I said. He nodded and walked back into the kitchen. I lifted the glass of tequila and said to Cora, "Cheers." It went down my throat like burning coal oil. I reached for the cup of coffee.

"What was that?" Cora asked.

"Mexican firewater. You wouldn't like it."

"Given the look on your face, I'm not sure you do either," she said.

I was about to deny it, but then I heard spurs and wooden heels again. The cantina doors opened, and another vaquero stepped inside.

Chapter 13

I recognized him. The third Mexican from the road. The young face with the cattle drive beard. He was duded up now, like the three who came in earlier. But we'd met before. He knew me instantly.

He spit out the word, "*¡Tú!*" Then he screamed, "*¡Pendejo!*"

He reached for his pistol. Cora turned in her chair.

I jumped up, knocking over my chair. I brushed my jacket aside and grabbed for the Colt. I wasn't going to make it in time.

A shot boomed in the narrow building.

The young vaquero collapsed against the doorframe and slid to the floor. He dropped his pistol and clutched at his side. A look of shock and pain spread across his thin, bearded face.

Cora was on her feet now, staring at the man on the floor. I stepped away from our table. My pistol finally free, I glanced to the left. The owner stood behind the bar with a gun in his hand—the big Navy Colt I had taken from the drunken cowhand last year. A puffy gray cloud of smoke floated above the bar's polished wood. He seemed inexplicably calm for having shot someone only a second ago. Maybe he'd done it before.

The cantina's patrons were silent for the briefest fraction of time. A single piece of flatware fell to the floor with a metallic ring. Then chairs scraped back and a stampede of boots on the plank floor began. The other three vaqueros rushed toward us.

Stepping in front of Cora, I aimed at the first one and shouted, "Don't." I shouted again, "Hands, hands," and to emphasize my point, I thumbed back the pistol's hammer.

Behind the bar, the owner yelled, "*Sus manos*," and pointed his revolver at the three men.

They got the message. None of them touched their guns. Instead, they pulled their wounded friend to his feet. He was bleeding from the lower stomach and his left side. It looked like a through-and-through shot in which the bullet had passed through him, coming to rest in the splintered doorframe.

Now the owner aimed his pistol again and yelled at all of them. The other customers were on their feet watching. Several people burst out of the kitchen to see what had happened.

The overdressed Mexicans helped their dazed friend out to the sidewalk. A splatter of blood and a pistol on the floor were the only evidence they left behind. I picked up the pistol and pushed open the doors to see where they were going. Two of them half-dragged their wounded friend down Larimer Street. The other man glanced back at me. I shut the doors.

Cora stood by our table, taking in the chaotic chatter among the customers and the serenity of the owner. "My God! It was the man from the stream. He tried to kill you." She glanced back at the front doors. The fingers of her left hand grasped the edge of the table.

I wrapped my arms around her and hugged her tight. "I'm sorry." It was all I could think to say.

I realized I was still holding two guns in my hands.

Easing away from Cora, I holstered my own pistol. I walked back to the bar and placed the vaquero's pistol on it. "*Uno mas*," I said to the owner.

He picked up the pistol and tucked it under the bar. Maybe he was assembling an arsenal down there.

We needed to leave. I didn't want Cora caught up in another fight with the Mexicans or some legal issue if the law showed up. I reached in my coat pocket for some coins to pay for lunch. The owner saw me and put his hand up.

In English, he said, "Next time."

I gave him one of his own silent nods and turned away. I led Cora outside and away from the cantina. We stopped and I looked around for the Mexicans. There was no one on the street but locals. Two of them gave us odd looks as they passed by.

Was I looking as wide-eyed as Cora?

"Where are we going?"

"Up Larimer, away from trouble, and then home. We'll grab a streetcar.

Almost breathless, she asked, "Should we summon the police or a sheriff?"

I don't think the Denver police will be interested. Not unless someone dies."

I led her back across the street, and we hurried up Larimer. A block away, I asked her to stop, and I leaned back against a brick building. I took a deep breath and hid my shaking hands in the pockets of my jacket.

Cora stepped closer and asked, "Are you all right?"

I nodded. Eyes closed, I said, "I think I need another shot of that tequila."

I felt her hand on my chest and opened my eyes again. I gave her the most reassuring smile I still had, took her hand in mine again, and we continued up the street.

Glancing at her, I said, "I should have shot all three of them when I had the chance."

On the way back to Avery's house, I asked Cora not to mention the vaqueros and the shooting. Not until she was on an eastbound train anyway. I didn't want any additional commentary from Mitchell or Avery.

"But you didn't shoot anyone," said Cora.

"Well, it wasn't for lack of trying," I said. "Still, they're likely to think trouble follows whenever I'm about. And I'd like to stay around a while longer."

"I'm sure they don't think that."

Then I told her about the bishop and his hat.

She laughed up to the corner and then gave me a look that was hard to read. The earlier cantina panic was replaced now with…what? Admiration for my having defended us against one last danger? Or admiration for my having defended Avery and Mitchell against a priest who probably owned a signed copy of Clarke's sex-and-education book?

Cora stopped us on the sidewalk again and held up two fingers. "Two lives left, Nolan the cat. Will you live through the week?"

I covered her two fingers with my hands. I nodded and said, "Yes. I promise."

****

We gathered again in Dr. Avery's dining room to look over the haul of daily newspapers for stories about the eclipse and Mitchell's tribe of Vassar astronomers. Cora and I had left our first collection of papers in the cantina. But Larimer Street was home to many of Denver's newspaper offices and presses, so we were able to buy more copies before returning to Avery's house.

Professor Mitchell, seated at the head of the table, put down a newspaper and said, "This is very good reporting of our presence here and of the eclipse in general."

She picked up another newspaper from the train station—the *Fort Worth Daily Standard*—and said, "Harvard's Fort Worth Eclipse Party reports a number of difficulties. Professor Waldo complains that the time signal from Washington was constantly broken in on by railroad agents. 'I was very much disturbed,' he is quoted. And Professor Willson says he lost fifteen seconds of viewing time because he forgot to remove his shade-glass."

There were knowing smiles among the Vassar women at this news. They had done everything right, even during Emma's panting count.

I glanced at Cora. She seemed composed, calm, engaged in the conversation around the table. What a story she'd have to tell on the train home or at some Eastern dinner party: being caught in the middle of a barroom gunfight in frontier Denver. I smiled at the idea. Cora turned just then to catch that lingering smile. She raised an inquisitive eyebrow. I inclined my head in Mitchell's direction.

Mitchell read, "Willson says he did not hear the time-keeper at the close of totality, and also lost the third contact. Light clouds then covered the sun to prevent observation of the last contact." She looked around the table. "We have been most fortunate in our own observations."

The professor picked up my copy of *The Democrat* and said, "This Wyoming story of Watson finding

Vulcan is, I think, a hurried claim of primacy which may not stand up to the sightings of other observers. I think I shall bring this point up later tonight."

"What is happening tonight?" asked Elizabeth.

Dr. Avery said, "We've arranged for Maria to give a public lecture on astronomy and Caroline Hershel's work at the Lawrence Street Methodist Church at eight o'clock this evening. The proceeds from the lecture will be given to the Colorado Equal Rights League."

I sat there thinking that of all the churches in Denver, Mitchell and Avery had found one only a block from the cantina Cora and I so recently vacated.

They couldn't find an empty schoolroom or a hotel ballroom? Can I slip a pistol into a Methodist church?

Professor Mitchell interrupted my plotting by holding up a telegram.

"Mr. Carter. We have word from your employer regarding the cost of transporting our telescopes and persons." She glanced at the telegram and said, "A complicated accounting which considers wagons, feed, trains, telegrams, and overnight accommodations."

Dr. Avery leaned over to look at the telegram. "Still, a not unreasonable sum, considering the circumstances. Do tell your company we shall send down the necessary funds."

"Well, Charles and Thaddeus will be happy to know that. I'll wire them tomorrow."

****

It was a short walk back up to the East Denver neighborhood. The early evening had cooled off; a soft breeze drifted down from the Front Range. Foot and carriage traffic was light by seven o'clock. Professor Mitchell and Doctor Avery led the way up the street. I followed them, surrounded by Cora and her colleagues. On the opposite side of the street, I spotted a couple of corner girls already out for the night, trolling for tourists and regulars. Mitchell and her fellow astronomers took no notice, but I was sure Dr. Avery must have been aware of them.

Near the church, a babel of voices spilled out from the wide-open front doors. We walked down an alleyway to enter through a rear doorway. I searched around, getting my bearings and looking for sombreros. Inside, we were met by one of Dr. Avery's friends, who directed all of us to a front pew and then led Mitchell and Avery up onto a low stage that also supported an unadorned pulpit to the right. The lights were up, and I spotted a few reporters—notebooks in hand—standing along the aisles. Ready to dash out to make the morning editions, I supposed. A few men took advantage of the absent choir and pastor to light up pipes. The sweet scent of burning Cavendish tobacco drifted our way. At eight o'clock, the packed pews quieted down, the pipes disappeared, and Dr. Avery took to the center of the stage to introduce Mitchell. Avery closed her lavish prologue saying Mitchell's work as a scientist had done a "service which all the women's rights pleaders on the continent could never dream of accomplishing." Applause broke out as Mitchell joined the doctor on stage. Then she took to the pulpit to begin her lecture.

She talked for an hour. Most of her lecture concerned a woman astronomer from the eighteenth century, Caroline Herschel, the sister of William Herschel who discovered the planet Uranus. In talking about Caroline's long hours at the telescope and her lack of professional recognition and poor pay relative to her brother, Mitchell actually was talking about herself and the young women who would follow her. She had had the same struggles Caroline Herschel had endured a century earlier, and now her former students likely were to follow a similar torturous path for recognition and equality in the sciences, in academia, and in any form of public life.

At the end of her talk, Mitchell took a few shouted questions from the reporters about the Denver eclipse and the contested sighting of Vulcan. One of the livelier newsmen jumped up on the edge of a pew, glanced at his notepad and shouted, "About the Vulcan planetoid, *The Washington Post* today declares, 'Should this body be discovered, it would be one of the greatest triumphs that astronomy could achieve.' Do you agree, Professor Mitchell?"

Mitchell stepped around to the front of the stage and looked over her audience. "It would be most interesting to find another body inhabiting the fiery environs between the Sun and Mercury. James Watson says there is one. Our Vassar group saw no such entity. We must await, patiently, the findings of other observers in other locations. But as to it being the greatest triumph of astronomy, yes, it might be. This year. But what about next year? The coming decade? The next century? Surely, many more triumphs await astronomy and those who practice it."

Mitchell gave a slight bow to the audience and turned to Dr. Avery standing off stage. The crowded church erupted in applause again. The audience came to its collective feet. A large M-shaped wreath of flowers was hauled onto the stage and presented to Mitchell. I clapped along with the crowded church, knowing I likely would have to carry that floral monstrosity back to Avery's house.

As the crowd flowed toward the front exits, Cora darted away. I followed her progress to the front doors where she stopped to talk to two men.

Emma came up beside me and I asked her, "Do you know those men?"

"Hmm, I think that's Charles Young on the right. He's from Princeton. His group has been here for two or three weeks, camped down in the Cherry Creek area. They received funds from a private benefactor. Plus, the American Express Company provided them with free transportation. Even the state of Colorado lent them a hand with camp equipment."

Emma turned back to me and said, "But us... Well, you know what our situation was just getting here."

She pointed a covert finger at the other man and said, "The other gentleman, I'm sure, is William Pickering from Boston. His older brother, Edward, is director of the Harvard Observatory."

She looked at me again and said, "Cora will be part of Edward's Harvard computer group. I think she's hoping to get some telescope time too. In between all of the computing and the cataloguing of stars." She gave me a mischievous smile and added, "Sometimes the computer group is called Pickering's Harem because of all the women he has hired this last year. He's very progressive."

Harem? I regarded William Pickering. He had a high, bald forehead and a thin beard and moustache. He wasn't very tall. I hoped his brother looked much the same. Only older.

Cora came back to the group with the news that

Professor Young had recorded the total eclipse at two minutes, twenty-eight and a quarter-seconds. Mitchell's group had counted twelve seconds more of totality owing to their observation site being two miles north of Young's party. Ben Franklin said time is money. For astronomers time is location.

****

Anna again had remained at Avery's house to prepare a late-night supper for our return. We gathered around Avery's dining room table, eating and talking. It was a peculiar kind of *salon* to which I added little. Yet in my muteness, I had the opportunity to listen to the easy flow of conversation from person to person and topic to topic. I learned a lot; not about astronomy or math *per se*, but about the women who practiced these arts and who wanted to make something of their lives and their knowledge.

I, on the other hand, had been squandering my time, my life, and whatever trade skills I might possess. The realization slid silently up against my conscience like a snake. And then it bit me. I actually flinched in my chair, embarrassed for myself. Cora glanced in my direction. Did she see the distracted look on my face?

I had led a privileged life. It was that privilege that allowed me to wander off into the West, play cowboy, almost get killed, roam up and down the Pueblo-Denver road hauling bags and bundles, and finally to shoot two men. I couldn't keep doing this. And looking at Cora sitting beside me, I didn't want to.

Professor Mitchell ended my private deliberations by announcing their midmorning departure. I knew they would be leaving shortly, but this long-expected announcement was another unwelcome jolt of reality.

"I hope all of you will consider packing tonight. The wagon for our baggage and equipment shall arrive at nine o'clock. The ticket agent informed me to expect a crowded train, as many of Denver's visitors will be heading home after the eclipse," said Mitchell.

She looked to me and said, "Mr. Carter. Perhaps you would be so kind as to assist with tomorrow's transportation of our telescopes? I shall remove the optics once again."

"Of course. Happy to help out." And earn my keep.

It was late now, and Emma and Cornelia drifted upstairs, taking along some of the local newspapers as souvenirs. Cora and Dr. Avery stacked our dirty plates and dishes and carried them to Anna in the kitchen. I followed them with an empty coffeepot.

In the kitchen, Avery asked, "Nolan, are you still comfortable in the carriage house?"

"Yes, thanks. Maybe by tomorrow night there'll be an empty room in a hotel."

I glanced at Cora, then opened the back door and stepped out to the garden. She followed a moment later.

I said to her, "Well, your Colorado adventure is almost done."

She looked pained and pale in the weak light of the late night. I wanted to tell her to stay. Or better, that I would follow her. But both were foolish, irresponsible ideas. She'd have no life here, and I had no prospects there. It seemed a cruel twist of fate that so many things—the Vassar astronomy column, the Philly Expo, the train war, my lost horse, and the hardship of our ride to Denver—seemed to pull us toward one another. Yet now, having met and been through so much, we had nothing to hold us together. Quite the opposite; we had become like two magnets whose similar poles could not stay in communion without some more powerful outside force.

She stepped up to me and asked, "You'll write to me, won't you?"

"I'm already composing letters in my head." I wrapped my arms around her and kissed her for the longest time.

"Nolan…"

She stopped and brushed her loose hair back. Her eyes were teary.

I hugged her again. Shadows moved in the kitchen window. "You should go in and pack. I expect tomorrow will be hectic." It hurt to breath. I wanted a glass of Avery's whiskey. We kissed goodnight. I let her hand slip from mine. She disappeared behind the kitchen door.

I looked up. The stars were out, and a thin sliver of the waxing Moon hung low in the sky. I raised my fingers to measure the distance between the Big Dipper and the North Star.

****

The train station on 16th Street was jammed with wagons, carriages, and harried pedestrians burdened with trunks and carpet bags. I left Barley hitched to a warehouse rail away from the crowded platform and dodged my way back across the street to help Avery's two hired men unload the telescopes and baggage. Having spent so much time worrying over those telescopes, I'd almost come to think of them as my property. Everything was loaded onto a wheeled cart, and one of the station porters pushed it down the line to a baggage car.

Dr. Avery and Professor Mitchell bought copies of

several Denver papers for sale along the platform and read snippets from the front pages to the Vassar group. I joined them on the passenger platform.

Avery surrendered her newspapers to Elizabeth and said, "I have appointments this morning, so it's time to say goodbye. It's been a wonderful time." She hugged Mitchell and said, "I'll see you in Rhode Island." She hugged each of the girls and then turned to me.

"Nolan, I'll see you back at the house."

I walked up to Cora, who was wearing her blue summer dress again. The small matching hat was absent. I had abandoned my coat and vest and rolled up my sleeves against the morning's warmth. "Got your ticket?" I asked her.

Cora waved a small yellow card with the words, Kansas-Pacific Rail, printed on it. She forced a brief smile.

"Emigrant?" I asked.

"Sleeper car. We'll be traveling in comfort once again."

We stared at each in silence for a second, not wanting, perhaps, to say out loud the things we really wanted to say. Certainly, it was true for me. That painful silence ended when a conductor called, "All aboard!" His summons was passed down the length of the train by two other conductors.

Professor Mitchell came over and said, "Mr. Carter, thank you very much for your steadfast assistance. Your youthful determination was essential to our successful observations here in Denver. I hope to see you again sometime."

She stuck out her hand and I shook it. "Perhaps in '89?" I asked.

She laughed and said, "That's an eclipse I am not likely to witness." She turned to her former students and said, "Ladies, we must board now."

But then she turned back to me and said, "You're not meant for hauling freight, Mr. Carter." She stepped into the carriage and disappeared.

I never saw her again, but I often think of her sitting out on the prairie, surrounded by a battery of brassy telescopes, her great gray curls shielded by her leghorn hat, waiting for the Moon and the Sun to merge into that spectacle of extraordinary light and shadow.

I got quick hugs and handshakes from Elizabeth and Phebe and the others, and then they hurried to the carriage doors. Cora lingered. We hugged. I felt her press against me. She looked at me through teary eyes and asked, "What should we do, Nolan?"

That question again. "I'll think of something. I promise." I glanced at the carriage door. "You need to get on board. Missing the train won't help."

I walked her to the door, kissed her again, and she stepped inside. A conductor walked by, closing the carriage doors as he passed. I waved through the glass. She put up a hand to wave, looked away, and moved deeper into the car. I lost sight of her. The engine whistle blew. The brakes released in a hiss of steam. The train pulled away. I watched it fade into the distance.

****

She was gone now. Cora and Mitchell and the others had done what they came here to do, and now they were headed home. The adventure was over. The eclipse came and went as the astronomers' formulas predicted it would, and the world returned to its everyday concerns and its normal pace.

And what of me? My job was done. I'd finished what I was contracted to do. I didn't want to do it again. I was tired of the West. Tired of hauling people's freight. Tired of playing cowboy. It was time to move on. Time to grow up. Time to find a place for myself in the larger world. Time to make something of myself. I wanted to follow Cora, and to do that, to be worthy of her and the life she wanted for herself, I needed a profession of my own.

I took my hat off and looked at the green ribbon encircling the low crown. It was spotted with dirt and a smear of blood. The silver pin holding the ribbon in place was tarnished.

Still lost in my anguished thoughts, a station agent walked by and asked what train I was waiting for.

"I missed it," I said and walked back across the street to reclaim Barley.

In the saddle, I remembered Cora had my old leather gloves. I didn't need them. Later, I learned she wore the gloves in the sleeper car, letting the scent of horses and prairie dust lull her to sleep.

Feeling hollowed out, I rode over to Baur's photography shop where I knew I soon would feel even worse. I stepped inside his shop. The photographer looked up from behind his counter. He smiled, pointed a finger at me, and said, "Ah, yes. With the astronomer ladies. Got it right here."

He reached under the counter and withdrew a photo of Cora and me standing by her telescope. In the tinted image I looked like I was guilty of something. Cora looked wonderful. She looked happy.

Baur placed two pieces of paperboard on the counter and said, "Ten cents."

"Worth every penny." I placed the photo between the protective paperboards and left with my treasure.

****

Dr. Avery returned to her house. I sat at the dining room table writing out details and impressions of Monday's eclipse. I had several long pages completed, relying on my own notes, comments from Mitchell's group, and some of the reporting from the Denver papers.

"You've been busy," she said. She pulled off a silk shawl and her hat and tossed them in a chair.

"That's a very interesting centerpiece you have," I said, pointing my pen at it.

Avery laughed and sat down across from me. She picked up the bishop's pointy purple hat and said, "I'd prefer his head, but his biretta will have to do." She set it back in the center of the table.

"You've met before?"

"Indeed, we have. Were you here in Colorado last year? You might remember the legislature added the question of female suffrage to the ballot."

I nodded, remembering the newspaper stories.

"Well, his holiness here"—she pointed to the bishop's hat—"called the idea of women voting absurd and revolting. He called some of our organizers old maids and claimed women going to the polls would be tantamount to abandonment of the family and the home. Machebeuf was, if nothing else, persuasive. The ballot lost two to one."

I nodded again. I had read newspaper stories about the vote. I looked at Avery and said, "We must keep pegging away."

She sat back surprised and let out a laugh. "You're

quoting me from the papers?" Now she took closer note of the papers spread about her table. "Are you also writing the news?"

I looked around at my work and said, "We'll see. My father might be inclined to publish some of this in Chicago. First-hand accounts of the Denver eclipse. I need to draft a quick letter and get all this on the next train." I looked up at her and said, "Who knows? This could become more press for Mitchell and her merry band of astronomers."

Avery said, "I'm sure she will appreciate that. Oh, I asked Anna to set up a room for you upstairs. You're probably tired of the carriage house, and now the house is empty again."

"Yes, thank you. She's put my things upstairs already. And I'll try to be out of your hair as quickly as I can. I have—"

"The house is empty. Stay as long as you need to. You've been no bother." She reached out and touched the bishop's pointy biretta again.

"Tomorrow I need to take the train down to Castle Rock to pay some debts. And send some telegrams. And close out my bank account here. Then I'm off."

"To where?" she asked, watching my face.

"Home. To Chicago."

"Chicago. Well, that's halfway." She got up and went into the kitchen.

****

At the Denver station, I handed my bundle of Chicago-bound letters to the man in the baggage car. He dropped them into a canvas mailbag, and then I walked across the platform to catch the morning train to Castle Rock. I traveled with only the clothes on my back, my pistol, my notebook, and a rolled-up Army poncho. Seated against a window, I opened the notebook and wrote down all I remembered about Davey and the ambush two months ago. He'd been killed by a random bullet fired by an anonymous man for reasons unknown. I didn't know it at the time, but that bullet also killed our Western adventure and killed whatever had been left of my childhood. Yet I had stayed out here, restless and wandering. I'm not sure I'd had a truly peaceful night's sleep since that dark, violent struggle in the foothills. And recent events only added variety to my fitful nights. Maybe now, writing down these words, I might find some meaning in it all, and maybe Davey's ghost might find the rest that still eluded me.

The train pulled into the Castle on time, and conveniently, Mr. Walsh, the station agent, stood on the platform checking his watch. I repaid him his two dollars and he invited me into the station office for a cup of coffee. Over black coffee and molasses sugar he told me the local Army detachment had returned from Pikes Peak and then galloped down to the burned-out town of Douglas. They found no Indians in the vicinity. Or any living residents. They buried five bodies in one large grave and erected a wooden marker. That seemed to be the end of the town called Douglas.

With one debt paid off, I walked over to the Western Union to send a message to Thaddeus. I stood at the desk, pencil in hand, and thought of Mitchell's words the other day at the train station: "You're not meant for hauling freight…" Perhaps not. But the job had been, if nothing else, a means to an end. That end was in sight now, and it was time to let go of the job and move on.

I wrote my goodbye to Thaddeus. I told him I was

needed in Chicago and asked him to forward any outstanding salary to the noted Chicago address. Thanking him for the job, I wished him luck against the railroads. It was a wordy telegram, but at least it was cheaper to send such a message from here than from Denver or Chicago.

And Travis? Should I send him a letter from Chicago? He had been a curious colleague and companion this last year. Taciturn for the most part, but there are worse people with whom to travel and work. And he succeeded where I had failed: he got Elizabeth and the telescopes to Denver.

I left the telegraph office, thinking whatever things I had at Mrs. Sullivan's boardinghouse in Pueblo were not important anymore; she could keep them. Then I thought of "Old Man" Frederick at the Pueblo stables wanting me to pay up last week before I left for Denver. He'd said, "You might not come back for one reason or another." Damned if he wasn't right.

I walked down to the livery to return the rubber poncho I had borrowed a few days ago. Inside the vast wooden structure, I found the kid mucking out a stall. I handed over the poncho and a nickel and thanked him for the loan.

He pocketed the money and said, "Mr. Goodyear ain't showed up for his blanket. Guess I can loan it out some more."

"Sounds like a money-making idea."

I headed back to the station to wait for the next Denver-bound train. My debts were paid. My ties to Pueblo were severed. I had but to take my leave of Dr. Avery and then I'd be on a train to Chicago. I looked around the busy street of Castle Rock. I felt like a balloon

279

cut from its mooring and now adrift on the wind.

As I passed the telegraph office again, the door banged open and the telegrapher yelled, "Hey, N. Carter. Got a telegram just come in for you."

Puzzled, I walked back over to the office. Who knew I was here but Dr. Avery?

At the door, the Western Union man handed me a message half-sheet, which read: "To N. Carter 1st Natl Bank, Denver. Blue at Larkspur."

"That damned horse," I muttered.

"Pretty smart horse that can send a telegram," said the amused telegrapher.

"You'd think so, but you'd be wrong."

Before getting on the southbound train this morning, I had stopped at the bank to close out my account. Chatting with the window clerk, I must have said I was heading down to the Castle. This telegram probably arrived at the bank right after I left and they sent it on to Castle Rock—leaving me to pay for the forwarded telegram, of course. Still, it was thoughtful of them to send the message.

I pushed my hat back, wondering what to do now. Blue complicated my travel plans. Once again.

"Looks like I need the wire again," I said to the telegrapher.

Inside, I sent a message down to the Larkspur stables asking if Blue still had his saddle. I couldn't ride him without one. I sent another message back to Denver, to Dr. Avery's house, telling her I might be delayed returning tonight.

After a quiet lunch, I stopped back in the Western Union office to find a one-word message from Larkspur: "Yep."

So I caught the next train to Larkspur and reclaimed Blue.

****

"Two fellas brung him in late on Monday. Said you'd pay his keep," the livery owner stated. "He's been no trouble, and his tack's over yonder."

"Been no trouble?" I shook my head. "You've no idea the world of trouble he's caused." I walked into the barn and found him in a back stall. "You skittish, cowardly creature," I said as I approached the stall. He glanced at me, but then turned away in what I hoped was an act of shame and contrition.

The bill paid, I saddled my brother's nomadic horse. Searching through the saddle bags, I found my small sacks of coffee and sugar were gone, along with the box of .44 cartridges. But carefully wrapped in a piece of burlap was my square of blue eclipse glass.

Soon, I was on the road again, heading back to Denver. There was no urgency this time. No weather or villains to dodge. But also, no Cora. I tried not to dwell on her absence, though I did wonder what she was doing right now and if she was still in New York or had already left for Boston. For the most part, I tried to enjoy the easy ride and the views of mountains and meadows, and the random appearance of mule deer and hawks drifting among the trees. I might not see these vistas again for some time.

It was eleven miles back to Castle Rock. In town, I spent the night in the hotel that Cora and Elizabeth would have occupied had our original travel plans held true. In the morning, I led Blue into the livestock carriage and then took an "emigrant" seat on the train to Denver. I waved to Mr. Walsh from the carriage window, and the train pulled away.

****

"Do you have everything?" asked Dr. Avery.

We stood on the 16th Street train platform two days after my return from Larkspur.

"Two horses, two guns, and a little money. Pretty much what I started this trip with," I said. I also had a newly developed photograph taken on the day of the eclipse, but I didn't mention the picture.

I reached into my vest pocket, pulled out a shiny dollar, and said, "Speaking of money, I'd like to make a small donation to the Colorado Equal Rights League."

She closed her gloved hands around my outstretch hand and said, "I'll make a donation in your name. Thank you."

Smiling, I dropped the coin back in my pocket and said, "Well, then, make it a big one." Then I asked, "Do you suppose the bishop was irritated Mitchell gave her talk in a church, or did he think the use of the church was further proof of how far the Methodists have fallen?"

Avery laughed. "He'd have had a proper stroke to know Maria's idea of the blessed Trinity is 'Observation, Reason, and Experience.'"

I nodded saying, "She's an interesting woman. I'm not sure, though, she ever really warmed to me."

Avery glanced at the train and took my arm, guiding me in the direction of the track.

"She liked you well enough. I imagine she thought it ironic that the person she asked to keep distractions at bay during the eclipse was himself the biggest distraction for her party."

I didn't know what to say to that news, but then she gave me a motherly hug and said, "Safe journey, Nolan.

Let me know what happens."

"I'm curious to know myself."

"Well, go." Avery pointed not at the train but to the east. She gave me a quick wave and walked back to her shay.

I had occasion to write to her, but I never saw her again.

****

My return to Chicago was in the stagnant heat of the late summer. Sweaty crowds and stinking stockyard cows were everywhere. From the passenger terminal, I rode Barley up to our house near Lincoln Park with Blue in tow. My mother was relieved to see me alive and whole, and she quickly settled in to harrying me about the dangers of the frontier, which to her mind was a vast wilderness of lawless savagery about a mile west of Michigan Avenue. She meant well. She was my mother. So, I told her only about ten percent of what I'd seen and done in Colorado and left out all of the adjectives and adverbs of my narrative.

Later in the evening, with Brian and my father at home, I poured myself a tumbler of my father's best whiskey and settled in a chair in his study to tell them about all the people I had met, the things I had done, the men I had shot or tried to, and the eclipse I had witnessed. Brian was impressed, but declared he was happy to have left Colorado when he did. My father, scribbling occasional notes, wondered aloud if my months in Colorado might be rolled into some kind of first-person adventure story for a Sunday edition.

I demurred, saying, "What of the pieces on the eclipse?"

"Already to press. Good stuff. Needed a bit of color,

283

but otherwise…very good. Who'd have imagined a whole group of women—in bonnets and bloomers—travelling to Colorado to study an eclipse," he said. "And that tale-of-two-towns piece—Glade and Douglas? Already on the streets. Like to have met that Mr. Glade character. Wonderful stuff."

Brian drifted off to bed, satisfied with the idea that Davey's death might have been avenged beside a Colorado stream and in a Denver cafe. My father stubbed out his cigarillo and flicked his fingers through his beard, checking for ash. I poured myself more of his whiskey and then poured some for him. For the first time since I was a child I was going to ask him for something I really wanted. I needed both of us relaxed.

I sat back down and said, "I need to move to Boston. I need a job there. Do you know someone I might ask?"

I'd surprised him. He was quiet for a moment. Finally, he asked, "Who's in Boston?"

I opened my notebook, pulled out a photograph and placed it on his desk.

Staring at the photograph of Cora and me standing beside her telescope, he asked, "Weren't you watching the eclipse?"

"Occasionally," I said.

He chuckled and leaned back in his swivel chair. He stared up at the plaster ceiling and said, "I know two editors whom I see occasionally in New York City. And I know a magazine publisher. Known him since the war. Good man. Always ready for an argument. Usually starts them."

My father picked up the photograph, glanced at it again, and passed it back to me. "I suppose you'd like me to make some inquires this week?"

"Tomorrow would be fine." I downed the last of his whiskey.

****

New Haven was cold and gray and smelled of low-tide mud and coal smoke. After seeing New York City, I did not imagine this little coastal town had much going for it beyond Yale and the Winchester Repeating Arms Company. I rode through the Green, and the Yale campus, up to the Winchester factory. A showroom and a sales office were attached to the main factory, and I stopped to look at all the variations of their famous rifles. A salesman tried to sell me a rifle, but I told him I already owned one and was glad for having had it.

Barley and I continued an easy ride along the west bank of the Connecticut River, stopping here and there to see a bit of New England. In Hartford, I visited the riverfront Colt factory and toured their museum of handheld firearms. In the showroom, I told another salesman I owned a .44 Colt and had used it in Colorado against a rattlesnake. He asked, half seriously, if I had had occasion to wield it in any barroom duels or gunfights with Indians. I told him such stories were just the stuff of dime-novel fictions. He seemed disappointed by this news.

Would he have believed me if I'd told him I had survived a late-night ambush, shot two men, was wounded by Indians, and sought to shoot a third cowboy but was saved by a man who seemed to be more gunman than barkeep? No. Likely he'd have thought me a liar, at best.

Later that day, I rode down Farmington Avenue to Mark Twain's house. It was a rambling red structure of wide porches and tall peaks and inspired chimneys. I found what passed for a front door around the side of the house and gave it a firm knock. A housekeeper answered and told me he was out for the day. Disappointed, I walked down to the corner of the lot to where Mrs. Stowe's less flamboyant house stood. I wasn't sure what I would say if she opened the door; I didn't have a copy of her book with me. An elderly woman answered my quiet knocking and told me she was engaged for the afternoon. Maybe she was having lunch with Twain.

Later, crossing into Massachusetts, I stopped in Springfield to see the famous Water Shops Armory. Emily Dickinson lived only a short ride up the river in Amherst, but now I knew I was stalling. Like a defendant rising to hear the court's verdict, I was both eager and hesitant to turn east toward Boston.

There's a job and a woman waiting for you, I told myself. *Go.*

So I ended my tour of the Connecticut River Valley and its armories and authors. At the Springfield terminal, I caught the afternoon train into Boston. I had not told Cora I was coming. I wasn't sure yet if I would be staying. Again, I fretted over imagining how I might be greeted.

****

I walked across the West Boston Bridge into Cambridge and jumped on the Broadway streetcar. I sat fidgeting in my gray wool sack suit and tight new shoes. Settled in my seat again, I unrolled an old copy of *Harper's* and glanced at the cover's illustration of "The Great Solar Eclipse." Even now, months later, the eclipse still was widely read news—with more information trickling out from artists and astronomers alike.

At Harvard College, I got off the streetcar, dropped

my hat back on my head, and walked up cobbled Garden Street to the observatory. The site was easy to find, with its several white-domed observation buildings clustered together like a patch of overnight mushrooms. I stopped a couple of Harvard students dressed in dark suits and ties and carrying book satchels. I asked them where I might find the astronomer, Cora Harrison.

One of them scratched his hairless chin and pointed to a three-story brick building in among the mushrooms. "Try the second floor. She still might be tutoring some freshmen."

"Thanks." I waved my notebook at them and walked over to the building.

Inside, climbing the front staircase, I was nervous all over again. She'd be surprised to see me. I hoped it would be a pleasant surprise; the kind of surprise I had imagined while traveling across the country, riding up the river, and rolling into Boston. We had shared a grand, sometimes harrowing adventure together, but I knew from other people and from books that such feelings of affection often faded with the end of the adventure and the danger. She left Colorado and the excitement behind a couple of months ago. We had written to each other, but a letter is no substitute for a presence.

On the Chicago train platform, my father had handed me an odd piece of mail that arrived at his office from the New Mexico Territory. It was addressed in crude penmanship to "N. Carter, Nat Denver Bank." On the back of the envelope were scrawled the words, "For the Profesor Lady." The Denver Bank forwarded it to my father's office from where he occasionally had wired money to the bank for my support. If nothing good happened at the Harvard Observatory this morning, I would at least be able to deliver this message in a bottle.

A woman's voice reverberated in the upstairs hall. I pulled open a heavy wooden door.

And there she was.

Cora had her back to the classroom and was chalking mysterious symbols across the face of a blackboard. Her hair was done up and she wore a black dress. A matching hat and jacket rested on an empty chair beside the blackboard. I stepped inside and sat down in one of the many empty chairs. Five students turned their heads to look at me. The slow-moving door slammed shut. Cora pivoted at the noise, a piece of chalk still in her right hand.

She saw me sitting there in my new suit and my old hat now tilted far back on my head. She stared at me for several seconds, as if not quite believing I was there. I held my breath, waiting for the verdict to be read out. Then she smiled a wide and welcoming smile. Pure joy was written across her lovely face.

That smile. I was cured magically of all my pent-up anxieties. I raised my hand and stood up; I imagined college students stood to ask questions.

"Sorry to intrude…Professor. Nolan Carter, reporter for *Harper's Weekly*. I'm writing a story about the recent solar eclipse." I traced an imaginary title in the air, "It's called, 'Star Queen of the Western Prairie.' I have a photograph and plenty of technical background, but I need a quote."

Her smile became a laugh. The five students stared at me and then back again at Cora.

"Nol-… You're living here in Boston…Mr. Carter?"

"For as long as necessary."

"Can you wait a few minutes? I just have to finish this tutorial."

I sat down and stretched out my legs. "Of course. We have all the time in the world."

Author's Notes

The Vassar Astronomy Group: The 1878 group consisted of Maria Mitchell, her sister Phebe M. Kendall, Emma Culbertson ('77), Cora Harrison ('76), Cornelia W. Marsh ('73), and Elizabeth O. Abbot ('73). In the words of Professor Mitchell: "We started from Boston a party of two; at Cincinnati a third joined us; at Kansas City we came upon a fourth who was ready to fall into our ranks, and at Denver two more awaited us; so, we were a party of six—'All good women and true.' Our party had three telescopes and one chronometer."

In Pueblo, they found themselves in the middle of the "railroad war" between the AT&SF and the DRG. They did, however, manage to get aboard a train and arrived in Denver on Wednesday, July 24. Unfortunately, their baggage, lens, and one telescope were missing.

"It was only five hours' travel from Pueblo to Denver, and we went on to that city. The trunks, for some unexplained reason, or for no reason at all, chose to remain at Pueblo," wrote Mitchell. The lost equipment and baggage was recovered in Denver on Friday, July 26. Mitchell writes that, "We haunted the telegraph-rooms and sent imploring messages. We placed ourselves at the station and watched the trains as they tossed out their freight; we listened to every express-wagon which passed our door without stopping, and just as we were trying to find a telescope to hire or buy in Denver, the glasses arrived."

It rained on Friday and through the weekend. But on Monday, July 29, the skies cleared, and the Vassar party set up on the McCullough Addition, across from St.

Joseph's Hospital. A local photographer took a stereophotograph of the six women with their three telescopes.

Maria Mitchell: The total solar eclipse of 1889 swept across the western United States and Canada on January 1. Maria Mitchell did not observe it. She had retired from Vassar College the year before and died in Massachusetts on June 28, 1889. She was seventy years old. Her comet-spotting Dollond telescope is on Nantucket Island at her family home near the Maria Mitchell Observatory. The non-profit Nantucket Maria Mitchell Association presents the annual Maria Mitchell Women in Science Award, which recognizes an individual or group whose efforts have encouraged the advancement of girls and women in the natural and physical sciences, mathematics, engineering, computer science, and technology.

The Railroad War: The war between the Atchison, Topeka and Santa Fe Railway (AT&SF) and the Denver and Rio Grande (DRG) began as a dispute over access to the Raton Pass leading into New Mexico. Lawyers and rival railyard workers created most of the early trouble. Then, in early 1878, the AT&SF hired local gunmen to end the dispute and claim the Pass.

Mitchell writes, "We had travelled so comfortably all along the Santa Fé road, from Kansas City to Pueblo, that we had forgotten the possibility of other railroad annoyances than those of heat and dust until we reached Pueblo. At Pueblo all seemed to change. We left the Santa Fé road and entered upon that of the Rio Grande. Which road was to blame, it is not for me to say, but there was trouble at once about our 'round-trip ticket.' "

Alida Avery: Beginning in 1865, Avery was a

professor of physiology and hygiene, and the resident physician at Vassar College. She resigned in 1874 and moved to Denver, where she became the first woman in Colorado to practice medicine. She was vice president of the Women's Suffrage Association of Colorado in 1876 and helped lead the 1877 referendum campaign for suffrage in Colorado.

Middle-aged and unmarried, Dr. Avery never got Bishop Machebeuf's hat or his head for her dining room table, but she was a regular target of his wrath. Machebeuf declared, "The class of women wanting suffrage are battalions of old maids disappointed in love—women separated from their husbands or divorced by men from their sacred obligations—women who, though married, wish to hold the reins of the family government, for there never was a woman happy in her home who wished for female suffrage."

Dr. Avery retired from medicine and moved to San Jose, California in 1887. She died there on September 22, 1908. The Nineteenth Amendment giving women the right to vote was ratified in 1920. In 1931, Avery Hall at Vassar College was named in her honor. In 2019, she was elected to the Colorado Women's Hall of Fame for "her leadership in securing Colorado women the right to vote."

Cora Harrison. Cora also missed the 1889 eclipse. From the *Vassar Miscellany* issue of January 1, 1889: "Died in Denver, Col., December 16, 1888, Miss Cora Harrison. After Miss Harrison's graduation [in 1876], she continued her studies in Mathematics and Astronomy, for which branches she had shown an unusual aptitude during her college course. She read mathematics with Prof. Pierce of Harvard College for a year or more. Prof.

Pierce spoke most highly of her ability and held her capable of original investigation. But soon the fatal disease, consumption [i.e., tuberculosis], which caused her death, declared itself, and ere long it compelled the laying aside of both labor and ambition. This thwarting of her hopes she accepted with a beautiful resignation and lost none of her interest in the work of others. In her death she remembered Vassar, whose welfare was always dear to her. She leaves her telescope to the Observatory, for the special use of the students of the department."

Nolan Carter. Nolan, his friends, family, colleagues, and horse are all works of fiction. On the other hand, the characters' language and cultural behaviors are real and typical of nineteenth-century America.

Vulcan. Astronomers and mathematicians had known since 1843 that there was something odd about the orbit of Mercury. During Mercury's orbit, its closest approach to the Sun advanced by a tiny amount each orbit. This advance is called "perihelion precession," but the observed value differed from the predicted value. The difference was assumed to be caused by the gravitational pull of an unknown planet—Vulcan— orbiting between Mercury and the Sun. The hunt for Vulcan began in 1859 and continued through 1908. In 1915, Albert Einstein published his theory of relativity, which predicted the massive gravity of the Sun would warp local space-time, thereby affecting Mercury's orbit. His theory was confirmed during the total solar eclipse of May 29, 1919, which lasted for six minutes and 51 seconds.

2024. The next total solar eclipse in the western

United States will be on April 8, 2024. It will sweep up from Texas and move northeast into Maine.

Books and Sources

Baron, D. (2017). *American Eclipse*. W.W. Norton & Company Ltd.

Sobel, D. (2016). *The Glass Universe*. Penguin Books.

Ruskin, S. (2017). *America's First Great Eclipse*. Alpine Alchemy Press.

Mitchell, M. (1896). *Maria Mitchell: Life, Letters, and Journals*. Lee & Shepard.

U.S. Naval Observatory. (1880). *Reports of the Total Solar Eclipses of July 29, 1878, and January 11, 1880*. Government Printing Office. Online at: http://www.worldcat.org/oclc/4759919.

Hein, R. Moon Shadows over Wyoming: The Solar Eclipses of 1878, 1889 and 1918. June 29, 2017. Online at: https://www.wyohistory.org/encyclopedia/moon-shadows-over-wyoming-solar-eclipses-1878-1889-and-1918.

Kent, D. The North American Eclipse of 1869. *Physics Today,* 2019;72(8):46. Online at: doi.org/10.1063/PT.3.4271

A word about the author...

Edward McSweegan is a writer in Rhode Island. He has had short stories published in several notable magazines and placed in at least two contests.

Shadow of the Moon is his debut historical novel.
Visit him at:

http://edwardmcsweegan.com

Thank you for purchasing
this publication of The Wild Rose Press, Inc.

For questions or more information
contact us at
info@thewildrosepress.com.

The Wild Rose Press, Inc.